Bath Ablaze

by

Maggie Rayner

The 'Bath At War' series:

'When Bombs Fell On Bath'

'Bath Ablaze'

PART ONE

CHAPTER 1

Bath, 1939

Susan Bishop pushed up the bottom part of the sash window in her bedroom, letting in the cold night air. Straddling the window-ledge, half-in and half-out, she said to her younger sister Ann,

'I'll only be an hour - I promised to meet him down by the gasworks. See you later!'

With practised ease she manoeuvred herself out the window and onto the roof of the coal shed, lowering herself to the ground then disappearing past the privy and out the back gate into the alleyway which ran between the rows of terraced houses. Eleven-year-old Ann, used to her sister's antics, sighed and shook her head. Shivering, she closed the window and went back to her book.

Susan ran the half mile from her house in Oldfield Park, a residential area on the West of Bath, to her rendezvous and found her boyfriend, Frank, waiting at the corner, his cigarette glowing in the dark. When she had recovered her breath he lit a cigarette for her, then they walked hand-in-hand towards the path that ran alongside the River Avon, sparkling in the moonlight. He was seventeen, a year older than her, and more worldly. When they reached the shelter of a tree they stopped and kissed, lingeringly.

'I love you,' he whispered in her ear, 'I want you so much, honey bunny…'

'Oh Frank, I love you too…'

His hand moved under her skirt and up her thigh to the point where her suspenders met the tops of her stockings. He knew that was as far as she'd let him go, although he lived in hope and there was no harm in trying.

After more fumbling in the dark Susan kissed Frank goodbye and ran home. She had just climbed back through the bedroom window when the sisters heard their mother, Pat, calling them downstairs for their night-time cocoa.

'Perfect timing!' said Susan.

As a youngster Frank Fowler was a quick boy, smart, lived on his wits - he'd had to. When his father had been killed in an accident at work his mother Mavis, unable to cope, had turned to drink for consolation and Frank had more or less brought himself up. He'd learnt when to act tough, when to turn on the charm, his eyes darting around, constantly on the look-out for opportunities, for survival. When he left school at fourteen he'd taken a job as a delivery boy for the local butchers, riding his push bike laden with its cargo of meat up and down the steep hills of Bath. Mr Drewitt, the owner, taught him his craft and by

'But Frank, you'll be away for months! And what about your Mum?'

'She'll be all right. I'll send money home and there's always someone in the pub will buy her a drink. I've asked old Mr Jones from the Church to look in on her.'

'Oh…'

She felt hurt that he'd been planning this for a while and hadn't said anything to her.

'Look, I didn't tell you before because I knew it would upset you. But I've got to go. And you mustn't worry, I'll be fine.'

The afternoon sunlight quickly faded and by the time they got back to Susan's it was dark and foggy, smoke from coal fires hanging in the air. He kissed her goodnight and walked away, leaving her on the doorstep feeling like the bottom had dropped out of her world, and not knowing what to make of it all.

In the new year Frank went to Plymouth to undertake his basic training. He wrote and told Susan he missed her, but she suspected her loss was greater than his - reading between the lines, he was having a great time. At the end of March she answered a knock at the door to see a sailor standing there, kitbag on his shoulder and a big grin on his face. He opened his arms and lifted her up in the air, saying, 'hello, honey bunny, I'm back!'

'Frank! I've missed you so much!'

They kissed, then she led him inside the house where her parents welcomed him.

'How are you, Frank? Tell us all about it!'

Susan watched Frank as he spoke, taking in all the little things she'd missed - his deep blue eyes, his lovely smile. And yet there were differences - he'd put on some muscle, looked more mature and spoke more quickly, using words that were unfamiliar to her - he'd got used to the banter with his fellow-sailors who had a language all of their own. He was alert, aware, enthused about his new job and his new life.

'...then we went dinghy sailing round Plymouth Hoe,' he was saying, 'it was brilliant! They said I was a natural - don't know how, coming from round here! Good job I was fit, mind - cycling up and down these hills all my life gave me a head-start I reckon. But enough about me! What's been happening here?'

Susan told him all the news while they drank their tea and he listened, although she couldn't help but feel he wasn't really interested.

'So how long are you here for?' Pat asked.

'Just for the weekend. On Sunday I'm catching a train to Portsmouth to join a frigate called HMS SALAMANDER, my first job as an Ordinary Seaman!' he announced, proudly. 'We're going to the Mediterranean, protecting convoys of merchant ships. I'll be away for a year or so.'

'A year!' cried Susan, devastated.

'I know, love - it's a long time. But it will fly by, and I'll write to you...And we are at war, don't forget!'

Susan and Frank spent Saturday together and in the evening they walked over to the gasworks where they used to meet before the war. Both of them were quiet, each thinking about Frank's imminent departure and neither wanting to talk about it. They suddenly became aware of a dull drone in the distance and looked up to see a squadron of German bombers flying in formation overhead, their metal wings glinting in the moonlight, heading West towards Bristol, thirteen miles away.

'They're for it tonight,' said Frank, watching the planes until they were out of sight.

'It's so horrible, we see more and more of them,' said Susan, taking his arm, then she added, 'I do realise, Frank, why you've got to go away - we've got to fight the Jerries and I'm so proud you're doing your bit.'

They walked for a while along the riverside path then he said, 'feels like ages since we used to come here, doesn't it?' He paused and gave a quiet laugh. 'And we're not on our own this time, are we?'

They could hear noises coming from the riverbank - the breath and sighs and giggles of courting couples in the darkness. Frank, aroused by the sounds of other people's love making, pulled Susan closer towards him.

'Do you hear that, honey bunny?'

He unbuttoned her coat and his hands began to travel over her breasts then down her back, squeezing her buttocks, and up her skirt. 'I've missed this, Susan. I'm not going to see you for ages. Come on, let me...I'll be gentle, I promise...'

Any concerns she harboured fled to the back of her mind. He was going away for a year, maybe more, and with the war you never knew what might happen...So she returned his kisses and together they moved over to a patch of grass and lay down. He grew more forceful, he pulled her clothes aside then he was inside her, moving, breathing hard, pushing against her, and it hurt, but it was okay. She felt his weight upon her, strangely reassured by the idea that other people were nearby, doing the same thing, then he stifled a groan, shuddered, and rolled off her, panting.

She lay there for a moment, looking up at the vast night sky. After the curiosity, the anticipation, she couldn't help but think, 'is that it?'

Then he said, 'are you all right, love?'

'Yes,' she said, trying to hide the disenchantment in her voice.

Suddenly they both felt the cold and got to their feet. He wanted a cigarette and lit one, then quickly put it out when Susan reminded him they weren't allowed to smoke in the black-out. He cussed under his breath, threw the match away and put the cigarette back in his pocket for later. They resumed their walk and at her door they kissed and he said, 'thank you for tonight. I love you.'

'I love you too.'

As he walked home he smiled to himself. He'd had his Susan at last, and now he couldn't wait to join his ship.

The next day Susan stood on the platform at Weston station among all the other wives and sweethearts saying goodbye to their loved ones as they went away to war. Her father, the Station Master, stood to one side, ensuring all the passengers were safely aboard while the train got up steam, hissing and puffing as it prepared to depart. Fred took his watch and chain from his waistcoat pocket and checked the time. Half a minute to go.

Fred watched the young men leaning out the carriage windows saying their farewells, feeling a shiver run up his spine as he suddenly saw himself doing the same thing on this very platform, twenty-five years ago. Then, it had been crowded with women in long skirts and high-necked blouses wearing their best hats, older men in flat caps and children being held aloft, everyone cheering and waving union jacks as the crop of Oldfield Park's young men went to fight the Hun. He remembered waving goodbye to his mother and his sister, Elsie, as the train pulled away, off to join his brothers on the Western front. He would be the only one of them to return.

Fred looked again at his watch. Time to send this batch of young men to their fate, he thought, grimly. He signalled to the driver and blew his whistle. With a blast of steam, hissing and shushing, the huge metal wheels began to turn. Susan blew Frank a final kiss as the magnificent iron and steel machine pulled out of the station, the women watching, powerless, as the train steamed away out of sight.

CHAPTER 3

Portsmouth, 1940

Portsmouth Dockyard was a hive of activity with sailors and dockyard mateys preparing ships for war. Frank located HMS SALAMANDER and climbed aboard in anticipation, excited about his new life and the challenges ahead. Straight from basic training he was the lowest of the low in terms of ranks at sea and soon found that he was treated accordingly. Along with the other new recruits he was directed to his accommodation - a hammock slung among many other tightly-packed sailors - then an old Able Seaman that everybody called Jack told them, 'we'll be staying here in Pompey for a month taking on stores, armaments and victuals, then doing trials in the Atlantic so don't think you're getting your holiday in the Med yet! Now, go to the Junior Rates mess and get some scran.'

As soon as they set sail from Portsmouth Frank was violently sick. The swell in the Channel was persistent and the weather grew worse by the day. Unable to work he was confined to his hammock, given a bucket to be sick into and told to stay put till he got used to it. After three days he felt a bit better and reported for duty - he'd had enough of the ribbing from the other sailors and was determined to show them what he was made of.

He quickly grew used to the daily routine, punctuated by bells and pipes in keeping with tradition, the former to mark the time, telling the crew when to change watches, the latter the prelude to a ship's broadcast. When not on watch the sailors would lie in their hammocks, sleeping, reading, smoking cigarettes, writing letters home and mending their kit. Frank wrote to Susan and his mother, assuring them he was safe and well, that the discipline on board was harsh but the scran ('the navy word for food,' he wrote), was good. He got to know his shipmates, mostly tough, working class lads like himself, from all over the country.

Frank was a seaman and his job was to be up on deck, watchkeeping and maintaining the ship in prime condition, cleaned and polished, 'ship shape and Bristol fashion'. As they sailed into the Atlantic he was on the look-out for hostile ships and aircraft. While undertaking trials they escaped enemy attention, but one day he noticed a threatening, dark shape just under the surface in the distance and alerted the Petty Officer on deck. Together they watched as the shape moved and swerved, then, with a mighty swoosh! Its massive, shiny, blue-black body and white underside leapt out of the sea, a spout of water exploding from its rounded head, its enormous tail fin flapping and slapping the surface. With an almighty splash it returned to the water, sending columns of spume high into the air. A few moments later the gigantic creature re-emerged to repeat its performance, landing with a smack on the surface then submerging, leaving the two sailors gazing in awe as the whale lunged away, into the depths of the ocean.

SALAMANDER proceeded to Gibraltar and docked, the massive Rock looming above them, the dominating presence on this British territory which safeguarded the entrance to the Mediterranean Sea. The harbour was crammed with vessels and air defence weapons were primed, ready for imminent attack. Frank looked at the massed ships of the Mediterranean Fleet, wondering how many would survive, hoping to be one of the lucky ones. He and his shipmates would need all the luck they could get as they embarked on their mission - to protect convoys of merchant shipping carrying vital supplies to the strategically important island of Malta, the British colony just south of Sicily, which was under siege by the forces of Nazi Germany and Fascist Italy.

Leaving Gibraltar, Frank was on watch in the warmth and bright sunshine of the Mediterranean, his blue uniform exchanged for tropical whites. He was relishing his new environment, feeling a million miles away from his old self, the butcher's boy from Bath. After four days' passage, looking to the horizon through his binoculars he sighted the shape of a rock shimmering gold in the sunlight, suspended between the blue sea and the even bluer sky.

'That's Gozo,' said the Petty Officer, 'it's a small island North West of Malta. Next we'll see Comino, another island, then Malta itself.'

They sailed past Gozo, then the coastline of Malta came into view, rocky, rugged, revealing steep cliffs and sandy coves washed by the sparkling sea. As they grew closer an almost Biblical scene unfolded with the odd farmhouse, gaily coloured fishing boats, scrubland with animals grazing, water towers and windmills. Malta itself was just fifteen miles long, and the ship reduced speed as they approached the Southern tip of the island. As they came within sight of larger towns they could see the damage that had been wrought by air raids, buildings reduced to rubble by war.

They sailed around to the Eastern side of the island, arriving at the capital, Valletta, where they entered Grand Harbour with its backdrop of tall, sand-coloured cliffs, its girdle of forts and watchtowers going back to ancient times. Crowds of people were gathered on the quayside, desperate for supplies. Getting food, water and shelter to a whole population under attack was vital and Frank felt a sudden surge of pride in playing his part.

They dropped anchor in Valletta harbour and remained there, guarding the merchant ships while they discharged their cargo. Even from off-shore Frank could smell the stink of rotting flesh, sense the despair these people must be feeling after days and nights of unrelenting bombing, trying to maintain their lives amidst their ruined city. He was struck by the contrast between the peaceful rural scenes they'd passed on

Gozo and the devastation of Valletta, the enemy's prime target.

Their task complete, SALAMANDER set course for their next port of call, Alexandria in Egypt, at the East of the Mediterranean. As they left Malta the Captain gave a ship's broadcast to congratulate his men on a job well done, with the reward of an extra rum ration.

As Frank downed his drink he said to another seaman, 'it was so real, seeing those poor folks there. We're doing a good job, aren't we?'

'Of course we are!' he replied, 'but don't get mushy over it, for God's sake. Here's to Alexandria and our run ashore!'

Bath, 1940

Susan was pleased to receive Frank's letters. She was also pleased when her period came, for although she'd heard the women at Bayer's say you couldn't get pregnant the first time she wasn't sure whether to believe them. She had no regrets about that night with Frank, though. She hadn't enjoyed it as much as he had but hoped the next time would be better.

Bayer's factory took on war work and the machinists were busier than ever, directed to produce vast quantities of utility clothing and items of uniform. Many of the women had sweethearts away in the Forces and they found solace in each other's company, going out to the cinema, enjoying romantic films and musicals with Fred Astaire and Ginger Rogers. The expert seamstresses would replicate the fashions they saw on screen in whatever material they could lay their hands on, creating their own versions of Hollywood glamour. All they lacked was the opportunity to wear them.

*

When he wasn't working at the station Fred kept busy on his allotment alongside the railway embankment in Oldfield Park. He was proud of his ability to coax fruit and vegetables out of Bath's unforgiving clay soil and had won many gold awards over the years for his produce at the local show.

Fred was busy gathering his early Summer harvest of lettuces and new potatoes when he heard planes flying overhead.

'It's all right, they're ours!' called out his friend Stan, as the two men stopped their digging and looked skywards.

'Funny how you get used to it,' replied Fred. 'Most nights now we hear the bombers flying over to Bristol and South Wales to do their dirty work.'

'It's getting closer, isn't it...and now we've been chucked out of Dunkirk they say Hitler's got us in his sights! Can you imagine, Fred, Nazi soldiers marching round 'ere, taking charge!'

'Over my dead body!' Fred exclaimed, thrusting his spade into the ground with renewed vigour, imagining he was attacking Hitler himself with a bayonet. He'd fight with every sinew to protect his land from the enemy and make sure his family didn't go hungry.

The Mediterranean, 1940

HMS SALAMANDER arrived safely in Alexandria, Headquarters of the Royal Navy's Mediterranean Fleet and a vital link in the transport of troops and ammunition along the Desert Road to Cairo. However, the strategic importance of the city was not at the forefront of the sailors' minds. On arrival the men were given a twenty-four-hour pass but before they were allowed ashore they were required to attend the 'VD talk' given by the Petty Officer in charge of the sick bay. He delivered his favourite line: 'you lot are going to put your private parts where I wouldn't put my walking stick!', then proceeded to show them graphic photographs of the results of unprotected intercourse before issuing them all with a supply of prophylactics.

Frank went ashore with a dozen or so of his shipmates and found Alexandria to be a real eye-opener, a cauldron of heat, dust and dirt, its streets full of beggars, boys in doorways polishing shoes, and flies everywhere. The Casbah was out of bounds to British forces but there were plenty of other attractions. The sailors made their way round market stalls where ancient, toothless men were selling their wares and after furious bargaining they each bought a few souvenirs. Then they went to one of the many cafés where they sat, sweating, writing postcards home.

A group of Arabs were sitting at a table playing backgammon, feral cats prowled and ceiling fans turned slowly overhead, having little effect on the stifling atmosphere. They tried the local cigarettes, which tasted horrible, and drank glasses of sweet, strong, black coffee.

Frank had made friends with William Wilson, a lad a couple of years older than himself who was known as 'Tug', because everyone in the Royal Navy whose surname is 'Wilson' is named in that way. Tug was an Able Seaman whose job was to man one of the Oerlikon guns on the upper deck. This was his third tour in the Mediterranean and he boasted to the others that he knew the best places to go to find what they wanted: drink and women. The war made it difficult to get good liquor in Egypt, but the club Tug led them to was run by an American who had an endless supply of bourbon, as well as ladies who entertained.

The sailors entered the stiflingly hot darkness of the club, sat down and ordered drinks. The owner, sensing the money burning holes in their pockets, came and welcomed them personally. When the dancers appeared Frank thought he'd died and gone to heaven. He'd never seen so much swaying, quivering female flesh on display and sat, bewitched, as the girls shimmied and shook their buttocks in the most alluring way. Dressed in sequined bras and flowing silk skirts hung from a tasselled belt they rippled their stomachs and gyrated their hips, fixing their audience with flashing dark eyes full of temptation. The drumbeat became louder and faster, the girls' movements more intense as they whipped their audience into a frenzy, then the dance ended and the girls left the stage.

'See! What did I tell you?' said Tug as Frank sat, stunned, wiping the sweat from his brow.

The sailors ordered another round of bourbon and the girls returned for a second performance. It was sensuous, hypnotic, the musky scent of their bodies and the rhythm of the music combining with alcohol, heat and cigarette smoke to create a thrillingly exotic atmosphere. When, after their final dance, the girls returned to the bar and sat on the sailors' laps there was only ever going to be one outcome. Couples disappeared upstairs and Frank spent the night with an extraordinary beauty called Fatima who, for a small fee, introduced him to erotic delights which he had never imagined in his wildest dreams.

Back on board Tug said, 'so you enjoyed your first run ashore in the Med, did you?', digging Frank in the ribs and laughing a filthy laugh.

Frank was still stunned.

Tug laughed again. 'And there's plenty more where that came from!'

SALAMANDER carried out two more successful passages East-West across the Mediterranean without serious incident, but there was no cause for complacency. On their next run, mid-way between Alexandria and Malta, Frank was on watch when he identified two Italian warships in the distance, supported in the sky by a squadron of Luftwaffe planes. He raised the alarm and the ship went to action stations.

With a deafening roar the first wave of planes, armed with torpedoes, flew low over the convoy setting fire to a destroyer and just missing one of the merchant vessels, then a second wave appeared, dive-bombing, blasting a hole in a frigate. Frank ran for cover, watching as Tug and his team fired the Oerlikon, scoring a hit on one of the aircraft which spiralled into the sea. The British and Italian ships exchanged fire, their guns booming, plumes of black smoke rising into the air. Frank watched as one of the Italian ships went down, then the other was struck and limped away. The aircraft made one last flight over the convoy dropping the remainder of their torpedoes but missing their targets. SALAMANDER escaped with minor damage which was patched up at sea, sufficient to get them back to Gibraltar where further repairs would be carried out. This time, thought Frank, they had been lucky.

Back in Gibraltar a batch of mail was waiting for them. Off-watch, Frank lay in his hammock, reading and re-reading news from home. One of the older Able Seamen was watching Frank and said, 'letters from your girl, eh?'

'Yes!'

'Got a picture of her?'

Frank showed him the photo of Susan that he carried with him and the sailor whistled.

'Nice looking lass. You'd better hope no one pinches her while you're away.'

Frank was alarmed. He'd had his fun in Alexandria, but that was different. It had never occurred to him that Susan might be attracted to somebody else.

'She wouldn't do that - she knows she's my girl.'

The sailor laughed bitterly. 'Never trust them!'

'What should I do, then?'

'Well, in my experience, the best thing is to get engaged. She'll be thrilled and won't stray, and you'll know you've got someone waiting for you at home.'

Frank thought about this for a moment, then said, 'but won't she want to get married? I don't want to get tied down yet...'

'She probably will, but you can put the wedding off till your next tour's done - and the one after that...and meantime you'll be free to go ashore and enjoy yourself!'

Frank reflected on these words of wisdom and before they set sail he wrote to Susan. Then he put thoughts of her to the back of his mind. Up on deck he would need all his wits about him to survive the next onslaught from the enemy and the sea.

CHAPTER 4

Bath, 1940

Susan was thrilled to receive Frank's letter. After a page about the weather, their skirmish with the foe and the ship's important role in helping the Maltese people, he came to the point:

...I really miss you, honey bunny and I've been thinking, you're my girl, and I hope you're still keen on me, and I'd like us to get engaged. Anyway, let me know what you think.

Susan caught her breath.

'Mum! Dad! Ann!' she cried, 'Frank wants us to get engaged! We're going to get married!'

The three of them looked at her in shock. Ann, knowing how much her sister loved Frank, jumped up and hugged her. Pat stood back as a wave of disappointment ran through her: so much for her dreams of a smart son-in-law with an office job. But Frank seemed to be doing well in the navy and her daughter was thrilled, so she put aside her reservations and hugged her too. Fred wasn't particularly enthusiastic - they were both so young - but it was wartime, and Susan was delighted.

'All right, love, as long as you're happy,' he said, giving her a kiss.

Susan wrote back to Frank straightaway, saying how much she loved him and was thrilled to accept his proposal. She would have to wait for an engagement ring but she didn't mind - Frank's word was enough.

The last months of the year saw a scattering of high-explosive bombs over Bath, damaging a number of properties. One night in November, Fred and Pat were woken by the louder than usual drone of enemy aircraft and, fearing the worst, looked outside to see wave after wave of bombers flying overhead. This time their target was Bristol, and to the West the sky was lit up in a bright orange glow. Over the next few days reports came in of a devastating attack on the city. In addition to the port and shipyards, swathes of the mediaeval centre had been wiped out and several churches destroyed, leaving many hundreds dead. Fred read the details in the newspaper in disbelief that such damage could be inflicted on the historic city, the familiar landmarks he had known since he was a boy, gone.

'Look, Pat, even the shops in Castle Street have been bombed!'

'But what did they want to go and do that for?'

She looked over his shoulder taking a sharp intake of breath at photographs of the destruction, thinking of the times she and Fred had gone there, happy days out, and her eyes filled with tears.

'All the more reason to keep fighting!' Fred said with determination. 'Let's just hope they don't come back to Bath...'

The Bishop family prepared for a modest Christmas, Ann decorating the back parlour room with paper chains made from newspaper and putting up a small tree with lights which, to Fred's relief, still worked. Frank sent the family some gifts he had picked up during his travels but what excited Susan most was the final sentence of his letter:

One other bit of news - I'm not allowed to say what the ship's programme is but if I tell you my tour is due to end around the time of my Mum's birthday then that should give you a clue.

Keen to know the answer, on Boxing Day Susan paid a visit to Mavis, Frank's mother, and Mr Jones the Church warden happened to be with her. Having established that Mavis' birthday was on the 23rd July, Susan's imagination took flight. It was wonderful to be engaged, but why not go the whole hog and get married? It was wartime and no one knew what the future held, so shouldn't they just get on with it? Several of her friends had done the same. She was sure Frank would be thrilled!

Mr Jones helpfully offered to have a word with the vicar to set a provisional date around the time of Frank's return. Mavis was keen, knowing Susan was a decent sort of girl, so, suitably encouraged, Susan returned home full of excitement and started designing her wedding dress. There was no time to lose.

The Mediterranean, 1941

Home seemed so far away, and when Frank received another batch of letters from Susan he didn't at first follow what she was saying. Maybe some letters were missing - but the more he read, one thing became clear - she had set the last Saturday in July as their wedding day. This wasn't what he had planned, at all. It was one thing getting engaged - he didn't want her to go with anyone else - but he'd never intended to marry her, at least not yet - he was only nineteen, for Christ's sake!

Frank didn't know what to do. He would feel mean refusing her, but he really hadn't reckoned on her getting carried away like this. And she sounded so excited about it all. In a more recent letter she told him something else of interest.

...I saw Julie Jenkins in town the other day, your friend Alfie's wife. They seem to be enjoying married life! Julie told me that Alfie's got a job at HMS Royal Arthur - you know, the training establishment near Corsham. I wish you could get a job somewhere like that, close to home! Julie was pleased to hear our news and said she'd tell Alfie about it...

So Alfie had got trapped too! This was all too much for Frank to take in and he actually felt thankful when the alarm sounded, warning of an attack.

Bath, 1941

During March and April some twenty people were killed when stray bombs fell on Bath and Fred decided it was time to take action. One Saturday morning Pat came back from the butchers to find her husband sitting on the floor in the back parlour surrounded by sheets of steel and wire mesh, lengths of wood and a miscellany of nuts, bolts and nails, looking quizzically at a sheet of assembly instructions.

'Fred! What on earth are you doing?'

'It's our new air-raid shelter - one of those indoor ones. Morrison shelters, they're calling them, after the politician. The Council delivered it while you were out.'

'But it's huge! Where are we going to keep it?'

'In here. Once I've put it together you can put a cloth over the top and we can use it as a table.'

'But we've already got a table!'

'Well, now we'll have another one! Let me finish, then you'll see.'

'Oh Fred...,' she said, doubtful about this new acquisition, 'well, I'll leave you to it. I've bought chitterlings for your tea - your favourite!'

'Thanks, love.'

Pat went into the kitchen and closed the door while Fred resumed his task. No one had told him the shelter had three hundred components and he'd need an engineering degree to work out how to put it all together. After two hours of banging, crashing and hammering Fred, wiping the sweat from his forehead, opened the kitchen door.

'I've finished! Come and have a look.'

Pat gasped at the steel cage which, at just over six feet long, four feet wide and two feet high with a solid steel top and wire mesh sides, dominated the room.

'I bet Herbert bloody Morrison didn't have to put his together himself!' said Fred, nursing his bruised thumb which he'd hit with the hammer.

Their daughters returned from a trip to Moorland Road, the main shopping street in Oldfield Park.

'What on earth is that?' asked Susan.

'It looks like a giant rabbit hutch!' exclaimed Ann.

'Look, it's an air raid shelter and one day it might save our lives,' said Fred, irritated at the lack of appreciation of his efforts. 'It's sturdy and safe - no bombs are going to get through that steel. See - you release these hooks here, then you lower the side down so you can get inside. You make it into a bed, put in some blankets and pillows and a flask of tea…and just lie there until the raid is over. It's a darn sight safer than hiding under a table or going outside to the public shelter.'

Pat sensed her husband's need for praise. 'Thank you, Fred, you've done well. Let's hope we never have to use it!'

CHAPTER 5

Bath, 1941

When July came Susan was on tenterhooks, hoping Frank would be back in time for their wedding. She was therefore beside herself with joy and relief when she opened the door on the Friday evening before the big day to find him standing there, large as life. And he wasn't alone.

'Frank!' Susan cried, flinging herself at him.

'I'm home!' He picked her up, swung her around and kissed her.

'You remember Alfie?'

Susan looked at the other sailor who was standing outside, waiting.

'Of course! Come in, both of you!'

Fred, Pat and Ann welcomed their guests with everyone talking at once. Frank sat down on the settee with his arm around Susan and said, 'I hope you don't mind me bringing Alfie along, but it was you gave me the idea, Susan! When you told me you'd seen Julie I thought, well I need a best man, and who better?'

Alfie laughed. 'I was surprised when I got your letter, Frank, but I'm very happy to be here. And isn't your Susan looking lovely!'

He ogled her in a way that made her feel uncomfortable.

'Julie told me you're at Royal Arthur.'

'Yes, suits me! And Julie loves it - home every night!'

'I wish you could find Frank a job there too!'

'Not so easy, I'm afraid,' Alfie said, giving Frank a wink, which Susan noticed but didn't quite understand.

'So where will you be going next, Frank?' asked Fred.

'I've got a second tour on SALAMANDER so it's back to the Med, but it will be shorter this time - I'll be home for Christmas. I'm leaving on Sunday evening. Sorry it's so soon,' he said, taking Susan's hand.

Frank told everyone about the important work they'd been doing at sea, remembering to say how much he'd missed Susan and was looking forward to their wedding tomorrow. Then he stood up.

'Well, thank you for the tea, Mrs B. We'd better be going now…'

Susan felt her heart sink. 'Why? Where are you going?'

'I haven't seen Mum yet, and Alfie's staying with us tonight.'

'Got to give him a bit of a stag night, haven't I?' said Alfie, grinning.

'Oh! But Frank, I haven't seen you for so long…'

'I know, love, but after tomorrow we'll have each other forever, won't we!'

He kissed her goodbye and as the sailors left the house Fred warned them, 'now, don't get too drunk, you two!'

'Course not,' said Alfie, 'you can trust me!'

'See you in church!' said Frank.

After they left the house Frank said, 'thanks, Alfie. You're a great pal.'

'Always happy to help an old mate. When I got your letter I thought, Christ, Frank needs to be careful here...'

'Yes...and thanks for your advice.'

'You're welcome. I hope it works out for you like it has for me and Julie - it is good to know you've got someone waiting for you at home, and you need somewhere to keep your kit. And as I said, as long as you keep getting jobs at sea you'll hardly notice the difference!'

'Thanks, Alfie, I'll remember that!'

'So, you're off back to the Med, lucky bastard. All those runs ashore!'

Frank chuckled. 'Hey - did I tell you about those belly dancers in Alexandria?'

'Yes, several times - but tell me again, will you?'

The wedding ceremony may have been a small affair but for Susan it was the biggest day of her life. She had spent months making dresses for herself and Ann, her bridesmaid, now a pretty blonde thirteen-year-old. Miss Daniels, Susan's supervisor at Bayer's, had managed to obtain a length of parachute silk and off-cuts of material, lace and ribbons. From these Susan had stitched and sewed, producing an exquisite, flowing white dress with long lace sleeves and a similar creation dyed in pastel blue for her sister.

Susan arrived at the local church with her father and Ann, all of them relieved to see Frank and Alfie there, looking smart in their uniforms. When Frank turned to see his bride walking up the aisle on her father's arm, carrying a posy of pink roses, the trepidation he had felt about being wed diminished. Susan looked beautiful, and when Alfie whispered, 'you're a lucky man!' Frank knew he was right. He suddenly remembered his hunger for her, down by the gasworks, and felt it again. Maybe being married wouldn't be so bad.

The vicar carried out the brief ceremony in front of the couple's family and friends. Pat watched her daughter, happy for her and wiping away a tear as memories stirred. Mavis sat with Mr Jones, proud of her son and his pretty bride, but in her mind she was elsewhere, remembering her own wedding day and the husband she had adored, so cruelly taken from her. Frank was almost as handsome, with those same deep blue eyes… She glanced at her watch. Not long now, then she could have a drink.

Frank gave Susan the wedding ring he had bought that morning, vows were made, the register signed, and it was done. Outside the church Mr Jones took some photographs then all the guests repaired to the Bishops' front parlour room for tea and sandwiches and a barrel of cider that Fred had managed to acquire.

There was a tiered cake - albeit made of cardboard - but it gave the opportunity to photograph the happy couple pretending to cut it.

Fred took his new son-in-law to one side and told him that his sister Elsie and her husband Edward had paid for Frank and Susan to spend the night at the Regina, a plush hotel in the centre of Bath. Frank was delighted, as he had neither time nor money to organise a honeymoon, and when at the end of the afternoon's celebrations he announced that they were going away Susan was overjoyed.

'Thank you so much!' she cried, kissing her husband, her parents, and thanking her uncle and aunt. 'I'm so happy!'

When the newly-weds were ready to depart Susan asked, 'but how are we going to get there? On the bus?'

'No,' said Frank, ushering Susan outside where Mr Drewitt had parked his Austin 7, decorated with a white ribbon.

'Your carriage awaits!'

When Susan awoke the next morning she lay there for a moment, looking around at the unfamiliar room. Smiling to herself she stretched out, enjoying the comfort of a decent mattress and quality bedding, then turned to look at Frank who was lying naked on his back beside her, his chest rising and falling with his breath. She had never seen him asleep; he looked handsome, young, muscular. Dark stubble covered his chin; she hadn't realised how quickly his beard grew.

She knew so little about him, and there was plenty she wanted to discover.

She was right; this time had been better than before. Being in a bed had helped, more comfortable than that night lying on the grass by the riverbank. And Frank had been nicer this time, gentler, more considerate. They'd made love as soon as they'd got to their hotel room, then gone down to dinner, a grand affair within the wartime constraints, and the first time they'd been out for a meal together. When she'd been able to take her eyes off her handsome husband, Susan looked around at the other diners. They included some well-off looking couples who, she later learnt, had de-camped from London to the relative safety of Bath and were living in the hotel for the duration.

Susan and Frank drank a bottle of wine - another first - and returned to their room, then - goodness - she blushed at the thought of what they'd done next. He was insatiable. They'd finally fallen into a deep sleep in each other's arms and now, here they were, together, the morning after.

Frank stirred and opened his eyes a fraction.

He looked at her strangely for a moment as if trying to remember who she was, making her feel quite odd, then he smiled and touched her face.

'Good morning, honey bunny.'

He rolled over and kissed her, and they made love once more before breakfast.

The newly-weds spent the day in Bath, walking hand-in-hand from their hotel opposite the newly-renovated Assembly Rooms, around the Circus and the Royal Crescent, enjoying the quiet of the Sunday streets. They walked through Queen Square where a huge air raid shelter had been built, big enough to take over a hundred people, then down to the Parade Gardens where they sat by the river, admiring the view of Pulteney Bridge and the weir.

'Look at us two, like a couple of grockles!' said Frank.

Susan laughed. 'Yes! It's nice to pretend we're on holiday. And what better place to spend our honeymoon?'

Even with sandbags piled high and posters with dire warnings about 'careless talk', the city still had a charm all of its own. Although they had both been born and brought up only a couple of miles away it felt like a different world from the terraced houses and alleyways of Oldfield Park.

'Thank you so much, Frank.'

'What for?'

'For coming back - for being here. And for last night!' she said, blushing.

'I hope you didn't doubt me!'

'Of course not! But I'm so pleased it worked out.'

Then she sighed. 'We've got so much to think about, Frank. Where are we going to live when you come back, permanently, I mean?'

He kissed her. 'Don't worry about that, love, it will be all right. We've got to win the war first...'

'But it will be over soon, won't it?'

'I hope so, love...I hope so.'

Towards the end of the afternoon they wandered back home.

Frank went to say goodbye to his mother then came round to Susan's for tea. Afterwards the couple walked to the railway station and waited for the evening train to Portsmouth that would take Frank away. The couple embraced and he had to prise himself from her to board the train.

'I love you, Frank,' she cried, as he leaned out the carriage window to kiss her one last time.

'I love you too, Susan,' he shouted, as the train gathered speed and steamed into the distance.

CHAPTER 6

The Mediterranean, 1941

By now Frank was a salty sailor, used to the routine and good at his job. There were times when he'd been scared rigid when under attack, and even in the Mediterranean there were storms and rough seas to contend with. But he found that the comradeship with his fellow sailors and the professionalism and pride instilled in them by the Royal Navy made up for all the troubles. The crew were back in their blue uniforms now; the intense Summer heat had dissipated and when they arrived in Malta the weather was mild and a little light rain was falling.

At this point of the war Malta had been under siege for over a year, bombed to ruins by an enemy determined to starve the Maltese people into submission by attacking its ports and cities. Hundreds of people had been killed and many more injured, military bases and homes destroyed, and the stench of death pervaded the island. The population was on the brink of starvation, totally dependent on the convoys which were battling their way through to Grand Harbour, laden with food, fuel and emergency supplies. This was what war meant, thought Frank - disease, hunger, poverty, hardship.

After witnessing such harrowing scenes it came as a relief when they set course Eastwards to Alexandria. On-board activity veered between action stations and periods off-watch when things were uncannily calm. To take their minds off imminent danger the crew amused themselves playing cards and reading. Frank noticed an old Able Seaman who was doing some carving and asked him about it.

'This is called scrimshaw,' said the man, whose name was Walter. 'An old sailor taught it me years ago when I was up in Greenland on the whalers. It's a good way to pass the time.'

Frank watched, fascinated, as Walter slowly and carefully etched tiny grooves into a piece of whalebone cut into an oval shape about two inches long.

'I've got the best stash of whalebone this side of the Arctic! The secret is to have a very sharp knife, a needle and a steady hand. When the engraving's finished I rubs Indian ink into the grooves so you can see the picture, then I gives it a good polish to make it nice and smooth.'

'What are you drawing?'

'A salamander - a little lizard - after our ship. I've done loads of them. The lads like to send them home to their sweethearts. They can be made into a pendant - see, I drills a little hole so they can thread a chain through it and wear it as a keepsake.'

Walter looked up at Frank and said, 'you got a girl at home, then?'

'Yes, Susan - my wife!'

It felt strange, saying that.

'You can have this one, if you like,' said Walter, 'I'll make it special for her.'

'That would be great!' exclaimed Frank, '...although I haven't got much spare cash...'

'That's all right, lad. Give me a few smokes, that'll do.'

HMS SALAMANDER docked in Alexandria where they were to stay for a week, taking on provisions. Frank went ashore with Tug and returned to the bar they had been to before, once more mesmerised by the belly dancers.

'Not sure if I should be here now I'm a married man!' said Frank, feeling a tinge of guilt.

'Rubbish!' replied Tug, 'you know what they say - when the pennant numbers are below the horizon, anything goes!'

Frank looked out for his favourite girl, Fatima, but couldn't see her. When he asked for her, a different girl by the same name appeared, not quite so pretty but equally accommodating.

The next day, comparing notes, Tug looked at Frank and laughed at him. 'Don't you see? They *all* say their name is Fatima!'

Frank felt daft but tried not to show it.

'It's all part of the game,' explained Tug. 'It's like - if anyone asks where you're from, you say 'London'. They think it sounds exciting and it's the only place in England they've ever heard of. Saves explanations…'

Frank suddenly felt six years old again, growing up without his father, having to live on his wits, picking up knowledge as and when. Listen and learn, he thought - listen and learn.

The ship made its return Westwards and one evening Walter called Frank over and presented him with the finished engraving. The work was exquisite: the salamander's body was twisted in the shape of an 'S', its four short limbs and feet splayed out at right angles to its body, with a rounded head pointing to the right and a long tail pointing to the left. The intricate pattern on its body was filled with black ink, standing out against the creamy white of the whalebone.

'It's wonderful!' said Frank, looking at the piece in awe and at the old man with respect. 'And what's that little squiggle there?'

'I've added that just for you. It's an 'S', for 'Susan'.'

'Thanks so much, she'll love it! I'll post it to her when we get to Gib.'

Frank had been putting off writing to Susan, his mind still full of exotic dancers. Still, this pendant gave him a reason to drop her a line and salve his conscience. Then he told Walter, 'I saw a whale in the Atlantic when I first joined. It was amazing, watching it swimming along then jumping out the water.'

The old man nodded his agreement. 'They are wonderful creatures. You can use every part of them, you know - the meat, the blubber, the bones…nothing goes to waste. Yes, we had a good time on the whalers.'

Bath, 1941

Susan was thrilled to receive the pendant. Her parents had given her a silver chain for her eighteenth birthday, so, as instructed by Frank, she strung the pendant onto it and fastened it around her neck.

She showed her mother. 'Look, isn't it lovely! Frank said he asked the old sailor to make it especially for me and to put the 'S' for 'Susan' on it.'

'That's wonderful, love!' said Pat, looking at her joyful daughter and admiring the pendant. Then Susan showed it to her father who was sitting in his armchair, reading.

'Very nice, lovely piece of carving. You're a lucky girl,' he said, returning to his newspaper.

Later, alone in her bedroom, Susan stood, holding the pendant on its chain in her right hand, feeling its smoothness. She thought of Frank and their passionate lovemaking on their wedding night and her left hand went instinctively to her belly. Tomorrow she had an appointment to see a doctor, but she already knew she was pregnant.

CHAPTER 7

Bath, 1941

Pat was at the local Post Office queuing to post a parcel when she happened to see a notice pinned on the board:

'Junior assistant required to run messages and help with office work. Enquiries to Miss Hill, Postmistress.'

Pat knew Miss Hill of old and asked to speak to her. That evening Pat told Fred about it, then she had a word with Ann.

'When you leave school I know you don't want to work at Bayer's, like Susan. Well, I think I've found something that might suit you…'

It was Ann's fourteenth birthday in December and although she would prefer to stay on at school and take exams she knew her parents couldn't afford it, and in any case it wasn't what girls round here did. She dreaded the prospect of working at a machine, day in, day out, so was quite taken with her mother's suggestion.

Within the week everything was arranged: Ann would leave school at Christmas and start work at the Post Office in the new year.

Pat may have sorted out one daughter's problems, but she hadn't anticipated the next event. One evening after tea Susan announced, 'I've got some news.'

Her parents and sister looked at her, waiting.

'I'm going to have a baby!'

There was a moment of complete silence, and Pat's face fell.

'That's your life over, then,' she responded, bitterly. 'Oh Susan, you're only eighteen, and that's it, now - you'll be tied up for the rest of your days!'

'Mum!' cried Susan, shocked, 'it's not that bad! It just happened a bit sooner than I would have wanted, that's all...'

'A honeymoon baby!' said Ann.

'Well, thank God you are married...' said Pat.

Fred kept quiet - this was women's talk. But he did say, 'you'll need to find somewhere to live, Susan - you can't stay here with a baby. You and Frank will have to find a place to rent. I'll start asking around if you like.'

'But Dad, the baby's not due till April! And Frank won't be back for ages...'

She was disappointed - no, - hurt, at her family's response.

'You're not going to throw me out, are you?'

'Of course not, but think about it - a baby here just wouldn't work, you sharing a room with Ann, and it waking us up at all hours...'

'I could help you,' said Ann.

Pat scoffed at that idea. 'And what would you know about looking after a baby?'

'Well I don't know anything either!' exclaimed Susan, 'and a bit of help from someone around here would be nice!'

She started to cry and ran from the room.

Ann got up to follow her but Fred said, 'sit down, leave her. She's got herself into this, and she'll have to find a way out.'

The Mediterranean, 1941

Frank read Susan's letter in disbelief. A baby! Surely not... Then he thought of how he'd got carried away with her on their honeymoon and it began to make sense. How the hell was he going to get out of this one? He'd gone along with the wedding, but this... He couldn't bring himself to write to Susan - he had no idea what to say to her. They were due to return to Portsmouth for Christmas leave and he would discuss it with her then. Meanwhile, he put the matter to the back of his mind. They were about to embark on their next mission to Malta and he had other, important, things to think about.

However, at sea nothing was predictable. Soon after they left Gibraltar there was a terrible noise, the whole ship shook violently and its engines ground to a halt. Divers were sent overboard to discover the cause of the problem: the propellor had struck an underwater obstruction and to make things worse a fishing net had become entangled in the blades.

The Captain broadcast the news to his disappointed crew: they would have to be towed back to Gibraltar where the ship would be put in dry dock, the damage inspected and the necessary repairs carried out. They would not return to Portsmouth and Christmas leave was cancelled.

'That's life in a blue suit!' said Tug.

The men were billeted ashore in a dormitory next to the hospital, cooped up like chickens but being on dry land made a welcome change. In the evenings they entertained themselves watching films in the Mess including old gangster movies which Frank enjoyed, reminding him of nights at the Scala with Susan. Thinking about her, and knowing he wouldn't see her at Christmas, he couldn't put off writing any longer. He needed some peace and quiet to think, so when he was off-duty he took himself for a hike up the Rock. At the top he sat down, looking across the Straits to North Africa and, at last, put pen to paper.

Bath, 1941

As Christmas approached Susan was becoming increasingly anxious about the future. Her bump was showing, things at home were uneasy and she still hadn't heard from Frank who could be dead for all she knew. She had told Mavis Fowler about the baby, and although she seemed pleased Susan had the impression that the past meant more to her than her future grandchild.

When a letter from Frank finally arrived, Susan cried with relief and took it upstairs to her bedroom.

Gibraltar, December 1941

Dear Susan,
I'm sorry I haven't been able to write to you for so long.
The ship had an accident at sea and we're stuck here in Gib, all leave cancelled. I was looking forward to coming back and seeing you for Christmas but now I won't be able to.
The news about the baby has come as a bit of a shock! That must have been some honeymoon we had…! I still can't believe it. We never talked about these things, honey bunny - everything happened so fast. You must take care of yourself. It's a good job you've got your family there to look after you.
I don't know what our programme will be and I can't say when I'll be home. But rest assured that I love you and I'm thinking of you.
Wishing you all a Happy Christmas,
All my love, Frank

Susan was dismayed that Frank wouldn't be coming home but understood that these things couldn't be helped. She was more concerned at his apparent lack of interest in the baby, and his letter didn't give her the comfort she craved. Were all men like that? she wondered. Hopefully he'd come round to the idea and things would be all right when he returned. She put the letter down and touched the scrimshaw pendant that she wore around her neck all the time.

'Don't worry,' she said to her bump, 'he loves us, and he'll be back.'

When one of Fred's colleagues mentioned that he had a room to let in Lower Weston, near the railway station, Fred thought it would be ideal for Susan. They went to see it and Susan was quite taken with the light and airy bed-sitting room on the second floor of a detached house, close to home but giving her the space she needed, and somewhere for Frank to come back to.

Susan gave up work, relying on her parents to help her out, and spent her time preparing her new home for the baby and getting to know her neighbourhood. She enjoyed walking up the hill to the local shops, passing a row of Victorian villas with wide bay windows, gables and front gardens. Certain houses, like the one she now lived in, had been converted into flats and bed-sitting rooms but others remained family homes for the better-off. She noticed a particular one called 'Eagle House' which had two stone eagles on pillars by the front gate, very grand, and was told that Dr David Roberts, an obstetrician, lived there with his wife. She saw him once as he left the house, a kindly-looking gentleman who beheld her heavily pregnant state and doffed his hat to her.

When Susan next went to her parents' a letter from Frank was waiting for her.

Gibraltar, March 1942

Dear Susan,
Great news, the repairs are finished and SALAMANDER is now back and ready for action! We've all had enough of Gibraltar and it will be great to be back at sea. Here is a photo of us they took the other day, I've sent one to Mum too.

Susan picked up the photograph of the ship's company. There was Frank, in the front row, squatting next to a lifebuoy with the ship's name on it, smiling broadly, looking the happiest she had ever seen him.

She continued reading.

The other great news is that I've been advanced to Able Seaman! I can't tell you how chuffed I am. It will mean more interesting work and more pay which I know will be handy with the baby coming along. I've arranged an allotment for you to be paid every month which should help with the rent on the room you told me about.

I hope you're keeping well and looking after yourself. We're resuming convoy duty now so I won't be able to write for a while. But I'm always thinking of you.

All my love, Frank

Susan showed her parents the photograph.

'Very good!' said Fred.

'Well, he looks happy!' said Pat.

'Yes, doesn't he…' said Susan, unable to shift the thought that he loved his ship more than he loved her.

After her stint at the Post Office Ann took to spending Saturday nights with her sister to keep her company. Getting to the cinema wasn't practical for Susan now and she'd rather lost interest in films, having other things on her mind - the baby was due in two weeks, at the end of April. They would chat and drink tea, and Ann asked Susan whether she'd heard from Frank recently.

'Not since the letter I got last month,' she replied, 'but it's odd - I had a dream about him the other night. I heard him calling out to me, as if he was in the next room, but when I went to look for him he wasn't there.'

'How strange!'

'But it's all right, he'll be home soon.'

The Mediterranean, 1942

The torpedo came from nowhere.

One minute Frank was up on deck surveying the convoy against the dark sky of a brewing storm, a day's passage away from Malta, the next he was blown off his feet, high into the air as a massive explosion tore the ship apart. Moments later a second torpedo smashed into the stern to finish the job. The men didn't stand a chance. Sailors, their clothes on fire, ran screaming from the chaos, hurling themselves overboard from the burning deck as the ship's superstructure collapsed.

Frank fled from the spreading flames, feeling the heat all around him, clinging to a warped metal stairway as the ship lurched violently. A red-hot piece of debris fell onto his left side, searing his skin. Now he was in agony, his face on fire, screaming, then with a massive groan the ship broke in half and Frank was propelled into the flaming sea. Floundering in fire and boiling oil he desperately tried to keep above water, struggling between burning and drowning.

For a moment he saw Tug, gasping for breath, but there was nothing he could do to save him and he watched as his friend went under.

Frank grasped a piece of flotsam and clung to it, desperately, then he blacked out.

It took just three minutes for HMS SALAMANDER to sink beneath the waves.

CHAPTER 8

Bath, 1942

Late one Saturday evening Ann was running up the hill in the blackout, desperately searching by moonlight for the house with eagles on pillars by the front gate that her sister had told her about. At last she found it and hammered frantically on the door until a woman answered.

'Is Dr Roberts in? We need help, urgently! It's my sister, Susan Fowler, she's gone into labour! She's in terrible pain, she's shouting the house down! Please, please can he come and help?'

'I'm sorry, my husband's away, but I can come - I have delivered a few babies in my time!'

Wendy Roberts, a nurse, called to her son to tell him she had to go out, grabbed her coat and medical bag and followed the panicking girl onto the street. They quickly made their way down to Susan's where they found her on the floor, crying with pain. Wendy helped Susan up onto the bed and examined her while Ann fetched hot water and towels.

'The baby's on its way, there's no time to go to the hospital,' said Wendy. 'You need to be very brave, Susan, but I'm here to help you. Ann, hold her hand, will you? Now, breathe…'

Around eleven o'clock the air raid siren began to wail but the women ignored it, used to hearing aircraft flying towards Bristol, but within minutes they could hear the drone of enemy planes closer than they had ever heard them before. The planes dropped chandelier flares and incendiaries, lighting up the sky with orange flames, and the women realised with horror that tonight, Bath was their target.

Susan would never have made it down to the shelter so the three clung together, terrified, as the planes flew over the city, unleashing their deadly cargo of high explosive bombs. The cacophony of war erupted around them, shaking the whole house and shattering the windows. Susan cried out in agony as waves of pain swept through her body.

Suddenly there was a huge explosion and a fireball lit up the sky.

'It's the gasometer! It's exploded!' exclaimed Wendy.

An hour went by as the planes flew low over the city, machine-gunning people fleeing in the streets. Susan was exhausted, her hair wet with sweat, her face contorted as Wendy helped her in the final stages of her labour.

'You're doing well!' she said, as yet another bomb ignited close by, 'now push! Breathe! Not long now…'

In Oldfield Park, Fred and Pat had taken refuge in the Morrison shelter.

'Summat's up,' said Fred, 'sounds like there's more planes than usual. They're out to get us tonight!'

'I hope the girls are all right! At least they're together...'

Suddenly there was an almighty crash nearby and the couple clung to each other in the blackness. With every bomb that dropped, Pat realised her husband was shaking more than she was, shivering and sweating, and she held him tighter.

In Fred's mind he was blinded by flashes of gunfire and deafened by bursts of artillery screeching overhead. He could hear the screams of his injured comrades, see their horrific wounds, smell the stench of cordite and blood. Now he could hear someone crying hysterically, writhing in fear and anxiety while a woman tried to soothe the tortured soul.

Fred realised that the person crying was himself, and the woman was Pat.

Just after midnight, with bombs raining down and Bath ablaze, the baby entered the world.

'It's a girl!' cried Wendy.

Wendy washed the baby, wrapped her in a towel and placed her in Susan's arms.

'Your daughter...you have a beautiful daughter!'

The planes finally droned away and just after one o'clock the all-clear sounded. Pat slowly released Fred from her arms and kissed him.

'I'm so sorry, love,' he whispered, 'I'm so sorry. I lost it. Those noises - it just brought it all back, as if it were happening again, right in front of me…Oh Pat, what must you think of me? I'm so ashamed, you must think I'm a proper coward!'

He was still shaking.

'It's all right, love, I'm here,' said Pat, putting her own distress to one side. 'I'm sorry you had to face it again. How you used to endure that night after night, week after week…You're not a coward! I think you are a very brave man, Fred - a very brave man.'

They climbed carefully out of the Morrison shelter and looked around them as the dust settled. Windows were broken but at least the house was still standing. Fred ventured outside to find the row of houses opposite alight, with firemen fighting to put out the flames. The air was thick with dust, the ground covered in bricks, stones and broken glass. Fred heard his neighbours screaming out in pain as rescue parties scrabbled amongst the ruins to free them. For some it was too late and in the light of the fires he saw bodies, and parts of bodies, laid out on the ground. The injured were being carried on stretchers from the rubble of their homes into ambulances and taken away to hospital. The battlefield had come to his own doorstep.

Pat was about to leave the house and, re-asserting himself, Fred shouted, 'stay inside! You don't want to see this.'

Fred spoke to one of the wardens who told him, 'it's even worse in the city centre - the whole place is on fire! Them Jerries didn't hold back. Thank God it's over now.'

After the all-clear sounded Wendy Roberts left Susan, Ann and the baby, desperate to know whether her own house was still standing and her family safe.

'I'll come back later to check on you and the baby,' she said to Susan, 'just try and get as much rest as you can...'

Ann took charge, making sure her sister was as comfortable as possible and sweeping up the broken glass. She looked out at the city, orange flames leaping into the sky, and thought, so this is war, and now it has come to Bath. She knew life would never be the same again; she was fourteen and had grown up overnight.

Then she said, 'Mum and Dad...oh God, I hope they're all right!'

There was little Fred and Pat could do until daylight and the warden advised them to stay indoors and try and get some sleep. But how could they sleep, with danger everywhere, and not knowing whether their daughters were safe? The water pipes had been hit so they couldn't make some much-needed tea, then Pat remembered the flask they kept inside the shelter. She was fetching it when the siren wailed again.

'Oh no, they're coming back!'

German aircraft were invading the skies for the second time. Bath was aflame, and the large number of fires which were still burning from the first raid guided them straight to their target. The planes released high explosive bombs, striking right across the city and diving low, aiming to disrupt the work of the emergency services who were out there, exposed to attack.

Back inside the Morrison shelter Pat held Fred tightly as the deadly planes flew directly over their heads repeatedly, dropping bomb after bomb after bomb, as if Oldfield Park itself was their prime target. The raid was vicious, unmerciful, terrifying. Suddenly, with a flash of light and a monstrous roar a huge explosion blew their world to pieces.

A mile away, Susan and Ann were holding each other, protecting the baby, as bombs fell and fires erupted all around them. Deafened by the blasts, the sisters quaked at explosions nearby, fearing for their lives and those of their parents. The raid continued, unrelenting, for an hour, then more, until at last, as dawn broke, the all-clear sounded. The two slowly released each other, thankful to have survived another onslaught, looking down at their little miracle, the beautiful new baby, born in the blitz.

Pat lay inside the shelter and tried to open her eyes but couldn't see anything. Next to her Fred stirred, coughing, trying to draw breath. It was pitch black. Fred's hand went to his forehead which hurt and he could feel blood. Both of them were covered in layers of dust, bleeding from cuts from broken glass and small pieces of debris that had penetrated the cage, their ears still ringing from the blast. They had no idea how long they'd been there.

'Pat?' he managed to say.

'Fred!'

After what seemed like hours they saw a chink of light and could faintly hear voices above them. They both shouted out 'HELP!' as loudly as they could, then heard a man say, 'there's somebody here! Keep digging!'

Time froze while the couple waited for the rescue party to clear the rubble and stone that had buried them. At last Pat looked up and could see daylight. The warden reached in and lowered the side of the cage, helping them as they climbed out, coughing in the dust.

'Where are we?' asked Pat, confused.

Fred wiped the blood and dust from his eyes and looked around. 'The blast must have blown us outside.'

'Sorry, sir,' said the warden, 'your house has gone. And if you hadn't been in that shelter, you would have gone too.'

CHAPTER 9

Bath, 1942

Leaving her sister in an exhausted sleep, Ann ventured outside on Sunday morning and didn't recognise her surroundings. Buildings were reduced to rubble, fires were smouldering and a smoky orange glow hung over the city. It was hell on earth and she prayed that her parents were still alive. Ann ran past firemen and civil defence workers quenching flames, clearing fallen masonry in the desperate search for survivors. She reached Oldfield Park, disorientated, familiar landmarks gone, row upon row of houses completely wiped out. Panicking, she found the bottom of her street and saw with horror the gaping hole in the terrace where her home had once stood. She screamed and collapsed to her knees.

A warden went to her and Ann cried, 'my parents! My parents! We lived at number twenty-four - where are they? Are they dead?'

The warden comforted her and told her to go to the church hall where survivors were being looked after. 'I hope you find them, my lover,' he said as she ran, tears streaming down her face.

Ann passed others desperately seeking their loved ones among the chaos. People were pushing prams stacked high with their remaining worldly goods and a mobile canteen had been set up where folk who had nowhere else to go were standing, shivering, drinking tea and smoking cigarettes. Children were playing in the rubble, wondering what sort of game this was. Water spurted from burst pipes and everything was covered in thick yellow dust.

Ann arrived at the church hall and was directed to a list of names, but before she could read it a woman said to her, 'you're Fred and Pat's girl, aren't you? Yes, they're here - they're all right!'

Ann could see them now, down at the far end. 'Mum! Dad!'

Crying with relief Ann pushed her way through the crowd to find them, still in shock, with blankets around them, drinking mugs of tea, refugees in their own city, battered and bruised but alive.

When they saw Ann they leapt to their feet and hugged her, then amid their cries of joy Pat said, 'but where's Susan? Is she all right?'

'Yes! And she's had the baby - right in the middle of the first raid. A little girl! You are grandparents!'

The three sat together, overwhelmed with emotion. News of the safe arrival of the baby was wonderful, but what sort of world had she come into where bombs were dropped on ordinary, innocent people, their homes destroyed, their lives shattered? They listened in horror as reports came in of the devastation of Bath, which had been attacked without warning and had no defences. Thousands of buildings had been damaged, from Georgian terraces, churches, businesses, historic and industrial sites to people's homes, shops and pubs. Part of the Royal Crescent was damaged by fire but it was the neighbouring area that had suffered the full force of the bombs intended to destroy the historic landmark.

Oldfield Park had indeed borne the brunt of the second attack, the enemy deliberately seeking out densely-populated areas in order to kill and maim as many people as possible. Explosions had rocked Moorland Road, destroying shops and the Post Office; Miss Hill, the postmistress, was found among the dead. But the news they found hardest to bear was that the large public shelter outside the Scala cinema had taken a direct hit. Stories abounded of the bravery of the wardens who had tried to help people trapped inside, the narrow escapes and the personal tragedies. More than twenty people lost their lives in the very place they had sought safety; the true number would never be known.

That day many people fled from Bath, hoping to escape any further attack. Those with relatives in outlying villages upped sticks and left, walking many miles to get to their destination. Those who had nowhere to go took to the hills, literally, their children and a few worldly goods in tow, to spend the next nights sheltering in fields, under haystacks, anything to get away from the dangers of the city. Ambulances and fire crews were sent from elsewhere to supplement the city's own, and anti-aircraft guns put in place in case of a third raid.

When Ann got back to Susan's her sister was sitting up in bed, nursing the baby. She was relieved their parents were safe but distraught to learn that their home had been blown apart, so many buildings destroyed and lives lost.

Just before midnight there was a knock on the door. It was Wendy Roberts, the nurse.

'I'm sorry, I meant to come round earlier but I've been so busy, seeing to people,' she said, looking exhausted. Thankfully her own family and home had survived both raids and she'd spent the day helping others.

Wendy examined Susan and the baby and declared that all was well.

'Thank you so much for all you've done, I'm so grateful,' said Susan. She picked up her wedding photo from the bedside table and showed it to Wendy. 'That's my husband, Frank. I wish I could tell him about the baby but he's away at sea and...'

Susan was interrupted by the wail of the air raid siren. The bombers had returned.

The three women stayed together, sheltering the baby, terrified and outraged that the enemy should attack them for a third time. The city was better prepared now; the anti-aircraft guns that had been brought in were deployed and RAF planes were scrambled from a local airfield. But it wasn't enough to stop the enemy planes on their deadly mission. In the bright moonlight they released flares and incendiaries, then began the main attack. The aircraft dived down, criss-crossing the city with their cruel weapons, again machine-gunning the streets. For two hours the bombs came raining down, the sky on fire, the noise ear-splitting. The booming and crashing seemed even louder than before, the rattle of machine-gun fire ever closer. Then with a massive roar a bomb exploded directly above Susan's home. Walls and ceilings collapsed, the floor gave way and the women fell down, down, down, sinking under the rubble as the conflagration took hold.

The next morning it was Pat's turn to go in search of her daughters. Leaving Fred to inspect what remained of the railway station she made her way through the wrecked roads to Susan's, only to see, with horror, that the house where she'd lived had been reduced to a pile of smouldering rubble. Pat ran towards the ruins where wardens were shifting the debris, searching for survivors.

'My daughters!' she screamed, and one of the wardens took her to one side to try and calm her down.

'Now, tell me their names,' he said, looking down his list while Pat waited, frantic with worry.

'Right, here we are,' he said at last, 'Susan Fowler and Ann Bishop, and a baby. They were taken to hospital, one with a head injury and one with a broken arm, according to this.'

'Thank God!'

Relieved to know that her daughters were still alive, Pat thanked the warden and half-walking, half running, made her way along the broken road to the hospital, a mile away. Among the hundreds of people who had been admitted she eventually found her daughters in the maternity ward, Susan in bed with a bandage around her head, the baby asleep in a cot beside her and Ann, her arm in a sling, sitting in an armchair. After a tearful reunion Susan said, 'so, meet your granddaughter - born on the 26th April, in the middle of an air raid. What a start to her life.'

Pat looked at the baby and her heart melted. 'She's beautiful! Oh Susan, thank goodness you are all right! I'm sorry I was so horrid to you about it all...'

'Don't worry, Mum, it's okay. I just wish Frank could see her...Heavens, I've just thought - have you heard anything about Frank's Mum?'

'Mavis? No, I haven't. I'll see what I can find out.'

Everyone was terrified that the Luftwaffe would return for a fourth raid, but thankfully, that night, they did not. The following day Susan and Ann were discharged from hospital and having nowhere else to go, joined their parents at the church hall. On their way they passed the remains of the house where Susan had lived. As she looked at the wreckage it dawned on her that she had nothing: her personal possessions, the things she'd bought for the baby - the pram, the cot - had gone up in flames. All she had were the clothes the hospital had given her, her wedding ring and the pendant around her neck.

Fred and Pat were relieved when their daughters arrived, Susan carrying the baby in her arms, wrapped in a blanket. They cooed over the new arrival, a ray of sunshine amongst the heartbreak.

Fred said, 'she's lovely, Susan. I'm sorry if I was a bit hard on you…What are you going to call her?'

'I'm not sure…I haven't decided yet.'

Susan passed the bundle to Pat who held her for the first time, rocking her back and forward. She gently stroked the baby's head which was covered with soft, downy, coppery-coloured hair.

'Look, Fred! She's going to be a red-head, like you!'

CHAPTER 10

Bath, 1942

The church hall was a haven, providing shelter, food and clothing for the newly-homeless. Among the volunteer helpers Pat spotted Mr Jones the Church warden and he approached them, looking sombre.

'I'm afraid I have bad news,' he began. 'The house where Mavis had her room took a direct hit. They found her, yesterday…'

As Pat and Susan offered him their condolences, his eyes filled with tears.

'She had her difficulties, but she was a good woman.'

'Poor Frank…' said Susan. 'I'll write and tell him.'

'Thank you, I would appreciate that.'

It occurred to Susan that Mr Jones may know about another person of concern.

'Have you by any chance come across a nurse called Wendy Roberts?'

'Dr Roberts' wife? Yes, indeed - she was working with us all day Sunday, treating the wounded. A wonderful woman, so kind. She was killed in the third raid, early on Monday morning. A tragic loss.'

Susan was stunned.

'...but she was with me and Ann! I thought she'd been saved, like we were. That's terrible news!'

'It is God's will,' said Mr Jones. 'We have lost so many good people. There is going to be a mass burial of the victims on Friday if you want to come and pay your respects.'

Mr Jones went about his duties while Susan, shaking, sat down with her mother.

'I feel awful, Mum! Wendy came back, late, to check on me and the baby. It's my fault!'

'Don't say that, Susan! She was a very brave lady who was doing her job. You mustn't blame yourself.'

Susan borrowed some paper and wrote to Frank, telling him he had a beautiful daughter but passing on the sad news that his mother had been killed in the raids, along with the brave nurse who had brought their daughter into the world. She kept the letter brief, feeling too emotional and unable to find the words to describe the devastation around them. She told him they were homeless, but thankful to be alive.

More news came in of what the Hun had done to Bath. Over four hundred people had been killed in the raids and hundreds injured including many children, some of whom were evacuees. The railway was in ruins and the Regina Hotel, where Susan and

Frank had spent their honeymoon, had been split in half by a bomb and many people had died there - Bath hadn't proved to be the safe haven the rich exiles from London had thought. The Assembly Rooms opposite the hotel were a smouldering shell. People across Bath were mourning their loved ones and their lost homes, knowing that life would never be the same again.

Leaving the baby in Ann's care, Susan went in search of a functioning Post Office so she could post the letter to Frank. She walked past the ruins which had been Mavis' home and stood, looking at the remains in disbelief. Some young boys were there, scavengers, looking for anything of value. It angered her and Susan shouted at them, telling them to clear off, which they did. In a pile of fallen masonry she spotted something, a piece of paper creased and charred at the edges, and carefully removed it. It was the photograph of the ship's company on board HMS SALAMANDER, and there was Frank, squatting next to the lifebuoy, smiling at her. Susan caught her breath and held the photograph to her breast. She had lost so much, but at least she had this.

Her thoughts were interrupted by a voice behind her.

'Excuse me, Miss...'

She looked around to see a Post Office messenger boy in his smart blue uniform.

'Can I help you?'

The boy replied, 'please, Miss, I'm a bit lost. I've got this telegram for number twelve, but...well, there's nothing here, is there?'

Number twelve was where Frank's mother had lived. Susan's stomach churned horribly and she felt nauseous. 'Let me see it.'

The boy handed her a telegram addressed to Mrs Mavis Fowler.

'She was my mother-in-law,' Susan managed to say, 'she used to live here - but it's all gone, and she was killed.'

With a mixture of sorrow and relief the boy said, 'I'm sorry. It's terrible. Er - is it all right if I leave the telegram with you?'

'Yes, of course.'

'Thanks, Miss,' he said, and went on his way.

Susan stared at the envelope, full of foreboding. Slowly, she opened it, took out the telegram and read:

'DEEPLY REGRET TO INFORM YOU FOLLOWING ENEMY ATTACK ON HMS SALAMANDER YOUR SON ABLE SEAMAN FRANK FOWLER IS MISSING AT SEA.'

Susan let out a howl of anguish and collapsed on the ground.

When she came round she was back in the church hall, having been rescued by a passing warden. She started screaming and her mother tried to calm her.

'But he can't be lost!' Susan cried, 'I was on my way to post a letter to him!'

Pat held her hysterical daughter while she wept, the unposted letter, the telegram and the photograph by her side.

*

On the 1st May the Bishop family, among hundreds of other grieving Bathonians, stood in the cemetery as the dead were buried and prayers said. The whole city was in shock, unable to believe what had happened, and those that remained were thankful to have survived. After the three raids the German bombers had turned their deadly attention to other cities, and everyone prayed that they would never return to Bath. Later, the raids became known as the 'Baedeker' raids, after the German guidebook which informed the plan to attack places of cultural and historic interest, a cynical Nazi ploy.

Fred and Pat remembered friends and neighbours who had died; Ann thought of Miss Hill and a schoolfriend who had been killed with her family in the shelter by the Scala. Susan held her baby close to her, unable to get Frank out of her mind, but today her thoughts were also with his mother and Wendy Roberts. She caught sight of Dr Roberts at the service, standing between two young men whom she assumed to be his sons; he looked bereft, empty - much as she felt herself.

That evening Susan asked her mother to watch the baby for a while.

'I'm going out, there's something I must do.'

Susan walked to Eagle House, knocked on the door and asked to see Dr Roberts. A woman in her thirties called Sonia showed her into the living room where he was asleep in his chair, and gently woke him.

'How may I help you?'

'My name is Susan Fowler. Your wife delivered my baby girl, right in the middle of the first raid, she was so brave, and I am so grateful. Then she came back and she was with me and my sister when the house was hit and…'

Susan stated to cry.

'Sit down my dear!' said Dr Roberts. 'Sonia, bring her some tea, will you?'

Susan dried her tears and said, 'what I want to ask you is, I would like to name my daughter 'Wendy', in honour of your wife. Would that be all right?'

Now Dr Roberts had tears in his eyes.

'What a touching thought. Wendy would be delighted. Of course, my dear, that would be wonderful.'

As Susan drank her tea, Dr Roberts - David, as he insisted she call him - asked about herself and her family. Mentioning Frank, the tears flowed again.

'My husband's missing at sea. We had a telegram just a couple of days ago…'

'I'm sorry,' said David, 'you've lost so much…'

'But so have you!'

They sat for a few moments in mutual sympathy, then Susan got up to leave, saying, 'I've taken enough of your time. Thank you, and I'm so sorry about your wife. She was such a lovely lady.'

David stood up and shook hands.

'Thank you, my dear. Take care of yourself and your baby - Wendy…' Then he added, 'do stay in touch, won't you? I'd be interested to know how you're getting on.'

'Thank you. Yes, I will.'

*

Fred had been doing some thinking. The raids had dragged up memories of the First War, but he had survived that, and now he would survive this. He still had his family to provide for and it was time to build new lives for them all, but first there was something they needed to do.

He led his wife and daughters to what remained of their old street and they stood, looking at the gaping hole where their house had once been.

'We've lost everything,' said Pat.

'I've lost Frank,' said Susan.

'We were so happy here, weren't we?' said Ann.

Then Fred said, 'yes, we've lost our home and our old lives have gone. But now we need to say goodbye to the past and look to the future, make a new start. The main thing - and the only thing that really matters - is that we've got each other.'

Then, looking down at the baby in Susan's arms he said, 'and now we've got Wendy, haven't we...our little Wendy.'

PART TWO

CHAPTER 11

Gozo, 1942

Nina Camilleri, sixteen years old, was walking along the beach at her home on Gozo, the small island just to the North West of Malta, enjoying the fresh early morning air before the heat of the day set in. A gentle breeze wafted in from the calm azure sea, a sharp contrast to the storm which had raged the previous night. There had been another battle a few miles out - they'd been able to hear the roar of the guns even above the bellows of thunder. Nina wondered which ships had been damaged or sunk this time, how many men killed and injured - it would take some days for the reports to filter through.

The girl wandered along the shoreline, enjoying the warm sea as it lapped over her bare feet. As usual, debris had been washed up and she looked here and there to see if there was anything worth harvesting. There were items of clothing - a shoe, some wood, pieces of metal, the detritus of people's lives on board ships. She picked up some cans of food which were undamaged and whose contents might be edible. Then something else caught her eye, half in and half out of the sea, the waves rolling over it - a shape, a form, the colour of flesh. She walked slowly towards it, dropped the cans and screamed as she saw the body of a naked man, lying face down on the sand. She looked towards her house and screamed again as her father and mother ran towards her.

'Stand back!' instructed her father, kneeling down and carefully turning the man onto his back.

The left side of the young man's body was raw, red and blistered, his face was burned, his hair singed. He was covered in scratches and bruises. Nina's father put his ear to the man's chest.

'Holy Mother!' he exclaimed, 'I can hear a heartbeat. He's alive!'

The three made the sign of the cross.

'We must save him!' cried Nina.

Together, they carried the unconscious man back to their house and laid him on a bed. Gozo's only doctor had been despatched to Malta when the bombardment started. They would have to look after the injured man themselves.

Nina's mother, Ester, had nursed fishermen and farm workers who had suffered accidents in the past, but had never seen anyone with wounds as extensive as this. She would need all her knowledge of the ancient remedies to help this poor man.

'Nina! Fetch me my medicine box.'

Immersion in seawater had kept the wounds clean, and now she had to protect him from infection. Ester mixed honey and resin to make a poultice and applied it to purify the man's sores and promote healing, then washed him with spring water, gently wiping away the blood and sand that covered his body.

'We must let him rest. We have done all we can. He is in God's hands now.'

'I wonder who he is?'

'Probably a foreign sailor. Did you hear the battle last night? It's a miracle he survived.'

Ester's husband, Alessandro, was a hard man who wouldn't normally put himself out to help a stranger. But something about this young man who had been swept to his shore drew his attention. Beyond his injuries he could see that he was muscular and strong, a fighter. Alessandro had a feeling that, if and when he recovered, he might be useful.

'For the moment, I think it's best we don't tell anyone he's here. You girls look after him and we'll see how he progresses.'

Ester taught her daughter how to dress the man's wounds and together they watched over him as he drifted in and out of sleep, convulsing and writhing with pain. Ester gave him water and her special potion of thyme, opium and belladonna to soothe him. The weeks passed and the young man lay there, dimly aware of the sounds around him, voices, children playing, shouting, waves breaking on the shore and planes flying overhead. The heat became stifling, the height of Summer. They put a mosquito net over his bed and closed the windows to keep out the sun. In the evening he heard the chirping of the cicadas and the warm air was filled with an earthy, herbal scent.

Gradually, in his waking moments, inch by inch the man became aware of his body, able to feel and move his right arm and leg but feeling pain all the way down his left side. He was aware of an unusual, sweet smell from the strange mixture they applied to his wounds. He tried to speak but the sound stuck in his throat. As his body and mind slowly began to heal, he started to remember. He was in the sea, on fire, his ship was sinking. He could hear men screaming, see the flames, feel the heat as the ship exploded. He must have passed out and washed up ashore, like a piece of driftwood, and these people had rescued him. He suddenly thought of his shipmates and saw them disappearing beneath the waves. Was he the only survivor? He cried out in distress and the women came running to him. Ester gave him her potion and he slept once more.

One morning the young man opened his eyes a fraction to find the father of the house sitting, looking at him. He spoke to him in English.

'So, you are awake! How are you feeling? You understand me?'

The young man gave a slight nod of his head.

The man lit a cigarette and exhaled a plume of smoke.

'I am Alessandro Camilleri. My wife and daughter have been looking after you. They saved your life. We found you on the beach, here in Gozo. I wonder who you are…? An Englishman…a sailor, probably…And who is missing you? Who thinks that you are dead?'

He touched his face, squeezing the flesh on his right cheek.

'You tell me when you're ready to talk, my friend, and I will be here to listen. Then we can decide what to do with you.'

He laughed, got up and left the room.

Bath, 1942

'This will be fine, Elsie, thank you so much,' said Pat, gratefully, as she looked around the bedroom with its view over the back garden. 'It's so kind of you and Edward to put us up for a bit till we get settled.'

'You're more than welcome. I said to Edward, I can't see my brother homeless when we've got rooms to spare. Ann can have the single at the front, and we'll put Susan and the baby in the dining room - there's a camp bed for her and we've brought our old cot down from the loft.'

Fred's sister and her husband had bought their brand-new three-bedroom semi-detached house in a pleasant square on Combe Down on the South side of Bath before the war. When the raids started the community headed underground, seeking safety down the mines where Bath stone was extracted. They emerged two days later into dust and destruction, but Edward and Elsie were among the luckier ones whose house suffered only superficial damage. Their own children had flown the nest and when Elsie tracked down Fred and his family, homeless in the church hall, she had to act. They were comfortably off - Edward held a responsible position as Head of Works for Bath City Council - and could afford to be generous.

Swathes of housing across Bath had been destroyed and the raids had left hundreds homeless. Danger was everywhere - many chimney stacks atop the Georgian terraces were askew and at risk of falling, collapsing through the buildings and onto the people below. Teetering buildings were demolished, covering everything in a thick film of dust and acrid smoke hung in the air. There was the danger of unexploded bombs and everyone learnt to look out for the chequered flags which marked their locations. Bath was in ruins and it would take decades to restore the city to its former glory.

Sharing a house was never going to be easy, but for the first six months the two families managed to get along. Fred was fully occupied getting the station back to order and supervising repairs to the railway, Elsie and Pat shared cooking and household chores between them, and Susan concentrated on looking after Wendy. Ann's job had gone up in smoke along with the Post Office, but on the back of the experience she had gained there, and without a trace of nepotism, her uncle found her a temporary job with the Council.

At first Wendy slept through the night, but when she began teething she took to waking and screaming the house down. Susan would do all she could to soothe her, but the more fraught things became the more the child refused to settle.

They were all very tolerant but one December morning, after a particularly bad night, Susan overhead Edward talking to Elsie in the kitchen.

'I'm sorry, I know he's your brother, but if that child keeps us awake one more night I'm going to go mad! I haven't had a decent night's sleep for weeks - it's worse than when we were being bombed by the bloody Germans! You'll have to talk to them, Elsie.'

'I know, Edward, but it will pass - remember what ours used to be like!'

'Yes, I do...but that was different. We should be past all that now at our age - nappies drying in front of the fire and all...and the kid will be crawling soon, getting into everything. I'm being serious, Elsie - I can't stand it any longer.'

'But Edward, Christmas is coming - we can't chuck them out now!'

'Why not?!'

'You know why! The least we can do is give her a month's notice, let her have a chance to find somewhere else.'

Edward wasn't happy.

'All right, Elsie. One month. But not a moment longer!'

Susan felt terrible. Her uncle and aunt had been so kind, but she had clearly outstayed her welcome. She needed to talk to someone outside the family that she could trust and sought out Miss Daniels, her old supervisor at Bayer's, who she had always got on well with. Miss Daniels, a feisty, independent woman in her thirties, was delighted to see Susan and offered her a job - Bayer's had suffered some bomb damage but was now back in business. Moreover, when Susan explained her predicament she said, 'I have a spare room - you can take it if you like. I could do with a lodger.'

When Susan announced to the family that she was moving out Edward looked visibly relieved and everyone tactfully agreed that it was for the best. The only person who seemed upset was Ann, who was close to her sister and would miss helping to look after her baby niece.

Miss Daniels had a two-up two-down terrace in Oldfield Park, near the Bishop family's old house, but hers had escaped the worst of the raids. The spare room had a single bed and space for a cot.

'Thank you, Miss Daniels, this is lovely!'

'You can call me 'Jean' when we're not at work! Now, there's a few things here belonging to my old lodger, I'll collect them up and put them in a bag for her. Then it will be all yours.'

'Oh dear - I hope we won't be in the way!'

'Not at all. Frances is in the Wrens - she's working down in Portsmouth.'

'I see…will she mind us having her room?'

'No, it's all right. We'll sort something out for when she comes back on leave…which isn't very often…' she added, regretfully. 'Now, get yourself organised then we'll have tea.'

Jean suggested that Susan arrange to leave Wendy with her neighbour during the day - 'she's got five young children so one more's not going to make much difference, and she could do with the extra money. She'll lend you a cot, too.'

Susan settled in well, but Wendy was still teething and woke at nights. After a particularly bad one when Wendy had screamed for England, Susan approached breakfast apologetically.

'I'm so sorry, Jean, I just couldn't get her to sleep. Look - do you want us to leave?'

Jean smiled.

'Don't worry, Susan, I never heard a thing. I have my special weapon - it's how I put up with the noisy machinery at work...' she said, taking something from the pocket of her dressing gown.

'Earplugs!'

CHAPTER 12

Gozo, 1943

The Maltese Winter, with rougher seas and welcome rain, had passed. The young man heard Alessandro say the siege had ended and the Allies were on the offensive; the war continued without him. Sleepy Gozo seemed to have escaped the raids, having no targets of military interest, and the family appeared to want for nothing, playing out their simple lives much as their ancestors before them.

Lying in bed the young man followed their days from cock crow to nightfall. They had a farm; he could hear the bleat of goats and smell their stench; there were sheep, and chickens. Alessandro was a fisherman and sat with other men on the shore while they mended their nets. The family went to church on Sunday and sometimes the women would kneel by his bed, praying for his recovery. There were some younger children but they kept them away from him. Once he opened his eyes a crack to see a little girl of about nine years old standing at the foot of his bed, staring at him, wide-eyed. When she realised he had seen her she gave a shriek and ran from the room.

As Spring approached he found he could open his eyes fully without pain, but his throat still suffered from the smoke he had inhaled. He watched the girl as she washed him, humming a tune to herself, happy in her work. She was dark, like her mother, an olive-skinned Mediterranean beauty with eyes the colour of black coffee. She shaved him, running the razor smoothly over the right side of his face. As she gently dabbed his face dry with a towel he opened his eyes and looked straight at her. She caught her breath. His eyes were the deepest shade of blue.

He struggled to sit up and she placed a pillow behind his head for support.

'Don't try and speak. We are looking after you. You've been with us for a year. My name is Nina.'

Nina felt responsible for the foreigner she had found on the beach, as if the Holy Mother herself had arranged for him to be there just for her. At first she had found his terrible wounds hard to look at, but guided by her mother she overcame her aversion and learnt how to tend them. She admired the strength of the young man, his will to survive, and as his injuries began to heal she felt a certain satisfaction, knowing she was helping to mend him. His deep blue eyes had been a revelation. Other people would look at his scarred face and maimed body and be curious, even repulsed, but to her he was beautiful.

Ester decided it was time for the patient to get out of bed. Propping him up on either side, she and her daughter encouraged him as he cautiously placed one foot in front of the other until he learnt to walk to the far side of the room and back. He realised how much his muscles had atrophied, how far he had to go to get fit again, and the left side of his body held him back, hurting as he tried to move.

Local people showed little interest in the stranger and knew better than to ask questions. The younger children - girls of eleven and nine - were told that he was a friend who had been hurt and needed looking after. Ester put a chair out on the terrace where he would sit during the day to get some fresh air and look at the sea, wearing one of Alessandro's hats and a loose shirt to protect his delicate skin from the sun. His favourite pastime was watching Nina as she walked along the beach, the sea washing over her bare legs, her long dark hair flowing down her back. Occasionally Alessandro came and sat with him, speculating out loud as to who he might be and where he was from, then he would get up, grip the young man's right shoulder and say, 'tell Nina when you are ready to speak to me,' and walk away, laughing quietly to himself.

The young man observed local fishermen as they worked, speaking in Maltese, a harsh-sounding language involving noises in the throat and spitting. It reminded him of the Arabs talking in the cafés in Alexandria. Some nights he noticed lights out at sea and heard voices in a different language, maybe Italian? But they were still at war and Italy was the enemy. He also observed occasional visitors, business types who came over from Malta to meet Alessandro in his study, the door firmly closed. They would emerge, smoking cigars, and after much shaking of hands, depart, all parties satisfied with their day's work. Evidently, Alessandro was more than a simple farmer and fisherman.

One morning the young man opened his mouth and realised he could speak without pain. But he also knew, in the same moment, that he needed to think carefully before he uttered a word to anyone.

Bath, 1943

In April a special service was held in Bath Abbey to commemorate the first anniversary of the Bath Blitz, as the raids had become known. The Bishops attended along with hundreds of other bereaved families. Baby Wendy's birthday would forever be linked to those terrible nights when Bath was ablaze, when Wendy Roberts and Mavis Fowler were killed, and Frank lost at sea.

A week after the service Susan took Wendy to visit David Roberts who was delighted to see them and listened as Susan told him about their new home at Jean's and resuming her job at Bayer's. He was still a man in grief and put all his energies into caring for his patients at the hospital. He shared his home with a family of German Jewish refugees, the Blumfeldts, who looked after him and Eagle House while his sons were away in the Services.

As Susan got up to leave David said, 'thank you for coming to see me. In these strange times it's good to see people doing the best they can, carrying on... We will always miss the loved ones we have lost, but we have to keep going - there is no choice.'

He gave her a kiss on the cheek.

'I've enjoyed your company today. Do drop by again, won't you - it's good to stay in touch.'

*

One evening Susan came back from work, collected Wendy from the neighbour's then went home to find an unexpected visitor in the sitting room.

'Susan,' said Jean, 'this is Frances.'

Frances, an attractive brunette in her Wren's uniform, got up and shook hands.

'Pleased to meet you, Susan. Jean's been telling me all about you and your little girl.'

'Lovely to meet you too! But you'll want your room back…'

Jean and Frances exchanged a glance and Jean said, 'no, it's all right, Frances is only here for the weekend and she can bunk up with me.'

They drank some tea and chatted, then Frances said, 'I hear your husband was in the Royal Navy?'

'Yes, he was an Able Seaman on HMS SALAMANDER.'

Frances nodded. 'I've seen her in Portsmouth, she was a fine ship. Such a tragic loss - I heard she went down with all hands.'

'Yes - I still can't believe it.' Then she got up to show Frances the scrimshaw pendant she always wore.

'All I have is this, my wedding ring and a photo of the ship's company. I lost everything else when the bombs hit.'

Wendy, who was crawling around on the floor, looked up and gurgled, as if to say, 'what about me?'

They all laughed.

'Well yes, I've still got you!' said Susan, picking her up and kissing her.

'She's a delight!' said Frances, 'I love the colour of her hair - sort of coppery-red, isn't it. And those green eyes - wow!'

'Yes, her eyes were blue to begin with, like her father's, then they turned to this wonderful green...'

'She's going to be a beauty, isn't she?'

'Yes! But a noisy one, I'm afraid...'

That night Wendy awoke crying in the early hours but fortunately quietened down when Susan comforted her in her arms. As Susan held her baby she became aware of other night-time noises coming from the next room - a creaking bed, sighs and moans of pleasure...

More curious than shocked, Susan realised that women could be more than friends with each other. It didn't help her, though - all she wanted was Frank.

CHAPTER 13

Gozo, 1943

It was time to confront reality, and the young man spoke his first words to Nina.

'Thank you for looking after me,' he said, in a gravelly voice.

Nina gasped.

'You can speak! I knew you would get better. I never doubted you.'

'You are an angel.'

She laughed. 'I am not, but I think our prayers to the Holy Mother have helped. What do you want?'

'A mirror. Could you bring me a mirror?'

'Yes…I will fetch one.'

Nina returned and the young man looked at his reflection. The skin on the left side of his face and neck was scarred and his hair and beard on that side had refused to grow back. His left eyebrow and eyelashes were missing. His face had an odd, lop-sided look and when he turned his head he saw that the top part of his left ear had completely burnt away.

He had grown used to the sight of his red and wrinkled arm and leg, but it came as a shock to see his face. He'd never thought of himself as a vain type but knew girls had been drawn to his handsome looks and felt a pang of sorrow that those days were over. He wondered what the hell he must have looked like when he was first washed up on the shore, and how brave Ester and Nina had been to take on the task of looking after him.

Nina took the mirror from him, sat on the bed and held his right hand.

'It is hard for you, but you will get used to it. Your body is healing well and in time your scars will fade. Mama and I will look after you as long as you need us. The main thing is, you are alive, and the person inside you is still there. And now you can speak!'

She was right, but he didn't want to say anything - the shock of his appearance had stolen his words away.

Ester put a wireless in his room so he could listen to news bulletins and music from Rediffusion Malta. He learnt that the Allies had taken Sicily, and Italy had switched sides and declared war on Germany.

He thought about the Royal Navy and its sailors at sea, doing what he used to do, and wished he could be back with them. Then he looked at his injured body and knew there was no longer a place for him.

What should he do? His mind was in turmoil.

At last his thoughts turned to home. Home! In his head the word triggered an avalanche of memories and emotions which he had been shutting out, unable to cope with the feelings they evoked, but he couldn't hide from them any longer. Home was Bath, rows of terraced houses on a hill, and his mother, slumped in her chair. And home was Susan.

He pictured Fred, Pat and Ann in their cosy house in Oldfield Park with Fred coming back in the evening from the railway station and Pat cooking chitterlings for his tea, Susan in the bed-sitting room in Lower Weston with a baby that must be - what - eighteen months old?

They would have sent a telegram, 'Missing at Sea' they called it, but everyone knew it meant 'dead'. He imagined Susan, the grieving widow, and wondered what tales she would tell the child about his - or her - Daddy. He had loved her, for a while, but everything was different now. She wouldn't want him back, looking like this - she was better off thinking he was dead. And he would have made a lousy father. Susan was a sweet girl and would soon find someone else to look after her and the baby. As for his mother, as long as she could get a drink she wouldn't miss him.

He considered his options. When he was more mobile he should go to Valletta and hand himself over to the naval authorities. If he didn't, he would be a deserter, the lowest form of man. But surely he'd suffered enough for his country? Let others take on the task of winning the war.

In any case he wasn't fit enough to serve so he would be discharged and repatriated, to face - what? People he'd known, staring at his disfigured face? A wife and a crying baby in a poky room? A boring job in Bath?

And then there was Nina...

Every time he saw her his heart filled with joy. He loved her gentle touch, the way she moved with such grace, her voice... She was totally devoted to him and he wondered what he had done to deserve her attention. He trusted her completely and didn't want to leave her. He finally admitted to himself that he was in love.

He started to think, what if he didn't go back? What if he stayed here?

Bath, 1943

Susan spent the Christmas holidays with the family on Combe Down, pleased to be in their company for longer than the odd afternoon she normally spent with them. Frances was home on leave so it gave her and Jean some privacy together.

Ann, who had just celebrated her sixteenth birthday, loved having Susan back and doted on Wendy. They bathed the child together and Ann said, 'I do miss you! It gets so boring, being with old people all the time - it's like having two sets of parents fussing over you. I wish I could go out more, have some fun like you did. Remember when you used to climb out the back window?'

'And look where it got me!' replied Susan, trying to wash a wriggling Wendy with soap and a flannel. 'It's different now, though, with the war - you can't expect to have the same freedoms nowadays. How's your job going?'

'Well, that's boring too...I spend most of my time making tea! And they're all old as well. I mean, I'm grateful to Uncle Edward for finding me something and I like working in an office, but I want to do more than that…'

'They might find you something interesting if you ask! Or you could always look somewhere else, find out what opportunities there are…'

'Mmm - I'll try,' said Ann, unconvinced.

The next Saturday, Susan met Ann in Bath to go to the January sales. With Wendy in the new push-chair Susan's parents had bought her, and armed with clothing coupons they had saved up, they started at the top of Milsom Street, window shopping in Jolly's, working their way down the hill to the stores which were more within their price range. In Plummer's, Susan bought a warm Winter coat - she needed it in the bitterly cold weather they were having - and Ann bought a skirt and blouse for work. They were just going next door to treat themselves to a cup of tea at the Old Red House café when they saw coming towards them a sailor and his heavily pregnant wife, pushing a pram.

'Is that you, Susan?' asked the woman.

'Julie!' cried Susan, 'Alfie! And who's this?' she asked, looking into the pram.

'This is Albert!' said Alfie, proudly, 'and as you can see he's got a little sister or brother on the way!'

'And this is Wendy,' said Susan, as her daughter stared up at Alfie and pointed at him. She hadn't seen a sailor before.

Rather awkwardly, Alfie said, 'we were so sorry to hear about Frank...I still can't believe it, poor bloke...'

Julie looked embarrassed. 'I'm sorry, Susan, we meant to get in touch when we heard, but we didn't know where you were, and...'

'He must have been very brave,' said Alfie. 'And are you managing all right?'

'Not too bad, and today I've got my sister to keep me company.'

'Ann, yes, I remember you from the wedding. You're a bit more grown up now!'

He ogled Ann in the same way that had unnerved Susan in the past.

'Your daughter's beautiful,' said Julie, 'I love her red hair! Frank would be proud of her. I hope we have a girl next time...'

'If not we'll keep trying till we do!' Alfie nudged his wife playfully with his elbow.

'Are you still at Royal Arthur?'

'Yes...keeps me out of trouble...'

They stood awkwardly for a moment then Ann said, 'we'd better get going, Susan.'

'Yes...well, it was lovely to see you all and good luck with the birth!'

'Thanks!' said Julie, as she and Alfie went on their way.

When they were out of earshot Ann said, 'I don't like him.'

Susan replied, 'do you know - neither do I!'

*

As Easter approached Jean said to Susan, 'I need to tell you something.'

Jean didn't beat around the bush, so Susan prepared for the worst.

'It's Frances - she's been offered a job in Bath, at the Empire Hotel with the Admiralty. There's something big going on - God knows what - and they want her to come and work here with the naval engineers. So…'

'She needs her room back?'

'I'm sorry, Susan - I've loved having you and Wendy here, but…'

'All right…how long have we got?'

'Frances starts her new job in April.'

'A month. Okay, I'll look for somewhere else - and we can always go back to my uncle and aunt's, they won't mind having us for a short while.'

'Thank you, Susan, I knew you'd understand. And…' She hesitated, uncharacteristically, '…I have appreciated your discretion. Thank you.'

Susan nodded. 'Frances is your sweetheart, isn't she?'

'Yes…she is. And it will be good to have her home again - Portsmouth has really suffered from the bombing, worse than we have, and I do worry about her.'

'She's a lovely woman - you're very lucky.'

'Yes, I am.'

*

Housing was at a premium in Bath after the bombings and Susan had difficulty finding a place that would accept a young child. After a month of searching she found herself back with her uncle and aunt, only temporarily, she stressed, as Edward reluctantly climbed into the loft to retrieve the cot (now only just big enough for Wendy).

But Ann had an idea. She showed Susan a job advert she'd read in a copy of the *Bristol Evening Post* her father had brought home from the station:

'LADIES WANTED FOR FACTORY AND
OFFICE WORK. EXCELLENT RATES OF PAY
AND WORKING CONDITIONS.
ACCOMMODATION AVAILABLE. APPLY TO:
WD & HO WILLS, MANUFACTURERS OF
CIGARETTES AND FINE CIGARS,
BEDMINSTER, BRISTOL'

'I've been speaking to someone at work who knows Bristol and they told me this company is a really good employer,' said Ann. 'They reckon that with the war people are smoking more, so the factory's expanding and needs workers. They have rooms to rent, very reasonable, and there's even a nursery! It would be perfect for us!'

'But why would you want to go and live in Bristol?'

'To get away from here! Don't you see, Susan, it would do us both good to make a new start and do something for ourselves. I know we'll miss Mum and Dad but we won't be far away, and we'll have each other. Have a think about it, won't you?'

Susan loved her home city, all the more so since the Jerries had tried to destroy it. Gradually, ruined buildings were being cleared away and plans made to re-build historic sites and provide housing on a massive scale when the war ended. No matter how many bombs fell on it, no matter the buildings lost to the blaze, nothing could take away Bath's own unique beauty.

And yet…Susan found it hard to walk around Oldfield Park without thinking about her old life and when she passed the empty space where their house had once stood she cried every time. One day, she thought, someone will live in a new house here and not even know it's where our home used to be. Working at Bayer's made it worse; she remembered the hours she had spent at her sewing machine, day-dreaming about Frank and his kisses. She missed him so much and seeing Julie and Alfie again had made her wonder how her life would have been if Frank had come home. He would have adored Wendy and perhaps she would be expecting another baby by now. Two years on she still found it hard to accept that she would never see him again.

She thought about Ann's suggestion to move away. This time, the war was offering her and her sister an opportunity and perhaps they should take it.

CHAPTER 14

Gozo, 1944

The young man listened to the wireless, learning about the great invasion called D-Day and following the progress of the Allied forces as they fought their way across Europe and into Germany. Sea battles continued in the Mediterranean where the Allies were attacking the enemy's supply ships, and now he heard Spitfires, Hurricanes and Beaufighters flying overhead. The war would soon be over, and what then?

The more he thought about it, the more obvious it seemed.

Why go back?

People at home thought he was dead. Here, nobody knew who he was. He could start from zero, re-invent himself, like a story from one of those old films he used to watch at the Scala with Susan. He'd spent all his life having to adapt to different situations, from losing his father to learning the trade of the butcher, then joining the Royal Navy and becoming an Able Seaman, and he could do it again. He could stay quietly here, on Gozo, till the war ended, and just not go home. He could become a new person with a new name. But who did he want to be?

Finally, he came to a decision and asked Nina to fetch her father. It was time to talk to him.

Alessandro joined them on the terrace and said, 'Nina, you can leave us now. Go and take a walk along the beach.'

When the two were alone the young man, in a rasping voice, said, 'Alessandro...thank you for everything you and your family have done for me.'

'My wife and daughter have nursed you well. So, you are ready to talk about your future?'

'Yes.'

Alessandro lit a cigarette. 'When the war ends, do you want to go back to England?'

'No, I want to stay here. I have nothing in England.'

They watched Nina as she wandered along the shoreline wearing a sarong, enjoying the warm sea as it lapped around her legs.

'I think you like my daughter.'

'Yes, I do, very much. She is the most beautiful girl I have ever seen.'

'In fact I think you are in love with her.'

What was the point in denying it?

'Yes...yes, I am.'

'Is she the reason you want to stay?'

A slight hesitation, then, 'yes.'

Alessandro exhaled. 'If you want to stay here and make a new life for yourself you will need papers - passport, birth certificate, identification documents. I can help if you wish.'

The young man nodded, slowly. 'And what would you want from me?'

Alessandro sat back, pleased they were beginning to understand each other.

'I may be a simple fisherman, but I have other interests too. I need an assistant, somebody I can trust. It is my biggest regret that I have no sons - I love my wife and my daughters, but women are no good at business, they get too involved, too emotional…Some of the decisions I have to make are very difficult and I need someone to work for me who will not flinch, who will do as I direct.'

The young man sensed danger, but if this was to be the price of his new life, he was prepared to pay.

Alessandro continued. 'War has offered many opportunities, and peace, which is not far away now, will bring even more. It is a foolish man that will not seize them. So, this is my proposal. In due course I will introduce you to my associates. We will tell them you came to Malta after the war to pursue your business interests. We met, and you fell in love with my beautiful daughter. You can marry her - I think it will make you both happy and I would welcome you as my son-in-law.'

'Marry Nina? But that would be wonderful!'

'All I ask is that you look after my daughter and do what I tell you.'

With the promise of Nina, this deal was too good to refuse.

'All right, Alessandro…all right. I accept. Thank you.'

'Excellent. I will explain the situation to Nina and arrange your papers. Now tell me, what is your name?'

After weeks spent pondering his future identity - places, movie stars and friends blurring into one - he had made his decision. He took a deep breath.

'My name is James Robinson,' he said. 'I'm from London.'

Frank Fowler was dead, but James Robinson was very much alive.

CHAPTER 15

Bristol, 1944

From its beginnings as a tobacco shop in eighteenth century Bristol, WD & HO Wills had grown into one of the largest international tobacco companies in the world. By the 1930s their factories in Bristol and around the country employed thousands of people, particularly women, whose nimble fingers and delicate touch were required in production of the popular cigarette brands of the day - Woodbines, Capstan - as well as pipe tobacco and fine cigars. Many said the war was fought on the back of Wills cigarettes, and tea.

With their excellent references from Bayer's and Bath City Council, the company offered Susan a job on the production line and Ann a position in the accounts department, and they both accepted. Fred and Pat were saddened to see their daughters and granddaughter moving away but understood their reasons and would look forward to their visits at the weekends.

Before they left Bath, Susan took Wendy to see David Roberts, passing on the way the empty space where her bed-sitting room had been. Although she'd only lived there a matter of months she felt sickened, knowing that the place where she'd given birth to her daughter had been destroyed, and Wendy Roberts with it. The scars of those terrible nights would stay with her forever.

David was delighted to receive them and listened with interest as Susan told him about her and Ann's new venture.

'It sounds perfect! I'm so pleased for you.'

It was over two years since the raids, and Susan told David yet again how awful she would always feel about the loss of his wife in such horrific circumstances.

'I miss Wendy so much,' he said, sorrowfully. 'I blame myself. I should have been here that night, but I was working in London.'

Hearing the name, toddler Wendy, sitting on the floor with a picture book, pointed to herself and said, 'me!'

Susan and David laughed.

'Clever girl!' said Susan, picking her up and sitting the child on her lap.

'Your flame-haired beauty! Wendy is your phoenix, rising from the ashes. You have lost so much, my dear, but you have an adorable daughter. She is the key to your future.'

*

The Wills factory in Bedminster was a welcoming community and Susan and Ann soon felt part of it. They were given rooms to rent, there was a place in the nursery for Wendy, free health care, a canteen, sports and social club, a library and, of course, discounted cigarettes which both girls took advantage of. On Fridays, pay day, the workers would pour out of the towering red-brick buildings onto the streets and spend their money in nearby pubs, shops and cafés. By the end of the year, Susan had been promoted to supervisor of the Woodbine production line and Ann had caught the eye of Brian, a young warehouse manager who made no end of excuses to visit the accounts department in order to chat up the pretty blue-eyed blonde. By all measures, their move was a great success.

The sisters and Wendy returned to Bath for Christmas (with holiday pay), full of praise for the company, pleased with their new lives and armed with gifts of cigarettes and pipe tobacco. When they had settled in and caught up with the news, Pat took Susan to one side and said, 'I have something for you. Last Sunday I went back to our old church and I saw Mr Jones, the warden. He gave me these.'

Pat handed Susan an envelope containing some sepia photographs of Susan and Frank's wedding.

Susan looked at the young girl in her white dress, arm in arm with the sailor in uniform, and stared at them as if they were strangers. Another picture showed the couple in the Bishops' old house, pretending to cut a cardboard cake.

Susan felt faint and sat down.

'Mr Jones thought you'd want them, knowing we'd lost our own copies. He's kept one of Mavis - he still misses her.'

'That's so kind of him. Of course I want them, although....'

She looked at her mother.

'Sometimes, Mum, I wonder if it ever happened at all - me and Frank. If it wasn't for Wendy…! And this…'

Her hand went automatically to the scrimshaw pendant.

'…but now I can look at these photos and remember that we really did get married. I'll write to Mr Jones and thank him.'

Each Winter of the war seemed colder than the one before, canals froze and became skating rinks, and with fuel being short, Susan, Ann and Wendy huddled around the only fire in their rooms to try and keep warm. But the end of the war was in sight. As 1945 gathered momentum great strides were made in Europe with the Allies crossing the Rhine and on St Valentine's Day the RAF bombed Dresden, killing over twenty thousand souls. At the end of April Hitler killed himself in his Berlin bunker and Germany surrendered.

In Bedminster, the 8th May, Victory in Europe Day, was a working day like no other. The Wills employees gathered in the canteen to listen to Winston Churchill's broadcast on the wireless which was relayed to them through loudspeakers. They cheered with joy and relief in celebration that the war in Europe was over, singing and dancing, everyone thankful that loved ones would soon be returning home, and that was when Susan finally accepted that Frank would not be among them.

Gozo, 1945

After a suitable interval following VE Day, Alessandro arranged for a priest to marry his daughter to James Robinson. Nina was ecstatic; she was deeply in love with this man whom she fully believed had been sent to her by the Holy Mother. James' thoughts flew briefly to another wedding, a long time ago, but he had been somebody else then. This was bigamy, but who would ever know?

After the ceremony Ester embraced her daughter and new son-in-law. Alessandro followed, hugging James and kissing him on both cheeks.

'Welcome to the family,' he said.

On their wedding night Nina came to James in what was now their bedroom. He looked at her while she slipped off her dress and underwear and got into bed naked beside him.

She put her finger to his lips. No words were needed.

She knew every inch of his body as well as she knew her own. She had dressed his wounds, she knew where he felt pain, where his injuries had healed, which areas were sensitive. She gently caressed the healthy side of his body, then softly kissed his scarred skin. She kissed him on the mouth, then carefully knelt astride him. He looked up at her, spellbound by her loveliness, her long hair tumbling around her shoulders and over her breasts as she slowly gyrated her hips. Clasping her by the waist he pulled her closer to him, the desire they had both felt for so long unleashed.

In the shadows of the doorway Alessandro stood, watching them.

CHAPTER 16

Bath, 1946

'Oh Fred, this is wonderful!' exclaimed Pat, 'look - our own bathroom! Better than the old privy. I love the kitchen - it's so compact - see this table here, it folds away into the cupboard. And everything's so *clean*!'

'First class!' said Fred. 'Two bedrooms - that will be perfect - one for us, and one for the girls when they come to stay...and look, at the back there's even a little patch of garden.'

'You'll take it, then, will you?' asked Edward.

'Of course!' Fred and Pat said, together.

Using his contacts at the Council, Edward had ensured that his brother-in-law and his wife were high up the list to be re-housed in one of the new pre-fabricated bungalows that were springing up in new estates on the South side of the city. This particular one in Twerton was ideal, close to their old neighbourhood and familiar faces.

Fred hired a small van to move their few belongings and some second-hand furniture they'd acquired. After nearly four years, with hugs and kisses of thanks, they said goodbye to Elsie and Edward, grateful for all they had done, and eager to make a new start.

As they waved them off Elsie said, 'so, we're back to just us two! I'll miss them, but I'm so pleased they've got their own home now.'

'So am I!' replied Edward, putting his arm around her and giving her a kiss.

The Winter of 1946 to 1947 was the worst of all. Roads were impassable, the railways didn't run, basic foodstuffs were still rationed and with the shortage of fuel, everywhere was freezing cold. Work continued in the factory as usual, but Susan and Ann weren't able to get back to Bath until the thaw began in the Spring. The sisters loved visiting their parents' prefab, but it was never going to be their home - their lives were in Bristol now, especially since Ann and Brian had got engaged.

In April when Wendy was five she started at the local infants school along with other factory workers' children. She was a bright, lively child and thrived, enjoying her lessons and making friends easily. When anyone asked about her Daddy she repeated what her mother had always told her: he was a brave sailor who had been killed in the war before she was born. She loved sitting on her mother's knee while Susan showed her the photographs of their wedding and the picture of Frank on board HMS SALAMANDER.

'He's the handsome one on the left, next to the lifebuoy,' Susan would say. 'He was so proud of his ship. He was an Able Seaman.'

Best of all, Wendy loved to hear the story about the scrimshaw pendant, the child tracing with her finger the special squiggle, the 'S' for 'Susan' that Frank had asked the old sailor to carve, uniquely for her.

Gozo, 1947

To begin with, Alessandro employed James on the farm. Season by season, as his body grew stronger, he was taught how and when to sow potatoes, pumpkins, melons and tomatoes, and to harvest fruit from the trees. The scorching earth was irrigated using water pumped from the ground, powered by a blinkered donkey condemned to walk in never-ending circles. Ester and Nina showed James how to look after the sheep and goats, explaining that shoats were a cross between the two. They kept poultry and rabbits, and one day when Ester was about to kill and prepare a rabbit for their meal James said,

'I can do that, if you like. I used to be a butcher.'

He took hold of the rabbit, swiftly broke its neck, then skinned, gutted and cleaned it, finally presenting the neatly-jointed meat to Ester, ready for cooking. He was pleased to have re-discovered his skills. Even old Drewitt would have been proud of that one, he thought.

Ester was impressed and told Alessandro.

'A butcher!' he exclaimed, 'and a very good one at that! You have hidden talents, my friend!'

The next part of James' apprenticeship, as he thought of it, took him to the seashore where he sat with the fishermen, mending their nets and gutting fish. He longed to get to sea, and as his mobility and balance improved the fishermen took him out in a traditional wooden fishing boat called a *luzzu*, a fifty-foot motor-powered vessel painted brightly in red, blue, green and yellow, with a pair of eyes drawn on the bows. They went out during the day to show James the areas they fished, according to the seasons, the currents and the weather. The boats were sturdy and stable even in stormy seas, designed with a high bow and stern rising above the rest of the boat in order to protect the crew from the spray.

James loved being back on the water, enjoying the movement beneath him and the smell of salt in his nostrils. Down at sea level the perspective was completely different from being up on the deck of a warship; here, James felt at one with the sea birds above and the fish below, grateful to the salt water that had bathed his wounds and the sea-Gods that had carried him safely to shore. As they travelled further out he remembered the first time he had seen Gozo, the golden island caught between the azure sea and the sky, never dreaming that he would one day become part of the ancient landscape, sitting with the fishermen on the beach and tilling the land.

During the Winter months James went with them at night, laying nets which drifted in the current, checking them every hour for their harvest of little tunny. Other nets would be set on the sea bottom and left to trap octopus and cuttlefish. At sunrise they would haul them in, ready to sell their catch at the market that morning. In better weather the boats would travel further out to sea, seeking horse mackerel and red mullet, attracting the fish with strong lights.

After another productive night, James took his turn steering the boat back towards land. Against the pink sky of dawn he was able to make out the early risers working on the farm, and next to the farmhouse he could see a new building, the house with a terracotta roof which Alessandro had had built for his daughter and son-in-law. When the fishermen reached the shore, Nina walked down to greet James with a smile and a kiss. She looked radiant - pregnancy suited her well. He put his good arm lovingly around her shoulders, holding her close, and as they walked up the beach towards their home he felt like the luckiest man in the world.

CHAPTER 17

Malta, 1947

During the war, spared from the raids, Gozo had been Malta's market garden. Clever farmers had sold produce to their besieged and starving brothers at a premium and were now looking to invest their profits, taking advantage of new opportunities that peacetime presented.

Alessandro counted businessmen, builders, politicians and councillors among his associates, several of whom went back many years and were known to his father before him. Alessandro had money to invest, and not just from farming and fishing - sufficient to say that certain deals he had concluded during the war had proved lucrative. He was ambitious and had a talent for spotting openings and seizing them. In the ruins of Valletta, where others saw buildings destroyed and holes where homes had been, Alessandro saw a thriving new city with modern housing, office buildings, hotels full of tourists and car parks.

'Car parks?' exclaimed one of his fellows. 'Hardly anyone in Malta owns a car!'

'But they will!' declared Alessandro.

After the war, the Maltese islands were self-governing but were still in effect a British colony. Although the Maltese people were forever grateful to Allied forces for breaking the wartime siege, and their own bravery had been recognised by the award of the George Medal, resentment was growing. Malta was a fortress economy, dependent on the British military for its wealth, and Alessandro longed for the day when Malta would re-gain its independence and open itself to the world, with all the money-making chances that would bring with it.

As Autumn approached Alessandro said, 'James, it is time for you to come with me to Valletta.'

They left early, catching the ferry to Malta then taking a taxi across the sun-burnt landscape until they reached the city. James had last seen Valletta from the decks of SALAMANDER but had never set foot there. Alessandro showed him around, walking with him through the ancient city streets, narrow and steep, with flights of stone steps. The upper storeys of the houses had enclosed balconies which overhung, almost meeting those of their neighbours opposite. Stray cats prowled around in the residual heat and the stench from the drains was appalling.

The devastation from the war was obvious. The worst areas had been cleared, leaving gaping holes in the city's structure, but other ruined buildings still stood, burned black from the fires that had raged.

Some empty spaces had been taken over by market traders selling dried meats, vegetables, clothes and lace. In the centre the roads were packed and noisy with trucks, motorbikes, carts pulled by horses and donkeys, a few cars, people shouting out to each other, and church bells tolling.

Alessandro led James to a leafy square where they sat at a pavement café and ordered coffees and the local favourite snack, *pastizzi*, a lozenge-shaped pastry filled with ricotta cheese. James looked around, fascinated: he had grown used to sleepy Gozo and hadn't seen so much activity for years. They watched people passing by and going into the church on the square, women dressed in black, covering their heads with scarves and crossing themselves. Beggars and barefoot children hung around, asking for money.

Alessandro lit a cigarette. James felt his lungs had suffered enough smoke and declined his offer.

'So, James, this is our future. There is much work to be done in Valletta and money to be made. My associates are coming to Gozo next week and it is time for you to meet them. But before that, now you have seen Valletta, tell me what you think.'

James looked around at the age-old, sand-coloured buildings and the massive church. He thought carefully, knowing a lot depended on his answer.

'I agree there are many opportunities here. Your country is ancient, and people will always come for its history and traditions. But you need to attract younger people too, with families - they would love the sun, the beaches and the sea. Make Malta a holiday island! And visitors want somewhere to spend their money - shopping at local markets, going to nice places to eat and drink, and entertainment - cinemas, music, dancing - give them some fun!'

Remembering Alexandria he added, '…and you need bars, and girls…'

As if in response to this horror the church bell started to toll loudly.

James snorted. 'Yes…I suppose your Catholic Church will need some convincing!'

'Our Church is a powerful force, but in this modern age even that may change…'

'Indeed. It's important to give people what they want. And things they don't even *know* they want!'

'Ha!' exclaimed Alessandro, 'my thinking exactly! So, this is my plan - we buy land and we build - hotels, shops, restaurants - then we rent them to people to run and take a share of the profits.'

'Sounds good!'

Alessandro beckoned to the waiter and ordered two whiskies.

'We will discuss this at our meeting next week, but I'm pleased we have a similar view. Let us drink to our new venture.'

'Our new venture!' said James as they clinked glasses.

Unfortunately, Alessandro's associates didn't see matters in quite the same way.

When the four visitors arrived, James, honoured to be invited to his first meeting, followed them into Alessandro's study and closed the door.

Their host introduced James whom the men accepted at face value - if Alessandro trusted him, so did they.

Alessandro unrolled a map of Valletta and spread it on the table.

'This is the land I want to buy,' he said, indicating an area close to the square where he had taken James, 'and this is what I want to build.'

The men listened as he outlined his plans, then sat back, looking doubtful.

'This is all very well, but where are these tourists going to come from to fill these hotels you propose to build? And how will they get here?'

'And do we really want our island to be overrun by foreigners? - pandering to their wishes, entertaining them? It's not what we, the Maltese people, do!'

'Our Church will never accept such sinful over-indulgence.'

The fourth visitor, a councillor from Valletta, said to his fellows, 'I understand what you say, but Alessandro is right. Things are changing and we will have to change also, whether we and our Church like it or not. But I must tell you, Alessandro, that other people have expressed an interest in buying this land - in fact we on the Council are currently considering a generous offer.'

'Who from?' asked Alessandro.

'George Galea.'

Alessandro looked at him and laughed, scornfully.

'George may have plans, but it is I who will buy this land.'

The men started talking at once, and Alessandro held up his hand for silence.

'James, tell us what you think.'

James took a deep breath. 'I agree with Alessandro - Malta needs to look to the future. I can understand your reservations, and I don't have answers to your questions. There is a risk involved with this investment. But I know one thing for sure - nothing stays the same. If you want to survive you have to accept change and adapt to it, otherwise you'll get left behind.'

'You see,' said Alessandro, 'my son-in-law has a good instinct - he has travelled, he knows about these things.'

Then he addressed the councillor. 'Marco, I will make a realistic offer for this land and *you* will ensure that my offer beats George Galea's.'

Marco fidgeted in his chair and looked uncomfortable, but said, 'very well.'

'Excellent!' proclaimed Alessandro. 'James - go and get some cigars, will you?'

When the men left Alessandro put his arm around James' shoulders and walked him to his house where Nina was waiting, holding their baby daughter, Elena, to her breast.

James ventured a question.

'Who is George Galea?'

Alessandro chuckled.

'The Galea family think they own Valletta, but they don't. We are going to show them we mean business! And you, James, are going to help me.'

CHAPTER 18

Bath, 1948

In December, on her twenty-first birthday, Ann married Brian, her first and only love. Ann felt strongly that she wanted to return to Bath for her wedding as a last goodbye to the city she loved before returning to Bristol and starting married life with Brian in their new house on the Wills estate. Pat got in touch with Mr Jones and arranged for the ceremony to take place at the same church in Oldfield Park as Susan and Frank were wed.

It was over six years since the bombing raids had wreaked death and destruction on the community. Many of the properties which had been damaged had been repaired or demolished, with new buildings taking their place. Pat and Fred came over from nearby Twerton, pleased to be back on their home territory in spite of all the changes. Much as they loved their prefab, it would never take the place of their first home.

Ann was a beautiful bride, wearing an exquisite white silk gown her sister had made for her using material provided by Jean Daniels, and six-year-old Wendy was a delightful bridesmaid in pastel pink. After the ceremony the wedding party repaired to the upstairs function room at a local pub for cider and a finger buffet. To thank her for the dress material, Ann had invited Jean and Frances to the wedding. They were pleased to catch up with the sisters and Wendy.

'Your daughter's beautiful!' exclaimed Frances, 'I knew she would be, with those eyes and that hair!'

'She's a clever girl too, aren't you?' said her proud mother while Wendy relished all the attention. 'She loves school and has made lots of friends, haven't you?'

Wendy nodded. 'I like school dinners, they're lush,' she said, making the women laugh.

Jean said, 'Frances is working in the Admiralty, at the Empire Hotel.'

'I was posted there just before D-Day, with the Wrens, then after the war they offered me a civilian post so I stayed there.'

'Good, I'm pleased it's worked out well for you both,' said Susan.

Elsie and Edward were happy to see their younger niece married and had bought her a three-piece suite as a wedding gift. (Brian had organised a honeymoon in Minehead and didn't need the help they had given Frank and Susan). At the end of the afternoon Susan went to help Ann change out of her wedding gown and into her going-away outfit, a smart tweed suit which would be of use in the office.

Ann said, 'thank you for today, Susan. I knew it would be difficult, with memories of Frank, but I really wanted to get married here. Like a final goodbye.'

'It's all right, I understand. It's your day, and Frank is long gone now. I'm going to miss you at home, though - it's just me and Wendy now.'

'But I won't be far away - I'll still see you most days!'

The sisters gave each other a hug. 'We've seen some changes, haven't we?' said Ann.

'Yes - but we really can look ahead now, you a married woman an' all. Brian is a good man and I wish you all the joy in the world.'

A taxi arrived to take the happy couple to the railway station and the guests threw confetti and waved goodbye. As the wedding party broke up Jean said to Susan, 'do stay in touch, won't you, and let us know how Wendy gets on.'

'Of course!'

Pat looked at the two women as they walked away, arm in arm.

'It was good of them to come, and to provide all that material for the dresses,' she said to Susan. 'But…there's something odd about them, don't you think?'

'I don't know what you mean!' she replied.

Malta, 1949

The building programme in Valletta was proceeding apace. Alessandro made James responsible for hiring and firing, giving him free rein to recruit local men to take charge of teams of labourers from North Africa who had settled in Malta after the war. James was on site every day, inspecting progress and quick to quell any sign of trouble, motivating his workers with stick and carrot, finding that they could work very well, but preferred to be lazy. The men accepted orders from this strange-looking Englishman with the scarred face, aware that he was a hard taskmaster and son-in-law of Alessandro Camilleri.

The buildings were rising high; this particular site would accommodate a ten-storey hotel with a swimming pool on the roof. A gang of Libyan workers were erecting wooden scaffolding and while they were having their break, squatting on the ground smoking vile-smelling cigarettes, James noticed a young Maltese man, a stranger, talking to them, but when he saw James he made a swift exit.

'What did he want?' asked James of Guiseppe, who was in charge of the scaffolding party.

Guiseppe shrugged his shoulders in typical Maltese fashion and held out his hands, palms upwards.

'He says we are not paid enough. He says he knows where we can find work with more money.'

'I see! And where might that be to?'

The man looked at his shoes. 'I don't know…on another site in the city…'

'Mmm…well let me know if he comes here again. I don't want him bothering us. And now you can get these lazy bastards back to work!'

That week, after they had collected their wages some of the Libyans didn't return. James wasn't concerned as there were plenty more who wanted jobs, but he mentioned it to Alessandro who said, 'you must meet this stranger, James - talk to him. Show him around so he can see what good work we are doing and how lucky our labourers are to have jobs with us. But be careful: building sites can be dangerous places…'

James understood. The next time the stranger appeared, Guiseppe brought him to James who greeted him and took him on a tour of the site, praising his workers and agreeing that perhaps they did deserve higher wages. Then he said, 'Guiseppe, I have to go to the office now but please show our friend the wonderful work our scaffolding team is doing.'

Ten minutes later James heard a scream as the man hit the ground. James called an ambulance and ran out to help, but it was too late - blood was oozing from a gash in the man's head and his dead eyes stared upwards.

It was an unfortunate accident.

Later, James gave Guiseppe a generous bonus.

Alessandro sent his condolences to the dead man's family, repeating what he had told James: 'building sites can be dangerous places.'

*

On Gozo, Nina was feeling frustrated. She only saw her husband at the weekends and missed him dreadfully, yearning for the warmth of his body in bed and their lovemaking. He needed her care, for although his burns had healed she continued to apply a balm to treat his scarred skin, and to massage away the pain he still suffered.

Their children were a delight: Elena, the eldest, was eighteen months old and most importantly she had recently given birth to baby Nikolai, the long-awaited son and heir, the grandson that Alessandro had longed for. Nina wanted more children but feared that James' time and energy were being spent in Valletta rather than with her.

Ester noticed her daughter's mood and said, 'I understand. Let me talk to your father.'

By the time James returned the following weekend, everything had been arranged. The family ate together on Friday night and Alessandro made an announcement.

'I am very pleased with the work James is achieving in Valletta and he will be there for a long time. You need to live together as a family, so I am going to have a house built for you in Malta. Ester and I and your sisters will miss you, but you will visit us, and your house in Gozo will always be here for you. I think this is for the best.'

Nina, delighted, rushed to her father and hugged him. James was stunned, but pleased, feeling slightly guilty at the realisation he'd been neglecting his wife. He, too, got up and hugged his in-laws and a night of celebration ensued.

'So where will our house be?' asked James.

'I have some land, on a point just round from St Julian's bay, near Valletta. It is quite remote, and private. Nina and her mother will tell me what they need.'

'I don't know how to thank you,' said James, shaking his hand.

Alessandro smiled.

'It is very simple, James. Just do as I ask, and make my daughter happy.'

CHAPTER 19

Bath, 1950

Eight-year-old Wendy was helping Fred who was turning over the small patch of ground at the back of his prefab, preparing for Spring planting. Her hands covered in muck she was happily digging into the clay soil with a little trowel when she noticed a flat, round piece of metal with an uneven edge. She called to her Grandad who told her to take it inside and wash it under the tap, then she dried it and showed him what she'd found.

'Good heavens! It's a Roman coin! A silver one, too! Can you see? - there's the profile of a man with a beard and a wreath around his head - and there's some writing round the edge. Well done, Wendy - that's quite a discovery!'

Wendy was very excited and went back into the garden to look for some more coins, but without success.

'Where do you think it came from?' she asked.

'Well…I expect two thousand years ago some Roman chap was walking around here with a hole in his pocket and lost it, and it's been buried ever since, waiting for you to find it! You should take it to school and show your teacher.'

Back in Bristol Wendy did just that.

'That's interesting, Wendy,' said her teacher, 'we're going to do a project on the Romans this term. You can show it to the other children and tell them all about it.'

When the Summer holidays came Fred and Pat offered to have Wendy to stay for a week, and there was only one place she wanted to go. Finding the coin had sparked her imagination, and a trip to the Roman Baths was top of her list.

The Baths had suffered some damage during the war but were now open to visitors. With Fred and Pat either side of Wendy they followed the guide, an old Bathonian with a rich, deep voice, who led them down stone steps to below street level. Wendy listened avidly as he told them tales of the Romans' daily lives, the Gods they worshipped and how the wealthier people kept slaves to do their bidding. It was like discovering a whole new world.

She learnt the remarkable story of King Bladud and his pigs who reputedly first discovered the hot springs and their healing properties. But, the guide said, that was just a tale - it was the Romans who were there first and developed the city in the bend of the river, naming the place Aquae Sulis - Waters of the Sun. Wendy looked around the ancient buildings in awe, feeling the stones beneath her feet as she walked in the shadows of the Romans who once bathed in the Great Bath, smelling the sulphur in the air, the hot waters bubbling up from miles beneath the ground.

They saw the gilt bronze head of the goddess Sulis Minerva which stood within the Temple beside the Sacred Spring, and in the museum there were pieces of pottery, bones and coins, 'just like the one you found!' said Fred. They drank some hot water from the spring, although, it had to be said, it tasted horrible. At the end of the tour Wendy spent all her pocket money on a book about the Romans in Britain - a proper, grown-up book which she insisted her grandparents read to her, absorbing every detail. When Susan collected her at the end of the week Fred said, 'she's been no trouble at all - I think you've got a budding historian there!'

Pat, who would have preferred her granddaughter to show some interest in making cakes and knitting, added, 'I expect it's just a phase. She'll soon be into something else!'

Malta, 1951

Alessandro's vision for Malta was slowly being realised. His first hotel in Valletta had opened to great acclaim and was fully occupied from the start, mainly with tourists from Sicily and Southern Italy who came over by ship, keen to enjoy Maltese hospitality and the exciting new restaurants and bars. James had proved his worth and Alessandro gave him funds to buy a parcel of land to build a hotel and restaurant in Sliema, a small town between Valletta and St Julian's. James was buzzing with ideas for this stretch of coast which was rocky but attractive to swimmers and sun bathers, ripe for turning into a tourist attraction.

In August James took a month off work and he, Nina and the children - Elena, Nikolai and new baby Maria - returned to their house on Gozo for a holiday. Nina was a wonderful mother, looking after her children's day-to-day needs, and James found to his surprise that he adored being a father, finding unexpected pleasure in his children's company, passing on his knowledge and having fun with them. Nina loved being back on Gozo with her mother and seeing her younger sisters who worked on the farm, carrying out the tasks that she used to do.

Towards the end of the day when the sun was less fierce, James would join the family on the beach. He had taken to wearing a Panama hat and always wore loose clothing to protect his scarred skin. Looking at the pleasure boats on the water he said to Nina, 'I'd like to get a sailing dinghy - I haven't sailed for years. I used to be quite good at it. It would be a nice thing to teach the children, too.'

'That's a good idea. I'll ask my father.'

'No, it's okay, I'll look around for one myself.'

Elena ran up to him and grabbed his hand.

'Please come and play with us in the sea, Daddy!'

James got to his feet. 'I'll race you, honey bunny!' and he chased her down the beach.

Bristol, 1951

Towards Christmas, Fred and Pat came over to Bristol to spend the weekend with their daughters. Ann and Brian had been married for three years and Ann was expecting a baby, much to their delight. Brian was working his shift, so the five of them - Fred and Pat, Susan and Wendy, and Ann - took a bus into the city centre. Fred and Pat wanted to see the area near Castle Street which had been the main shopping district before it was heavily bombed.

Fred knew Bristol well, from the days when he first worked on the railways, and he had often taken Pat there when they were courting. They were prepared for a shock, but it was only when seeing it for themselves they could appreciate the scale of the devastation. Ten years after the raids which had erased mediaeval buildings and more than a thousand lives the place had a strange atmosphere, as if ghosts from the past lingered there. Bulldozers were at work clearing acres of ravaged land. The Council had decided not to re-build but to lay the area to parkland and keep the ruins of the church as a memorial to those who had lost their lives on those terrible nights. A new shopping area was being developed in Broadmead.

Shaken by what they had seen and feeling the cold they needed a walk, so headed towards Broad Quay where Fred bought them hot soup and rolls at a café. Afterwards they hiked up College Green towards the university. Susan saw a sign to the Wills Memorial Building which had also suffered significant bomb damage.

'Is that the same Wills as owns the factory?'

'Yes, it is,' answered Fred. 'It's money from the Wills family that made the university possible - they were major benefactors to Bristol. They funded churches, theatres and museums. The city wouldn't be what it is without people like them.'

'So where did their money come from?'

'The tobacco industry. They were among the first to import tobacco on a large scale from the West Indies and America. It's all linked to the slave trade, of course.'

'Really?'

'Well, no one really knows whether it was

slaves that grew the tobacco that the Wills imported, but it was all going on at the time,' said Fred, matter-of-factly. 'You've heard of the triangular trade, haven't you?'

Susan looked blank.

Fred sighed. 'Didn't they teach you anything at school, Susan? Our ships sailed from Bristol to West Africa with goods like guns and brandy which they exchanged for African people. They took them to the West Indies where they were sold as slaves, and with the proceeds they bought rum, sugar and tobacco which they shipped back to England to sell. Like a triangle,' he said, drawing one in the air. 'Do you see?'

'But wasn't it cruel?' asked Wendy, who was listening, horrified.

'Well, yes, it was. Many of the slaves died on board the ships before they even got to the West Indies. And of course once they were there, some were treated badly. But that was how things were done in those days.'

'It's horrible!' said Wendy, shivering.

'But this was over a hundred years ago. It's not like that now!'

'Come on, let's go and have a cup of tea,' said Pat, who'd had enough of the history lesson. 'There used to be a nice café in Whiteladies Road, let's see if it's still there...'

Fred and Pat stayed over at Susan's. In the evening, after Wendy had gone to bed, Pat commented on how well Ann was looking, then said, 'and what about you, Susan - have you found yourself a young man? Frank's been gone a long time now and you're nearly thirty - if you want more children you'd better get a move on!'

'Mum!' exclaimed Susan, 'for goodness sake…Well, no, I haven't got a *young man*, and I'm not sure I want one, either. Wendy and I are very happy as we are, thank you. Anyway, even if I did there aren't many around - most of the men who came back from the war were engaged or married, and single ones don't want to take on a kiddie.'

'Ann did well to find Brian.'

'Yes, she did. But as I've told you, Mum, it's mostly women I mix with at Wills, especially now I'm supervising the cigar line.'

Susan loved her new job. They'd all heard the old story about cigars being rolled on the thigh of a Cuban maiden, and although that wasn't strictly true the process nevertheless required a gentle touch. Only the best workers were chosen, the pay was better, and the women were proud to think that the cigars they made would be enjoyed by the richest, most important men in the land.

'Well, I'm just saying…' said her mother. 'You'll want someone to keep you company as you get older and Wendy won't be at home forever!'

CHAPTER 20

Malta, 1952

James was pleased with his new hotel in Sliema which had just entertained its first guests. The restaurant next door was nearing completion and his plans for a cinema were well-advanced. His own family had enjoyed the sailing dinghy he'd bought last Summer so, using part of the funds intended for the restaurant, he had purchased six boats for hire, keeping them in a boathouse he'd had built on the sea front. It was satisfying to have organised this boat project on his own initiative, not involving Alessandro.

Every evening James went home to his lovely house at St Julian's and his gorgeous Nina who was pregnant with their fourth child. One night, baby Maria awoke crying in the early hours and Nina went to comfort her. Looking out the window she noticed something strange around the point in the direction of Sliema. The sky was lit up in orange and she could hear the wail of sirens in the distance. She caught her breath and rushed to her sleeping husband.

'James! Wake up!' She shook him. 'James! There's something happening - Sliema's on fire!'

James awoke, jumped out of bed and went to the window.

'My God!' he exclaimed, 'I'd better get over there straight away. You stay here with the children.'

He quickly got dressed, ran to his car and drove round the bay, his heart in his mouth. He arrived on Sliema sea front fifteen minutes later to find his boathouse ablaze, along with the building adjoining it which he used as an office. The fire brigade cordoned off the area and two fire engines were in action, trying to douse the flames.

'Let me through!' James cried to the fire officer in charge, 'this is my property!'

'Sorry, Signor, it is too dangerous. Please stay here and let the crew get on with their work.'

'But…'

James stood back, powerless, feeling the heat of the fire, hearing the crackle of burning wood and aware of a strong smell of gasoline. For a moment he was back in the sea, fighting for his life, his face and body searing in the heat, and he couldn't stand it, he had to get away. He ran back to his car and stayed there, crying with the pain he could feel down his left side all over again, watching helplessly as all his work went up in smoke.

At sunrise the firemen finally put out the worst of the fire. The boathouse and the office were in ruins, a smouldering heap of burnt-out wood and metal.

James went over to the fire officer.

'Somebody did this and the police had better get them!' shouted James, furiously.

The fire officer shrugged his shoulders and said, 'we will investigate and send you a copy of our report. Do you have insurance?'

James hesitated. It was one of those jobs he hadn't got round to…

'No.'

The fire officer shrugged again.

'We will be in touch, Signor.'

Nina was anxious and telephoned her father to tell him what had happened. 'Please come, Papa, I'm scared…'

Alessandro left Gozo and arrived at his daughter's the next day. He kissed her on the forehead, saying, 'don't worry, Nina, everything will be all right, I'm here now.' He was calm and reassuring and saw no need to go and inspect the damage. Then he put his arm around James' shoulder, firmly, and said, 'we need to go for a little walk.'

James, still full of anger, told Alessandro what had happened. 'Somebody did this, and I'm going to find out who!'

Alessandro replied, softly, 'we know who did this, James. The question is, what are *you* going to do about it?'

James turned and looked at Alessandro.

'I don't understand.'

'No you don't, do you, my stupid English son-in-law.'

Alessandro never raised his voice and was all the more menacing for it.

'You think you know what you are doing, James, but you don't. You have no idea…'

Confused and frustrated, James said, 'tell me what you mean!'

Alessandro put his hands on James' shoulders, gripping them tightly, hurting his left side.

'Listen to me. If you insist on not consulting me, this is what happens. Never forget, I am in charge here.'

He let him go and sighed, then, as if speaking to a child, said, 'it is very simple. In Sliema the sea front is the Galea family's territory. They run the cafés and shops, and if anyone is going to hire out boats it is their affair. With your boathouse you trod on their toes and this is what they have done, to teach you a lesson. So now, James, do you sit back and accept it, and let them try to take more? It could be your hotel next, up in smoke. Or do you show them you mean business?'

James felt out of his depth, caught between these rival families.

'If you had asked me I could have warned you, but you insisted on going it alone…'

'You could have said something!'

'That's not how it works…'

James was exasperated. 'So, what do you suggest?'

'Give me a few days and I will tell you all you need to know. Then it will be up to you to act.'

Alessandro left and James went back to his house, furious and humiliated. He found no comfort at home, either.

'You have let us down,' said Nina. 'I am going to sleep with the children until you have sorted this out.'

At their next meeting Alessandro gave James a name and address.

'This is the man you want. Every Saturday morning after the market he visits his Mama at her cottage near Dingli, on the West coast. The cottage is very remote. Be careful when you go there, James - the road near the cliffs is steep and can be dangerous.'

*

On Saturday, Mario Vella drove up to his mother's cottage in the new truck he'd just bought with the bonus that Signor Galea had paid him. He'd had a successful morning at the market and was looking forward to his mother's home-made *pastizzi* and an early glass of wine. He parked the truck outside her cottage, she greeted him at the door and he went inside.

An hour later, Mario said goodbye to his mother and took the coast road back to his home in the South. He steered the truck around the bends and down the hills, then realised with horror that the brakes weren't working. As the truck gathered momentum he panicked, thrusting the brake pedal down to the floor to no avail, the truck going faster and faster, out of control, and at the next bend it sped off the road.

Mario screamed in terror, wrestling with the steering wheel, trying to turn the truck back but it continued its path over the bumpy scrubland that led to the edge and plummeted over the cliff. The truck fell through the air as if in slow-motion, then smashed onto the rocks below, exploding with a roar as the fuel caught light.

Half-way back to Sliema, a pair of bolt-croppers safely in the boot of his car, James heard the *boom* behind him and glanced round to see black smoke rising into the air.

The next day Alessandro called on James.

'I have had a talk with Signor Galea. You can keep your hotel in Sliema, and the restaurant, but stay off the sea front, and he wants your cinema too. I have agreed this with him, reluctantly.'

Then he added, 'at least now you have proved you can do as I ask. Don't make the same mistake again.'

He put his hands on his shoulders and kissed him on both cheeks.

'Welcome back, James.'

That night, Nina returned to his bed.

CHAPTER 21

Bristol, 1952

When Wendy came home from school with a letter, Susan said, 'what have you done? I hope you haven't been naughty!'

'No! But Miss said to give you the letter and she wants to talk to you.'

The next day Susan asked for time off and went along to the school, feeling nervous. Miss Finch, Wendy's teacher, welcomed her then asked, 'have you given much thought to Wendy's future?'

Susan was taken aback.

'In what way?'

'Wendy is a bright girl, Mrs Fowler. I would like to put her in for the 11-plus exam next year. I can help her, give her some tuition so she knows what to expect, but she is a very capable child and I'm sure she'd sail through it!'

'Really? You think she'd pass?'

'Yes, I do! She would gain a place at Colston's Girls' - the Grammar school. It's a great opportunity for her. She'd qualify for a bursary so you wouldn't have to pay any fees. There would be the uniform of course, and money for clubs and outings - but hopefully that's not a problem for you?'

Susan laughed. 'Well yes, it would be a problem. It all sounds wonderful, but I just don't have money like that…'

Disappointed, Miss Finch said, 'that would be a great shame. At least give it some thought, will you, Mrs Fowler?'

At home, Susan told Wendy what Miss Finch had said, but made it clear they couldn't afford the extras that would be required.

'I'm not worried, Mum. I don't want to leave my friends and go to the posh school anyway!'

Wendy didn't want to upset her mother so kept her secret to herself. The discovery of that Roman coin had sparked in her a thirst for knowledge about the ancient past - in fact it had become an obsession. She had read books about people called archaeologists who dug amongst ruins and found out about people's lives, long ago, and she knew that this was what she wanted to do. It would mean studying, and visiting libraries and museums, and having teachers who would encourage her - all the things that grammar school would make possible.

But she knew that path wasn't open to her, and she would likely spend her days with her friends in Bedminster, making cigarettes.

*

During the October half term Susan took Wendy to stay with her parents for a few days. They enjoyed being together in the cosy prefab and Pat was glad that Wendy was at last showing some interest in baking, in addition to insisting on visiting the Roman Baths yet again.

On the Saturday, Susan and Wendy called on Jean and Frances who were delighted to see them. Wendy told them all about the Baths and her interest in Roman history.

Jean said, 'you've got an enthusiast there, Susan. I can't see her wanting to spend her life at a machine in a factory!'

Frances added, '…or as a housewife! It's so important for girls to be independent.'

'The younger generation is going to have opportunities we never dreamt of!' said Jean.

Addressing Wendy, Frances continued, '…and don't let men get the better of you - you're just as capable as they are. You can be whatever you want to be!'

Later, walking back to Twerton, Susan said to her daughter, 'I think you've just had your first lesson in feminism!'

'What's feminism?' asked Wendy.

*

David Roberts was sitting at his desk in his study at Eagle House, smoking his pipe, working his way through the pile of correspondence in front of him. Among the routine letters were a number of Christmas cards. He opened one postmarked from Bristol and read:

Dear David,

I hope this finds you well and wish you all the best for the festive season.

We are all in good health. I am still working at WD & HO Wills, making cigars, so next time you smoke one you can think of me! My sister Ann had a baby girl in June, she and her husband are thrilled. They've named her Elizabeth, after our new Queen.

Wendy is growing quite tall now, and her hair is as red as ever. She's doing very well at school. Her teacher wants to put her in for the eleven plus and says she would flourish at the Grammar school, but that's not for the likes of us! We couldn't afford the bus fare let alone the uniform!

Please give my regards to your family and the Blumfeldts.

With our very best wishes

Susan and Wendy Fowler

David read Susan's message with interest, glad to know the family were doing well. He knew it couldn't be easy for a woman bringing up a child on her own. He wondered what the prospects would be for a bright girl like Wendy - another worker for Wills, probably. He got up and put the card on the mantlepiece alongside the others he had received then sat down and re-lit his pipe. He was thoughtful for a few moments, then returned to his correspondence.

*

In the new year Fred came home from work, looking ashen.

'Fred! What on earth is the matter?' asked Pat.

Fred sat down, his worried wife kneeling next to him and putting her arm round his shoulders.

'It's the station - it's going to close. They've

146

decided it's not 'economical' - that's the word they used - not 'economical' to keep it open. People are using the buses more, it seems, so they're going to cut back on local trains. So - no need for the station.'

'Oh Fred, that's awful!'

'Short-sighted, I say - it's getting busier on the roads every day and this is going to make it worse!'

'So what about your job, Fred?'

'They've offered me assistant station master at Bath Spa, so that will be all right - it's a busy station and I'll have a lot to learn. But it won't be the same as being in charge of my own patch - I thought I'd see my time out here. I'll have to get used to having a boss again - and he's younger than me, too!'

'At least you'll have a job, though. And you'll be up to it - there's no substitute for experience.'

'I hope you're right, love. Funny, isn't it - as soon as everything seems settled, something comes along to change it all…'

*

Susan answered a knock at the door to find a man in a dark navy uniform and a peaked cap standing there.

'Mrs Fowler? Letter for you.'

For a split second she recalled the messenger boy giving her the telegram about Frank, but this time it was the postman with a registered letter that required her signature. Susan signed the receipt and took the manilla envelope into the kitchen where she sat down and examined it, curiously. The envelope was postmarked from Bath and stamped on the back with the name of a solicitors' office in Queen Square.

She opened it carefully to find a letter typed on good quality headed paper which read:

Dear Mrs Fowler,

We are instructed by our client to forward you the enclosed Postal Order for One Hundred Pounds. This is to cover uniform and sundry expenses in respect of your daughter, Wendy Fowler, in anticipation of her gaining a place at Grammar School. Six further payments of the same amount will be made to you annually.

Our client wishes to remain anonymous and requests your discretion in this matter. He asks us to convey the following message:

'For Wendy'

Yours sincerely etc…

Susan was stunned. She gasped, re-read the letter then read it a third time.

This money - a fortune! - would enable Wendy to go to the grammar school up to the age of eighteen, giving her opportunities Susan and her sister could never have imagined.

She suddenly remembered her throwaway remark in the Christmas card she'd sent to David Roberts. She would never have dreamt of asking him for money and felt embarrassed to think her message might have come across in that way. But she knew David was a kind and generous man, and the only person she knew who could afford to make such a gesture. And he had always been fond of Wendy.

She felt incredibly thankful, completely indebted, but also discomforted - he had chosen anonymity so she could never thank him, nor tell her daughter the name of her benefactor. How would she explain her sudden windfall?

Susan made a cup of tea to calm herself while thoughts raced in her head.

She read the letter over again. Here it was…the chance for Wendy to have a decent education, to mix with the best, to follow paths normally closed to a girl from her background.

How could she refuse?

David Roberts reflected on the trip to see his solicitor and was satisfied with his course of action. As he stared into the orange glow of his fireplace he recalled that terrible night when the bombs fell on Bath and he hadn't been here to save his beloved wife. He could never forgive himself for that, but he did have the means to help somebody else who deserved a better chance in life. He wanted no fuss or thanks over it, for this was in tribute to his own dear Wendy.

He felt a gentle hand on his shoulder and as he reached up to touch it he heard a woman's voice, saying, 'that's wonderful, darling. Thank you.'

But when he turned his head to look at her there was nobody there.

CHAPTER 22

Malta 1953

James was relaxing on the terrace of his home at St Julian's with its view out to sea, reading a copy of the *Times of Malta* which had a photograph of Her Majesty Queen Elizabeth II on the front page. This year would see her Coronation and the local press was already speculating about when Her Royal Highness might pay the island a visit. As Princess Elizabeth she had lived in Malta while her husband, Prince Philip, was stationed there with the Royal Navy, but her next visit would be as Queen.

James read about the preparations underway in London, looking at photographs of the Mall and Buckingham Palace under grey skies. It struck him as ironic that although he told people he came from London he'd never actually been there.

Reading on, he came across another article of interest. As part of the Coronation celebrations Winston Churchill, the Prime Minister, had announced an amnesty for war-time deserters from the forces. James reflected on this for a moment. This was remarkable, given that deserters from the Great War had been shot. So, that particular slate was wiped clean!

He had chalked-up plenty of other offences, though. Hardened as he was to the Camilleri way of doing business he felt a pang of guilt about the deaths in which he was implicated, but that was the path he had chosen, and he was in far too deep to ever get out. And what was the alternative? A return to his old life in Bath, the wife and child he had deserted, and the damp, dreary streets and terraces of Oldfield Park?

Nina came out onto the terrace and sashayed up to him, carrying Alfredo, their new baby son, on her hip. She looked delicious. He wasn't going anywhere.

Bristol, 1953

Colston's Girls' School was in Montpelier, a half-hour bus ride from Bedminster but a world away from the life that Wendy had known. She approached her first day in trepidation, feeling self-conscious in her uniform of a navy-blue gym slip and white blouse, felt hat, navy-blue coat with the school badge, and her hair in plaits.

When Susan told her a kind friend had given them some money to enable her to attend grammar school she was delighted and wondered who it might be. But whoever it was, she was immensely grateful that someone, somewhere, had recognised that she had dreams and given her the means to pursue them.

As Susan waved goodbye she felt more nervous than her daughter, but was sure she was up to the challenge. Wendy could look after herself and had a streak of toughness in her which she must have inherited from her father.

She would need it.

Wendy hated her first day. There was a clear divide between the fee-paying girls and those whose places were funded by the government and they quickly learnt who was in which category. Wendy was immediately picked on for her red hair and freckles and was told she was common. She hated the food at dinner time (*'lunch time*, you mean!' said a girl, scornfully), and although the school was in Bristol, Wendy seemed to be the only girl with a local accent for which they teased her unmercifully.

At last four o'clock came and Wendy caught the bus home, only to be taunted by the children in her street who sniggered at her uniform and called her a snob.

Wendy ran to her mother in tears, worried that she'd let everyone down. Susan tried to comfort her, saying, 'it will be better tomorrow,' whilst wishing David Roberts had kept his money to himself.

The next day was even worse.

At break the girls were talking about their fathers.

'And was does your Daddy do?' asked a girl whose name was Hilary.

'He's dead,' said Wendy, speaking the lines her mother had taught her, 'he was killed at sea during the war before I was born.'

'Was he in the Royal Navy?'

'Yes,' she said, proudly, 'he was an Able Seaman!'

Hilary looked at her in horror, then shrieked with glee, her friends joining in until Wendy was surrounded by a wall of derisive laughter.

'*An Able Seaman*!' parroted the girl, scornfully, 'you mean, a *rating*!'

Wendy didn't understand and her embarrassment grew.

'Well, my Daddy's a Lieutenant Commander,' said Hilary, 'and I don't think he'll be very happy to know that you're in the same form as me! We'll have to get you moved.'

'But why should I move?' cried Wendy.

'Well, you're a junior rank so you'll have to do as I say!'

Wendy wasn't having any of this.

'NO!' she screamed, throwing herself at the girl and pushing her to the ground. They wrestled together, shrieking and pulling each other's hair while the other girls looked on, until a horrified teacher arrived, broke them up and marched them to the Headmistress' office. Both girls were told to explain themselves and were given detention and a letter to take home.

'In School, it doesn't matter who your parents are,' the Headmistress told them, firmly. 'You are all equal in our eyes and you must learn to be tolerant of each other. Don't let me see either of you in here again!'

The following day a girl called Pamela came up to Wendy and said, 'don't worry about Hilary, she's a bully. If it wasn't about your father she'd have picked on you over something else. I'm sorry your father died, he must have been a very brave man.'

'Thank you, yes, he was.'

'We can be friends if you want.'

Pamela was tall, fair and skinny and although she spoke with a posh voice, Wendy liked her.

'All right.'

Making friends with Pamela helped, but

Wendy still hated school and resolved that if things didn't improve by the end of the week she'd tell her mother she wasn't going back.

On Friday the history teacher announced, 'this term we will be studying Roman Britain. Now, who can tell me something about that? Have any of you been to the Roman Baths?'

Wendy's hand shot up, her heart thumping.

By the end of the lesson she'd decided that she might stay, after all...

In the Summer holidays Wendy's friend Pamela invited her to stay with her family at their holiday home in Devon, by the sea. Wendy was keen and Susan was pleased for her, although while she was away she missed her daughter desperately. They acted as a couple and Susan was aware that things were changing - she would have to get used to her daughter becoming independent.

When Wendy returned from her holiday Susan detected a change in her and she was even speaking with a different accent.

'We went sailing!' she cried, 'they've got a dinghy and Pamela's father taught me how to sail. It was super!'

To Susan it sounded like another world, but one she was more than happy her daughter had the chance to join.

The new school year began and with the next postal order Susan bought items of uniform to replace those Wendy had outgrown, a satchel and a lacrosse stick. Susan mused how she and Ann had ever managed to get through school without all this kit. She ran up a dap bag on her sewing machine - at least there were some things she could make herself - although Wendy objected to the name.

'They don't call them daps here - that's a Bath word! They're plimsolls!'

Susan sighed. Even her native vocabulary wasn't good enough anymore.

Wendy's art mistress took her pupils to Bristol Museum and Art Gallery which was near the university, a mile or so away from school. The girls looked with interest at the paintings on display including some by members of the pre-Raphaelite Brotherhood, showing beautiful, ethereal women with cascading red hair, green eyes and pale skin. To Wendy's embarrassment the teacher singled her out, saying, 'see, Wendy! You'll look as gorgeous as these women when you grow up!'

They went on to look at the Georgian rooms where Wendy recognised scenes of Bath with its famous terraces and crescents, but what she loved most was the Antiquities section which contained rows and rows of glass cases displaying ancient Greek and Roman relics. She found the artefacts and the stories of how they had been discovered utterly fascinating and asked the curators endless questions. At the end of the afternoon her teacher had to drag her away, but one of the museum staff, seeing her enthusiasm, said to her, 'we are open at the weekends. Come and see us whenever you want.'

From then on, it became her favourite place to spend her time.

Wendy settled into the school routine and with each year her confidence grew. The divide between the fee-paying girls and those with funded places narrowed as the school's ethos took hold and the pupils learnt to accept each other's differences. She made her own set of friends, majored on the subjects she was good at, and flourished academically.

Every morning, just inside the front door to the school, they passed the large statue of their founder, Edward Colston, the seventeenth century philanthropist who gave money to many of Bristol's schools, almshouses, hospitals and churches, helping the great city to prosper. Once a year, together with Colston's Boys', the pupils attended a service in his memory in Bristol Cathedral, celebrating the man who had done so much to make their city great, and from whose legacy they were all benefitting. None of them ever questioned how Colston had accumulated his wealth.

CHAPTER 23

Malta, 1958

Alessandro had reached an uneasy truce with the Galea family, dividing up Valletta and Sliema between them. At this particular time they were joined in having a common enemy - the British government. There was a groundswell of resentment among the Maltese population against what they regarded as the colonial ruling class, and banners strung from balconies reading, 'BRITISH GO HOME!' and 'MALTA WANTS INDEPENDENCE!' had become a common sight.

At their next meeting Alessandro told James, 'I think it would be wise if you were to keep out the way for a while. Things are happening here which you don't want to be involved in. Take my advice - stay at home with Nina and make some more babies...'

Everything became clear a week later when the political arguments over the future of Malta erupted into violence. Dom Mintoff, who had led the Maltese government, resigned in protest at the breakdown of talks with Britain over the future of the island and workers declared a general strike. The day of protest led to ugly scenes on the streets of Valletta and other towns and a state of emergency was declared. Angry protestors pelted police with stones, an army jeep and a naval tug were set on fire and the cables of the Rediffusion radio service were cut.

After the day of violence the British Prime Minister suspended the constitution and imposed direct colonial rule, creating fertile ground for Maltese demands to be an independent state.

Due to the prevailing anti-British feeling James took Alessandro's advice and kept a low profile. He was beginning to realise what a mix of contradictions the Maltese people were. They could be brave - during the wartime siege they had showed immense fortitude and suffered enormously from the attacks on their island. And yet they were strangely ungrateful to those who had rescued them. James recalled the many ships that had been sunk, as well as his own, the hundreds of lives lost in the convoys whose mission had been to protect the merchant vessels bringing supplies to the stricken island and its people. Now the mention of Britishness was met with scorn and resentment, a struggle against colonial masters, with an inference that it was only because the islands were British that they had been attacked in the first place.

Bristol, 1958

Wendy came home from school, full of news.

'Miss Burton, our Latin mistress, fell when she was horse riding and broke her neck! She's in hospital and they say she might never walk again!'

158

'That's terrible!' said Susan.

'Yes!' said Wendy, relishing the lurid details rather too much - Wendy loved Latin but Miss Burton wasn't her favourite teacher.

'...And...,' Wendy continued, 'because we're preparing for 'O' levels they're getting a replacement and it's going to be a MAN!'

'Really?'

'Yes! He'll be the only male teacher in the whole school! We're borrowing him from Bristol Grammar - the boys' school. We're all wondering what he'll be like...' she said, dreamily.

'Well, as long as he's a good at his job and can get you through your exams...'

The following week Wendy came home looking disappointed.

'What is it?' asked Susan.

'Mr Johnson started today - the new Latin master. But he's so OLD! He hasn't got much hair, and wears one of those tweedy jackets with leather patches on the elbows, but it's all worn and fraying round the edges. He looks like a tramp!' she said, with disgust.

Susan laughed. 'I'm sorry he's not Rock Hudson! But what's he like as a teacher?'

'...all right, I suppose...'

At the parents' evening the Latin master was easy to spot. Susan approached him, a man of medium height, balding, with a reddish-brown moustache and a self-contained air about him. He looked at Susan with kind, brown eyes.

'You're Wendy's mother, of course - she's doing very well, Mrs Fowler, and should have no trouble getting the top grade. I would recommend she studies Latin at 'A' level, she has an aptitude for it and it's helpful for her interest in ancient history.'

'That's wonderful. I do wonder where she gets her brains from!'

'They say the fruit never falls far from the tree…'

Wendy laughed, then asked, 'and how long will you be staying at Colston's, Mr Johnson? Would you take Wendy for 'A' level?'

'Well, I'll carry on until Miss Burton recovers, though I fear that may take some time. So yes, I would take Wendy next year.'

'You must find it strange, being surrounded by women all day! What on earth does your wife think?'

He hesitated. 'Actually, my wife is dead - she was killed during the war. There's just me and my son. We live in a house in the grounds of Bristol Grammar - they've let me keep it while I'm seconded here.'

'I'm so sorry, I didn't mean to intrude…'

'That's all right. Wendy has told me about her father - how he died at sea. She's very proud of him. She's a bright girl, Mrs Fowler, you've done a good job raising her. It's not easy, on your own.'

'As you well know…! Thank you, Mr Johnson, that is kind of you to say.'

They stood rather awkwardly for a moment, then another parent came to talk to him and Susan turned away.

One Saturday morning in January, Susan and Wendy had just got off the bus in Whiteladies Road and were heading towards the museum when they bumped into Mr Johnson and his son.

Mr Johnson raised his hat. 'Mrs Fowler! How nice to see you, and Wendy. This is my son. Say hello, Tom.'

Tom, a sullen-looking boy of about fourteen, murmured 'hello,' and looked down at his shoes.

Wendy felt embarrassed.

'Wendy's going to the museum. You spend practically all your weekends there, don't you!' Susan said, turning to her daughter.

'Yes, I love it!'

The museum staff, recognising Wendy's interest, had taught her the basics of identifying and cataloguing artefacts and she was currently helping to sort out boxes of broken pottery. Her ambition to study archaeology was stronger than ever.

'And I'm off to the shops!'

'That's nice,' Mr Johnson replied, 'we're on our way to the barber's to get a haircut, aren't we, Tom.'

Wendy suppressed a giggle, thinking that was about the last thing Mr Johnson needed.

'Of course, you're local, the boys' grammar is just up the road, isn't it. I'm surprised we haven't bumped into you before!'

'Indeed! Well, it's very good to see you,' Mr Johnson said, with a smile that lit up his face, '...and hopefully we'll meet again. Good day to you both.'

'Good day,' said Susan, watching as they walked away.

Once a month Susan met Ann to go round the new shopping centre in Broadmead, have tea at a café and catch up with their news. They both led busy lives and were always pleased to see each other. Ann's daughter Elizabeth was six and had a little brother, Mark, and number three was on their way.

'I always imagined I'd be the one with lots of children, and you'd be working in an office somewhere,' said Susan.

'Yes, me too! Funny, isn't it. But I do enjoy being a mother, and Brian's a wonderful Dad.' She watched her two as they sat at the table, wrestling with doughnuts and getting jam all round their faces.

'We went to see Mum and Dad last weekend,' said Susan. 'They love to see Wendy - they're so proud of how she's doing at school. It's funny, when she's with them she reverts to her Bath accent, at home she's more Bristol and with her school friends she's posh!'

'Very versatile - she's a survivor!'

'And Dad's doing well - he still misses Weston station but he's getting on all right in Bath. Mum told me he struggled at first but she's great at boosting his confidence. I think she keeps him going.'

'She's good, isn't she. I sometimes think we didn't appreciate her enough, growing up - it's only when you've got your own kids that you think about it.'

'Yes, you're right. She's got herself a job at the grocer's now, she was getting bored at home all day on her own.'

Then Ann said, 'So have you met anyone yet, Susan?'

'You're as bad as Mum! No I haven't. Wendy and I are perfectly happy as we are, thank you. It's not easy being a single parent, but you find ways to cope. I was saying as much when I was talking to Wendy's Latin teacher at the parents' evening. He told me how he lost his wife, right at the end of the war, leaving him with a baby son.'

'Really?'

'Yes - he was nice man, very understanding.'

'So you like Wendy's Latin teacher?'

Susan giggled. 'Not in that way, you berk!'

Wendy knew she had to approach her mother carefully with her next piece of news.

'The school's organising a trip during the Summer holidays and I'd really like to go...'

'Where to?'

'Rome! And it includes a special tour to the ruins at Pompeii. Oh Mum, it would be so interesting - I'd love to go and see all the places I've been reading about, and it would really help me in my exams. But I'm worried we can't afford it.'

'How much would it be?'

Wendy gave her the details.

'Let me have a look.'

Susan had received the final payment from the solicitor in Bath. She had managed the funds very carefully, not wasting a penny, only buying uniform when essential and keeping a tight rein on Wendy's social activities. Susan went upstairs to her bedroom and opened the case where she kept her important papers. Looking at her Post Office savings book there were just enough funds to cover the trip. None of this - nothing of what Wendy had achieved - would have been possible without those annual postal orders.

Susan came back downstairs and said, 'there's just enough money, Wendy - so yes, you can go!'

'That's fantastic!' cried Wendy, flinging her arms around her mother's neck, 'thank you so much!'

'It's not me you have to thank...'

In July Susan received a succession of postcards from Italy showing pictures of the Colosseum, the ruined city of Pompeii and views of the Bay of Naples with Mount Vesuvius emitting a plume of smoke against a deep blue sky. Wendy's enthusiasm was uncontainable; she was having the time of her life, visiting a foreign land under the hot sun, making new discoveries and enjoying the company of her fellows. It stirred a memory in Susan from long ago, and then she realised.

It reminded her of Frank.

CHAPTER 24

Bristol, 1960

One Saturday, with the rain tipping down, Susan left Wendy at the museum and was walking to the shops when she literally bumped into Mr Johnson coming the other way, their umbrellas clashing. Recognising each other they laughed, then Mr Johnson said, 'shall we go somewhere to get out of this rain? There's a café just up the road, let me buy you a coffee.'

They were both grateful to get into the dry. They spoke about the weather and ordered their drinks, then Wendy took a packet of Woodbines from her handbag and offered one to Mr Johnson.

'No thanks, I don't smoke.'

'Really? If everyone was like you I'd be out of a job!'

'Of course, you work at Wills...Wendy mentioned it. Oh, it's just one of those things - I never fancied smoking, even when I was in the Army, but I don't mind if you want to.'

'It's all right,' said Susan, putting the packet to one side, 'I'll have one later.'

The waitress arrived with coffees. They chatted about Wendy's progress, then Susan asked, 'and how is your son?'

'Tom's at home today. He's…he's not terribly well, you see…'

Susan tilted her head to one side, happy to listen.

'He has difficulty relating to people - a sort of shyness, but worse than that. He's all right physically and he's an intelligent boy, but - it's hard to explain, it's as if he's built a shell around himself and won't come out. I thought he'd improve as he got older, but he hasn't. I think it goes back to when he lost his mother…'

Susan nodded sympathetically.

'It was just before the end of the war, in March '45. Vera - my wife - had gone to London to see her sister - we thought it was safe, then. She took Tom with her - he was only a baby. A V2 rocket exploded nearby, hitting their house. Vera and her sister were killed instantly. They found Tom in the ruins, the next day.'

'How terrible!'

'People said afterwards, how frightening it was - to hear that wailing sound above you which just stops, suddenly, then those few seconds of silence before it explodes…'

He took a deep breath.

'I was in Italy, with the Eighth Army, looking forward to coming home and getting de-mobbed. They sent me a telegram…'

He stopped for a moment, then continued.

'…Vera's parents took Tom in for a while, but

they were elderly and when I got home I wanted to look after him myself. I started teaching, and we haven't done too badly, all these years.'

The waitress appeared and they ordered another coffee.

'I'm so sorry,' said Susan, touching his hand, 'it must have been very hard for you.'

He nodded, then said, 'but you have suffered too. Tell me about yourself, and Wendy.'

The time flew by until they realised they were the only ones left in the café. The waitress was making impatient noises.

'Oh dear, we'd better go!'

Susan picked up the packet of cigarettes which lay, unsmoked, on the table, and put them back in her handbag.

'It's been so nice talking to you today, Mr Johnson.'

'Christopher, please, call me Christopher. We must do this again soon.'

'Yes, thank you, I'd like that.'

Wendy was excited about Colston's traditional end of term ball. As well as from Colston's Boys', invitations had been extended to a group of Royal Navy cadets from Dartmouth who were staying in Bristol as part of their training programme. They had a reputation for being handsome and daring and the girls couldn't wait to meet them. Wendy scarcely knew any boys - the ones she'd grown up with in Bedminster were working and thought she was a snob, and those she'd met from the Boys' school she found unbelievably boring. Tonight, though, she was determined to enjoy herself.

Susan had made her daughter an exquisite strapless evening gown in green silk, matching her eyes and showing off her slim figure. Not wanting to travel on the bus in her ballgown she was grateful to Pamela who asked her father to make a detour via Bedminster to give her a lift. As Susan watched Wendy leave the house she couldn't believe how grown-up her daughter had become, and how attractive. She wondered what Frank would have made of her.

The two girls arrived together and joined their friends who lined one side of the room while the boys stood on the other. At last the Headmistress gave some words of welcome, then the band struck up and the dancing began. Wendy danced with some non-descript boys, then one of the cadets approached her. He was tall, fair-haired and handsome, immaculate in his uniform, with piercing blue eyes and a winning smile.

He looked at her red hair cascading around her bare shoulders and said, 'my pre-Raphaelite beauty. May I dance with you?'

She smiled at him and they danced together for the rest of the evening. He was the best-looking of the bunch and Wendy could feel the eyes of the other girls jealously upon her. For his part, despite his apparent self-assurance, his insides were like jelly and he couldn't believe his luck in dancing with the loveliest girl in the room.

When the cadets were marshalled to leave he said to her, 'I'm joining my ship next week, but may I write to you?'

'Yes!' she said, attracted by his looks and flattered by his attention.

They swapped addresses, then he was gone.

With excellent exam results and a bursary, Wendy secured her place at Bristol University to study archaeology. Pamela headed to Oxford to study Law and the two promised to stay in touch. During the Summer holidays Wendy took a part time job at Wills, aware that it kept her feet on the ground as well as earning her some cash.

The next time they were in Bath, Susan said, 'I want us to go and pay a call on someone important. It's time you knew, Wendy. Those postal orders we used to get, for your education - the donor was anonymous, it was all arranged through a solicitor, but I'm sure it was David Roberts, the doctor. We must go and thank him.'

Wendy was surprised. 'Really? I always thought it might be one of those ladies - Jean and Frances. They always seemed interested in what I was doing.'

'Goodness! I must say, that had never crossed my mind. Jean and Frances have always kept an eye on you, but I don't think they would have had much money to spare. Well, we'll soon find out!'

David was delighted to see them both, saying what a fine young lady Wendy had grown into, then, prompted by her mother, Wendy told him about the degree course she had embarked upon.

'That's marvellous! And it's all down to your hard work.'

'Well, not quite...' said Susan. 'Without the help of a kind and generous friend, Wendy would never have got to grammar school in the first place. David - please tell - was it you?'

David sat back and sighed. 'I thought you'd probably guess, but I just didn't want any fuss. I'm very pleased it worked out well for you.'

Susan nodded. 'We can't thank you enough.'

'Thank you, Doctor Roberts!' said Wendy, and gave him a kiss.

After his guests had gone David sat and lit his pipe, and thought of his beloved wife.

Wendy took to university like a duck to water, loving the lectures, mixing with the other students and spending hours at the library and museum doing research. She and her mother enjoyed this new phase of their lives, with Wendy grown-up and independent whilst still living at home.

Wendy wrote to her new friend Cedric, who was serving as a Midshipman on a destroyer patrolling the Far East, and he sent her a formal photo of himself taken at Dartmouth. She remembered the thrill of dancing with him at Colston's ball and enjoyed reading his news from exotic places. They were getting to know each other through their letters. She learnt that he was nearly a year younger than her, they were both only children, born in Bath, where his widowed mother still lived; they had family connections to the Royal Navy and had both lost their fathers at sea during the war. When Wendy received Cedric's letters she would run upstairs and lie on her bed reading them.

Susan had a feeling of déjà vu.

CHAPTER 25

Bristol, 1961

Christopher Johnson took to calling on Susan on Sundays and they would go out together, discovering the delights of Bristol. He bought a Morris Minor and their outings took them further afield, to Bath, to meet Fred and Pat, and to the coast at Weston-Super-Mare. As their friendship developed Susan learnt that in spite of his rather old-fashioned looks he was actually only five years older than herself, and when he smiled at her she felt a glow inside. He had a way of drawing out the best in people.

Miss Burton the Latin mistress had recovered sufficiently to return to work, and Christopher resumed teaching at Bristol Grammar. To mark the change, rather self-consciously he asked Susan, 'would you mind coming with me to the tailor's? I think it's time I bought a new jacket and would appreciate your advice…'

His main worry was his son Tom. His classmates accepted him for the eccentric he was, but he didn't really have any friends. Christopher didn't like leaving him for too long and when he went out for the day he would ask the school Matron to keep an eye on him.

Susan asked, 'what's Tom interested in? Does he have any hobbies?'

'Just maths, really - he loves anything to do with numbers. He has a fantastic memory - he could memorise the phone book! It's people he can't deal with. Oh, and he loves trains - fascinated by them. The best day out we have is train spotting at Temple Meads!'

'Really? That's given me an idea…'

Standing on the platform at Bath Spa station, Fred took out his pocket watch to check the time.

'Right, Tom, one minute and it will be here!'

Tom stared intently up the railway line. The seconds ticked by and then they saw it approaching - *The Bristolian*, flying down from London Paddington. As the train neared they felt the pressure of the air as the mighty steam engine thrust towards them, the noise rising to a crescendo until with a whoosh it rattled past them, its whistle blowing, the whole station shaking, then they turned and watched as it thundered away, onwards to the city of its name.

'Magnificent!' said Fred.

'Yes!' said Tom, recording the details in his notebook. 'Which ones are coming next?'

'There's a Castle class due at 12.54 and one of the new diesel trains is coming through at 1.09. After that you can come up to the office, if you like. We've got all the timetables in there.'

'Timetables! I would like that. Thank you, Mr Bishop,' said Tom, almost smiling.

Malta, 1961

Since the disturbances of the late '50s the political situation in Malta had calmed down. James had followed Alessandro's advice to the letter, resulting in another daughter, Alessia, named in his honour, and there was another baby on the way. James was now ready to re-emerge into the world of Maltese business and both he and Alessandro were pleased to find that the new Governor's plans for economic development based on tourism fitted nicely with their own ideas.

However, there was a problem.

At Alessandro's next meeting with his associates he said, 'I had a conversation yesterday with Signor Galea which gives me cause for concern. As you know, our two families reached an understanding some time ago, but there is now a newcomer in our midst: an Italian called Massimo Moretti has moved to Valletta and started to meddle in our affairs. I have agreed with Signor Galea that he must be stopped before he goes any further.'

'What's he done?' asked the businessman.

'He has opened some bars in Valletta, bringing in girls from North Africa, and now he has his eye on Sliema front which, as you know (he glanced at James) is the Galea's territory.'

'So what should we do?' asked the builder.

'We have agreed a joint strategy. The Galea's will invite him to Sliema, and the Camilleri's will ensure that he does not return.'

Then, fixing James with a commanding stare, he said, 'this will be your job.'

*

Massimo Moretti was pleased to accept the Galea family's invitation to look at potential sites for bars along Sliema front - there was more than enough business to go round and they all agreed that having some new blood would help the rapid expansion of the Maltese entertainment industry. After a long lunch with copious amounts of wine the Galea's showed Massimo their growing boat-hire business which was proving lucrative. They had recently invested in a cabin cruiser with its own bar, nicely combining both sources of recreation. What better way to end the day than go for a jaunt to see if it fitted within his portfolio of interest?

They took Massimo to the cruiser and introduced him to its Captain, James Robinson, who steered out to sea, pointing out landmarks ashore, and invited Massimo to help himself to a bottle of whisky from the bar. As the boat nudged through the waves James offered his guest a turn at steering. Leaving him to take the wheel, James went below to fetch a sharp knife, returned to deck, stole up behind Massimo and, quietly and efficiently, slit his throat.

James heaved the dead man overboard, leaving him to the sharks who had recently been spotted in the area, then mopped up the blood. He threw the knife and his own bloodied clothes into the sea and changed into clean ones.

When he returned to Sliema he went straight to the coastguard's office, distraught, telling them about the dreadful accident that had occurred and his attempts to save his guest who had unfortunately slipped after drinking too much and toppled overboard.

His body was never found.

CHAPTER 26

Bath, 1961

Wendy's heart was thumping as she walked from Bath Spa railway station to the balustrade above the Parade Gardens where she had arranged to meet Cedric. They hadn't met since the night of the ball, over a year ago, and she felt as if she were on her way to a rendezvous with a stranger.

As she approached she saw him waiting for her, a tall, slim figure with a short back and sides haircut, wearing a sports jacket, a check shirt with a maroon cravat and light grey trousers. He looked nervous, smoking a cigarette, and threw it away when he saw her. They didn't quite know what to say and looked at each other awkwardly.

'Wendy!'

'Cedric!'

It was the first time she'd seen him in civilian clothes and she thought he looked very old-fashioned. She preferred him in uniform.

Wendy was wearing an orange shift mini dress with a white collar.

'You look…colourful!'

They laughed, and he said, 'let's find a café where we can talk.'

Sitting at a table drinking frothy coffees, Cedric told Wendy about his adventures in the South China Sea, swimming in shark-infested waters, talking of places with exotic names like Malaya and Burma. As they relaxed she remembered his charming smile, his keen blue eyes, and when he turned his head she noted his handsome profile, made for having a pair of binoculars perched on his nose, up on the bridge of a warship. For her part she enthusiastically told him about her studies, describing her fascination with how the ancient Romans saw the world in a completely different way, with different values and morals from the modern day. But she also talked about the latest pop music and the fun she had with her friends at the students' union.

'You won't be interested in me anymore, I'm far too boring,' he said.

'You do look rather like a fuddy-duddy!'

He was offended. 'These clothes? There's nothing wrong with Dog Robbers!'

'What?!'

'It's what we call them in the navy - the rig officers wear when we go ashore. Don't ask me why!'

'How peculiar!' The navy was obviously a different world.

After a pause Cedric said, 'look, Wendy, we're both changing. I'm enjoying my job - it's what I was born to. And you love digging around in muddy fields and wearing modern clothes when you go out. We are different. If you don't want to see me again I'll understand.'

She stared into her empty coffee cup.

'I don't know, Cedric - I mean, I did enjoy writing to you - we seemed to find a lot in common, on paper anyway...'

'I think we did, and I enjoyed writing to you too.'

He looked into her vivid green eyes.

'And I still think you're the most beautiful girl I've ever seen,' he said.

She blushed. For all of it, she still liked him.

'All right. We could see each other here next Saturday, if you want.'

'Super! I'll take you to meet my mother!'

Rosamund Mason, Cedric's mother, lived at The Oaks, a spacious detached Edwardian villa on Lansdown Hill, one of the most expensive parts of Bath, with a maid and a housekeeper. Cedric met Wendy at the railway station and together they walked up the steep hill to the house where the maid showed them in, then scuttled into the kitchen to prepare tea. Mrs Mason came forward to greet them. A formidable woman of about sixty with her white hair up, she was wearing a navy blue, high-necked knitted dress with a string of pearls and looked more like Cedric's grandmother than his mother.

Mrs Mason looked disdainfully at her visitor, raising her eyebrows at Wendy's short dress and the expanse of leg she was showing.

'Mother, this is Wendy - Wendy Fowler.'

'Miss Fowler,' she said, giving Wendy a feeble handshake, then indicated the way into the drawing room where they were invited to sit down in uncomfortable armchairs. In the background a grandfather clock marked out the seconds.

Wendy looked around the room which was ornately furnished with Edwardian artefacts and a portrait of a stern-looking naval officer.

Mrs Mason noticed Wendy staring and said, 'my late husband, Captain Mortimer Mason, killed in the Battle of the Atlantic in '42. He died before Cedric was born.'

'I'm so sorry,' said Wendy. 'My father…'

'Wendy's studying archaeology at Bristol,' interrupted Cedric. 'You're a real enthusiast, aren't you?' he said, looking at her.

'Yes, I am! It's fascinating…'

The maid brought some tea, then left.

Mrs Mason carefully poured the tea while the clock ticked, then said, 'Cedric tells me you have people in Bath.'

'Yes, my grandparents.'

'Wendy was born in the middle of the Bath Blitz!' said Cedric.

Mrs Mason softened slightly.

'An extraordinary time. I will never forget it…'

A wistfulness crossed her face, then she asked, 'did you lose anyone close?'

'Yes - my father's mother. And my mother and her parents lost their homes.'

'I'm sorry to hear that. I was here at the time - I was lucky, the house was only slightly damaged. I couldn't bear to live anywhere else. Where do your relatives live now?'

'I live with my mother in Bristol, and my grandparents live in Twerton, in a prefab.'

Mrs Mason almost dropped her teacup.

'*Twerton*? In a *prefab*?!'

178

'Yes,' said Wendy, 'they're very happy there.'
'I see!'

Cedric swiftly changed the subject, then it was time for Wendy to leave. She paid a visit to the lavatory and when she came back she overheard Mrs Mason saying, 'Cedric, I thought the navy would have brought you into a better class of girl than that. How on earth did she get into Colston's? Next time please bring one with a better pedigree!'

'Now don't be nasty, mother,' replied Cedric, 'she really is a wonderful girl. She can't help where she's from!'

'She'd better learn to hide it, then.'

Biting her lip, Wendy said goodbye and Cedric walked her down the drive. Away from the house, Wendy exploded.

'*Pedigree*? What does she think I am, a horse, or a dog? I'm sorry, Cedric, but your mother is the rudest person I've ever met!'

'She doesn't mean it...'

'Oh, I think she does! I hope you're not going to turn out like her!'

'Of course not!'

But Wendy had her doubts. At the end of the driveway she said goodbye, and walking alone down Lansdown Hill she wasn't sure whether she ever wanted to see him again.

*

Susan and Christopher were strolling along the front at Weston-super-Mare. As usual the sea was nowhere to be seen but the breeze was refreshing, clouds were scudding across the sky and it felt good to be away from the city. They stopped to look at the view of the Bristol Channel, leaning on the white rails lining the prom.

'I so enjoy coming here!' said Susan, breathing in the salty air.

'So do I!' said Christopher. 'In fact, these last few months have been the happiest I've spent for a long time...'

'Me too.'

He turned and looked at her, brushing back some loose strands of fair hair which had blown across her face. He'd waited long enough. Slowly, he drew her towards him and kissed her on the mouth, softly at first, then more fervently as she returned his kisses. She put her arms around him and they held each other close for a long time, lost in their own world. Day-trippers, sniggering teenagers and children with buckets and spades passed by, unaware of the miracle of love that was unfolding in front of their very eyes.

The couple drove back to Bedminster in happy silence. When they reached Susan's house Christopher leaned towards her and they kissed again.

'I don't want to leave you,' said Susan.

'And I don't want to go!' sighed Christopher. 'But I'd better get back to Tom, and it's school tomorrow!'

'Till next weekend, then.'

'Till then, my love.'

On Sundays Wendy was away at the museum all day and Susan had the house to herself. Much as she and Christopher loved their trips to Weston-super-Mare they had discovered other pleasures and for weeks to come the Morris Minor travelled no further than Bedminster.

Having been celibate for many years in widow(er)hood, the pair made up for what they had missed. The passion unleashed was beyond their understanding; they couldn't get enough of each other. Christopher bought condoms in industrial quantities (discreetly, through mail order), and Susan was unable to disguise the utter bliss she felt, totally confident and relaxed in a sexual relationship built on love, trust, and lust.

One Sunday afternoon Wendy came home from the museum early and was surprised to see the Morris Minor parked outside the house. She wondered why the couple hadn't gone out and opened the front door, expecting to see Mr Johnson and her mother having tea, only to hear moans and groans of delight coming from upstairs.

She made a swift exit, walking the streets until the coast was clear. Wendy had to say something and in the end it came out as, 'if you want each other, why don't you get married and have done with it?'

Susan couldn't hide the truth from her daughter.

'I'm sorry, Wendy - it's all a bit of a shock, isn't it? But goodness, I do love him. You're right, we should marry - but would you mind?'

Wendy shook her head. She still struggled to see her ex-Latin master as a rampant lover, but there was obviously more to him than she'd realised.

'Of course not, Mum! I can see he makes you happy…'

Although Wendy was pleased for her mother, she was also rather jealous that she had found love for the second time in her life when she, Wendy, was struggling to find it at all. She had given up on Cedric; he had written, apologising profusely for his mother's behaviour and assuring Wendy he did not share his mother's views. He was about to go to sea again and hoped it was still all right for him to write to her.

'He can write what he likes,' said Wendy to herself, still furious, 'it doesn't mean I'm going to read it!'

*

Lying next to each other in post-coital contentment, Christopher said, 'I think we should get married.'

'So do I,' said Susan.

The following Saturday, Christopher bought her a diamond solitaire engagement ring.

Back at Susan's he put the ring on her finger, then said, 'there's just one thing I ask. Your necklace - the one Frank gave you. Would you mind not wearing it now?'

Susan's hand went to the scrimshaw pendant. She'd grown so used to it she'd forgotten it was there.

'No, that's all right - I don't need it anymore.'

He leant forward, carefully unhooked the clasp and gently placed the chain and the pendant in the palm of her hand.

'I'll put it away in a drawer for now,' said Susan, then added, 'perhaps Wendy would like it.'

'Good idea,' he said, and kissed her.

CHAPTER 27

Malta, 1962

At the age of forty James Robinson was feeling satisfied with life. His health had improved remarkably; the potions that Nina continued to apply to his skin worked wonders, reducing the appearance of scarring, his left side had strengthened and even his damaged lungs were able to tolerate the occasional cigarillo. He had a beautiful wife and six wonderful children - the latest, a daughter named Leah, had just been born - and with the slash of a knife he had gained the respect of his father-in-law and the Galea family.

He learnt to use his unusual features to his advantage, knowing that they scared men and intrigued women. His status and power within the Camilleri family business were growing. Forever watching and learning, James developed his prowess in conducting business negotiations, always keeping Alessandro informed, and he concluded some lucrative deals.

Proud of his protégé, Alessandro introduced James to his influential contacts - powerful people who would play key roles in Malta's future government which must surely come soon, with calls for the country's independence growing louder. Now, the Camilleri's were ready for their next venture.

Alessandro and James had plans to develop an area of St Paul's Bay, on the North East coast of Malta. With cheap flights becoming more common they anticipated an increase in the number of tourists coming to the island and building a resort in a new area was timely. The Galea's had no objection - they were concentrating their efforts on Mellieha Bay, further North. Alessandro and James went to visit the ancient harbour of St Paul's, a peaceful village of yellow stone, a looming church and colourful fishing boats bobbing in the water.

'The bay is named after St Paul himself,' said Alessandro. 'He was shipwrecked at sea and washed ashore - rather like you!'

Together they met local property owners, councillors and landlords and worked with architects to draw up plans for hotels, restaurants, shops and bars. Everyone knew the Camilleri's were not to be messed with; the best thing was to let them do what they wanted and they would look after you. After several meetings prices were agreed, permissions given and work began.

Back on Gozo they held a family party to celebrate. Alessandro, surrounded by his adoring wife, children and grandchildren, thanked God for his good fortune and whispered a prayer to the Holy Mother, for, like Nina, he had come to believe that it was she who had arranged for James to be swept to his shore, just for him.

Bath, 1962

Wendy was pleased when her mother and Christopher announced their engagement and went with them and Tom to Bath where they shared the happy news with Fred and Pat, who asked many questions to which Susan had no answers. There was so much to consider, but at the end of it Pat said to her daughter, 'he's a kind man and it's clear that you love each other. I'm sure things will work out for you.'

Tom showed little interest in his father's marriage plans but enjoyed seeing Mr Bishop again and they arranged a date for Tom to pay another visit to Bath Spa station.

When Susan told her sister the news Ann said, 'the Latin teacher! I knew it!' Ann was happily pregnant with number four and delighted that Susan was at last on the route to finding some domestic bliss of her own.

Gradually, decisions were made and things began to fall into place. Christopher took Susan to meet the Headmaster of Bristol Grammar who was charmed and wished the couple every happiness.

'And you will be moving to the schoolhouse?' asked the Headmaster.

'Yes,' replied Susan, 'it suits us all and we don't want to disrupt Tom, especially now he's starting his degree in Bristol.'

'Yes, I heard about that, it seems you have a mathematical genius there! I'm sure he will do well.'

'He's always been a clever boy,' said Christopher. 'Susan's been a terrific help for him, and she's keen to be involved in school activities.'

'Excellent! We could do with a woman's touch around here!'

Wendy was sad to leave the house in Bedminster where she had grown up and didn't particularly like the schoolhouse. It had always been just her and her mother, and much as she was learning to like Mr Johnson it was strange having a man about the place - she had managed without a father figure in her life and didn't want one now. But it was only a temporary arrangement - she planned to share a house in the city centre with other students when she began her final year at university. She was going to spend the Summer holidays at a dig in Cirencester, well-known for its Roman remains, and couldn't wait to get away, looking upon this whole period as a fresh start.

Susan gave up work a week before the wedding. Her workmates gave her a good send-off and her boss recognised her eighteen years of loyal service to Wills with the gift of a silver cigarette lighter, engraved with her new married name. Ann and Brian came to wish her well, making Susan quite emotional, remembering when she and her sister had first arrived in Bedminster during the war, knowing no one.

'Now, don't get all maudlin!' said Brian, always a cheerful type, still completely in love with his wife, and newly promoted to a management position in the Wills company. 'You've got your new life with Christopher ahead and we all wish you the best of luck!'

Susan and Christopher married in July in a quiet ceremony at Bristol Register Office with close family present. They celebrated afterwards at a restaurant then, leaving Tom under the watchful eye of Matron, the happy couple set off for a brief honeymoon to the place that would always be dear to their hearts - Weston-super-Mare.

Susan loved life with her new husband and they settled into a pleasant domestic routine. It struck her that she and Frank had never lived together as husband and wife - in fact they'd hardly spent any time together at all - and she thought yet again that if it hadn't been for Wendy she would have almost forgotten about him.

Susan offered to make costumes for the end of term school play and one Sunday afternoon towards Christmas she was attending a dress rehearsal when Wendy came over to see them. Tom was in his room so while Wendy waited for her mother to return she found herself alone with Christopher.

Aware of a slight awkwardness, Christopher made some tea, then said, 'so, Wendy, have you thought about what you're going to do after you graduate?'

She shifted uneasily in her chair and said, 'I think about it all the time, but I still haven't made up my mind.'

He nodded, understandingly. 'I know, it's so difficult. It's as if the whole world is open to you and the hardest thing is to decide which path to take.'

Wendy recognised that Christopher was the only member of the family who had this kind of experience, so she ventured, 'what did you do?'

'Well, I graduated in 1939 so the decision was made for me - I joined the Army!'

'Of course...so how did you get into teaching?'

'It wasn't my first choice! Rather like you, I was fascinated by the ancient world. With my Classics degree I really wanted to go to Greece and explore the history there. I dreamt of travelling, writing books, learning more about the great philosophers, even becoming a professor.'

'So what happened?'

'The war - as I said - and then I got married in '43, just before I was sent to Italy. Tom was born in '44 so I didn't see him till after the war ended - after my wife was killed.'

'How sad! It must have been awful for you.'

'Yes…so after all that I needed to make a secure home for Tom. I went back to College for a year, qualified as a teacher and started at Bristol Grammar.'

'The war changed everything for so many people, didn't it.'

'Indeed. But those days are gone, now. You see, Wendy, you must grasp chances that come your way - do something thrilling, go somewhere exciting while you can! Be open to opportunities and they will come to you.'

Wendy paused to take all this in, then said, 'I loved our school trip to Rome and Pompeii. My first and only time abroad! It was so interesting exploring the ruins and experiencing a foreign country.'

'Yes - new languages and cultures are so inspiring. You should try and find an archaeological dig overseas. Be ambitious! You don't have to restrict yourself to Bath and Cirencester.'

Wendy nodded, thoughtfully. 'Thank you, Mr Johnson, that's very encouraging. I'm lucky having you to talk to about all this.'

'Not at all. And for the last time, call me Christopher!'

*

In April Wendy celebrated her twenty-first birthday. Cedric sent her a card - she must have told him her birth date at some point - but she still couldn't bring herself to write to him, and in any case she was having a fling with one of her housemates, a fellow student.

In the morning she went to the schoolhouse to see her mother, looking forward to receiving her birthday gift - a gold chain necklace. Then Susan said, 'I wondered if you might like this?'

She gave her the scrimshaw pendant and Wendy held it in front of her.

'Oh Mum! Do you remember, when I was little and you'd show it to me, with the photo of Dad on his ship…And there's the special squiggle - the 'S', for 'Susan'. Thanks, Mum, I'd love to have it.'

Susan threaded the pendant onto the gold chain and fastened it around her daughter's neck.

Wendy spent the rest of the day celebrating with her friends in the city centre. She returned to the schoolhouse in the evening, and while Susan was busy in the kitchen Christopher said to Wendy, 'I see you're wearing your mother's pendant.'

'Yes, she gave it to me this morning. I've always been fascinated by it. My father's ship was called HMS SALAMANDER.'

'Yes…You know what a salamander is, don't you?'

'Some sort of a lizard?'

'Well, strictly it's an amphibian. Extraordinary creatures - there's a host of myths about them. Of course, their association with fire first appeared in ancient Rome. Are you familiar with Pliny the Elder's *Natural History*?'

'No - not yet!'

'He wrote about the salamander's ability to withstand any heat. It secretes a liquid in its mouth which is so cold they say it can put out fire. And they are capable of regenerating themselves - they can grow back lost limbs and repair damage to their bodies.'

'Like the phoenix rising from the ashes?'

'Yes! But you have to beware because some species contain a powerful poison - they're colourful but deadly.'

'Fascinating!'

Wendy touched the pendant. 'I don't think I'll ever look at it in quite the same way again!'

Wendy's graduation ceremony took place in Bristol, her mother, aunt and grandparents bursting with pride at seeing the first member of the Bishop family gain a degree, and a First Class Honours at that.

Susan was delighted to send photographs of her daughter in her cap and gown to David Roberts, Jean Daniels and Frances, knowing they would be interested in Wendy's success, while Fred and Pat told anyone who would listen how Wendy's passion for archaeology had all begun with the discovery of a Roman coin in their back garden.

Susan said, 'what on earth would Frank have made of all this? He'd be so proud of you!'

A few weeks later Wendy arrived at the schoolhouse, brimming with excitement.

'I've got a job! I'm going to be a Field Assistant on a new project to excavate a Roman site - I saw it advertised in the Archaeology Journal at the museum and my professor gave me a reference. They've given me a two-year contract. I can't believe I'm going to get paid for doing something I love!'

'That's wonderful, Wendy, I'm so pleased for you!' said Susan, getting up and giving her a hug.

'Congratulations!' said Christopher.

'So, where is this site?' asked Susan.

'Well, that's what's so thrilling...I'm going to need a new Summer wardrobe, Mum. I'm going to Malta!'

PART THREE

CHAPTER 28

Malta, 1963

The plane touched down at Luqa airport and taxied to a halt. As soon as the doors were opened there was a rush of hot air and a distinctive earthy smell, part fragrant herbs, part dung. Wendy felt as if she were stepping into an oven. In the arrivals hall she was met by a short, fair woman in her forties holding up a piece of paper with Wendy's name on it.

'I'm Sandy Smith. Welcome to Malta!'

They walked over to Sandy's car, a timber-framed Morris traveller, and set off, Sandy chatting all the while.

'Hold onto your hat, the roads around here are pretty treacherous!' she said, crunching the Morris into second gear.

As they veered around narrow, twisty roads heading inland Wendy took in the scenery as it unfolded around her, the sun blindingly bright, the earth scorched, animals grazing on scrubland under an azure sky. After a bumpy half hour of a ride they arrived at a small village near Mdina, the island's ancient capital, coming to a halt in a cloud of dust outside a stone cottage with chickens clucking about in the yard.

'So, this is home,' said Sandy.

A man aged around fifty with a shock of grey hair emerged from the cottage.

'Wendy! Graham Fletcher,' he said, shaking hands, 'so pleased to meet you! Your tutor gave you a glowing reference. Come inside.'

Wendy followed Graham out of the bright sunlight and into the cool of the cottage. It was basic, with a stone floor, thick walls and small windows to keep out the Summer heat and retain warmth in the Winter. The remnants of lunch were still evident on the kitchen table and Graham offered her some bread and goats' cheese and a cup of black tea.

Afterwards Sandy showed Wendy to her room which was simple but comfortable enough with a single bed, a chest of drawers, a desk and a hook on the back of the door with a couple of wire coat hangers. It wasn't exactly luxury, but she hadn't come for that.

'Don't forget to put the mosquito net over the bed at night - they're vicious buggers. It's very free and easy here - we pool our money and take turns to buy food, cook and clean the place. You'll soon settle in!'

In the evening Wendy enjoyed the meal cooked by Sandy and met the other members of the team - a married couple, Ronald and Helen, and a tall blonde around Wendy's own age called Emily. They all spoke enthusiastically about their work and while Graham was out of the room, commented on how easy going and unstuffy he was for a renowned Oxford professor. It all sounded very promising, but Wendy was exhausted from her trip so left the party early, fixed the mosquito net and fell into a deep sleep.

The next day Graham took Wendy to the site they were excavating near Mdina where a Roman villa and outbuildings had once stood, home to a family, its workers and slaves around the second century. Evidence of their lives lay just beneath the surface, waiting to be uncovered. The team had already traced the outline of a mosaic floor, much like those Wendy had seen in Pompeii, and Graham showed her the human and animal bones, fragments of pottery, coins and figurines they had found so far. He explained that Malta's long and varied history provided a treasure trove with its sheer number of megalithic monuments, ruined temples and tombs.

'It's very exciting because in searching for a particular civilisation one comes across another. Just the other day Sandy was working here on this Roman site and found a relic from the Phoenicians!'

'How wonderful!' exclaimed Wendy, 'I can't wait to get started!'

At the weekend in the sweltering heat, Ronald and Helen took Wendy to explore Mdina, known as the 'Silent City' due to the loss of its prominence to Valletta as well as to the calm atmosphere that pervades its walls. They explored the ruins of the Domus Romana, the residence of a rich Roman aristocrat which had been excavated some years previously, then visited St Paul's catacombs with its miles of underground galleries and tombs.

Wendy was in Roman heaven.

Helen explained that these were only some of the catacombs that could be found across Malta. She told Wendy how, during the siege of Malta in the Second World War, hundreds of people had used them to shelter from air raids, describing the hardships they suffered, living underground for months on end in the filthy, rat-infested burrows with no privacy and near to starvation. Many had died.

'They say Malta was the most bombed place on Earth! It was the bravery of the Allied forces bringing aid that saved them.'

'My father was in the Royal Navy and he served in the convoys,' said Wendy, 'he was killed when his ship was torpedoed.'

'Oh, I'm sorry…'

'I never knew him, but being here, I can see why what he was doing was so important. What a dreadful time it must have been.'

Once a month the team went to Valletta to collect mail from their poste restante address and have a taste of city life. They walked through the bustling streets, busy with traffic, horns blazing and people shouting out to each other. Wendy turned up her nose at the stench coming from the drains. They found their way to a café in a shady square and sat reading their letters while eating *pastizzi* and drinking ice cold cola.

Wendy was pleased to catch up with the news from home. There was nothing from her ex-boyfriend - the fling with her housemate in Bristol hadn't survived after graduation - but her mother had forwarded a letter from Cedric. Wendy had to admire his persistence - it was two years since she had last seen him but he still wrote occasionally, even though she never replied. She opened the letter and, despite her misgivings about him, read his news with interest.

His ship was sailing along the East coast of the USA to the West Indies and he concluded,

New York Harbor is a sight to behold. I'd love to tell you all about it one day. I often think of you Wendy. We still have a lot in common and I am really keen to stay in touch. Please write to me - I'd love to hear how you're getting on.
Yours, Cedric

The bells of the nearby church began to toll loudly, making Wendy jump.

'Island of bells, smells and yells,' said Ronald, 'that's what Byron called Malta.'

'I can understand why!'

After lunch the group split up and Wendy wandered alone through Valletta's steep, narrow streets, ancient buildings side by side with modern apartment blocks and hotels, building sites and cranes. The British presence was very much in evidence in the number of military personnel, red pillar boxes and the names of the streets and shops, 'The Colonial Stores' being a favourite. She bought some postcards and, because he was on her mind, on a whim she sent one to Cedric.

She wandered through Upper Barraka gardens, a tranquil haven of colonnades and fountains, admiring the vivid colours and scents of the oleander and bougainvillea, until she reached the balustrade overlooking Grand Harbour. It was a magnificent sight, framed by golden cliffs, crammed with Royal Navy ships and small craft gliding around in the calm water, and cranes on the dockside loading and unloading cargo from merchant vessels. Admiring the view on this peaceful September day Wendy tried to imagine how it must have been twenty-odd years ago when ships were bringing aid to people under fire, and she thought again of the terrible sights her father must have seen. At least in his career Cedric would never have to endure anything as horrific as that.

Wendy and Emily got on well together and gradually told each other about their lives. Emily had also fallen in love with archaeology as a child and had been going out with a fellow historian at Oxford when he had unceremoniously ditched her and run off with an air hostess. She had come to Malta at Graham's invitation to take her mind off it and loved every minute, saying her ex had done her a favour.

Emily was curious about the letters Wendy received from all over the world and was impressed when Wendy showed her the photo of Cedric at Dartmouth that she had brought with her from home.

'What a dish! And you don't reply to his letters because...?'

'Because his mother is the most horrible woman!'

'But you're not going out with his mother, are you?'

'No, but...'

Emily shook her head. 'In your position I'd snap him up before somebody else does!'

Bristol, 1963

Susan had been up half the night finishing costumes for the end-of-term school play, a joint production of *The Mikado* with Colston's Girls'. She'd found it hard work this year for some reason, unable to concentrate and feeling weary. She was on stage at the dress rehearsal making last-minute alterations to Yum-Yum's kimono when she felt lightheaded and fainted.

The English master ran over to her and shouted to one of the boys to fetch Mr Johnson. By the time he arrived Susan was sitting on a chair, sipping a glass of water, the colour gone from her face.

'It's all right, I came over dizzy but I feel much better now,' she said, weakly.

Christopher, who had been concerned about his wife's health for a while, insisted on taking her home, saying, 'you must go and see a doctor, I'm worried about you.'

Susan made an appointment for the following week, not wanting a fuss, but at last forcing herself to acknowledge that all was not well.

On Christmas Eve Susan returned to the doctor to get the results of the tests he'd carried out. When Christopher came home that afternoon he found Susan sitting in the lounge on the settee, pale and still. His heart went to his mouth. This woman meant the world to him and he couldn't bear to think that there might be something seriously wrong.

He sat down, put his arm around her and said, gently, 'what is it, Susan? Please - whatever it is, just tell me!'

She couldn't speak.

'Susan!'

She looked at him.

'Christopher,' she said at last, 'my darling man - I'm pregnant!'

CHAPTER 29

Malta, 1964

Wendy missed being home at Christmas but the archaeology team had become her second family and together they all had a fabulous time with good food, Italian wine, cigarettes and dancing around to the Beatles' latest hits played on Emily's dansette record player. The weather was mild and on New Year's Day they went over to the deserted white sands and cool, clear waters of Mellieha Bay for a swim to cure their collective hangover.

They went to Valletta to fetch their post. Wendy read the letter from her mother with astonishment. A baby! She and Christopher sounded surprised but pleased about the news, so Wendy tried to be pleased for them too, although it was a shock, and she found it hard to imagine them raising a child at their age. She had a sudden yearning to be with her mother and wrote to her straight away, giving her love to Christopher whom she was sure would make a caring and patient father, as he had been to Tom.

When Susan and Christopher told Tom the news he asked, 'will the baby have its own room?'

'Yes, we'll convert the spare room into a nursery.'

Tom nodded, then said to his father, 'I think you are pleased about the baby.'

'Yes, I'm very pleased, but I am surprised!'

'No,' said Tom, 'I've read about it. Condoms are only 98 per cent effective.'

Susan looked at him in shock, then laughed, and Christopher said, 'yes, that 2 per cent was bound to catch us out sooner or later!'

Ann and Brian were thrilled with the news.

'That's wonderful!' said Ann, now with two boys and two girls of her own, 'and don't worry about he or she being lonely, they'll have their cousins to play with!'

The parents-to-be made a special trip to Bath to tell Fred and Pat who were astounded.

'At your age!' said Pat.

'I know, Mum,' said Susan. 'I hadn't been feeling well and I thought it was the change, or something worse, but…'

'Well, we're delighted for you both,' said Fred. 'Another grandchild! And when's it due?'

'In June,' said Susan. 'I've written to tell Wendy. Oh, how I wish she was here…'

While they were in Bath, Susan and Christopher visited David Roberts who was happy for them but had some words of caution.

'You're not elderly primigravida,' he said to Susan, 'but you must take care of yourself.'

'Elderly what?!'

'Primigravida,' he said, 'it's the medical term for women over thirty-five who become pregnant for the first time. But you've had Wendy, of course.'

'Yes - twenty-two years ago!'

'Indeed…a long gap between pregnancies. You should be fine, but don't over-exert yourself, eat a healthy diet, and cut down on smoking, too!'

'I've more or less given up, actually,' she said, glancing at Christopher.

'Pleased to hear it! The latest research shows that it can harm babies in the womb, reducing their birth weight. I have observed this in some of my own patients at the hospital here, in Weston. Anyway, make sure you attend all your check-ups - the staff at Bristol are very competent, and I'm sure your husband will look after you!'

'Of course,' Christopher replied, smiling, taking Susan's hand in his and raising it to his lips.

Malta, 1964

Wendy shared the news of the expected baby with her colleagues who took a passing interest, and she wrote and told her friend Pamela. However, she needed another outlet to express her feelings and at last she decided to write to Cedric. Emily's words were ringing in her ears - perhaps she had been a bit mean to him, and he still sounded keen on her. Her letter was a lot longer than she intended and she ended up telling him all about her life in Malta as well as the family news, but there, it was done: she felt better for having written it, and posted it on her next trip to Valletta.

Graham temporarily returned to Oxford and Sandy took charge of the team which continued its work near Mdina. Wendy was working meticulously on the mosaic floor with her pointing trowel and brushes, gradually revealing its colour and pattern, stone by stone. In ancient Rome mosaics were symbols of wealth and status, made to adorn villas and impress guests, and this particular one was placed perfectly in the vestibule of the villa. As she worked, Wendy imagined the generations of Romans who had set foot there, wondering about their lives, loves and losses, reflecting on how much had changed in the last two thousand years, and, in human terms, how little.

In her spare time she explored the island using Malta's unique transport system with its post-war buses painted in different colours according to their route. It was quite an experience, embarking on a journey which began with the driver saying a prayer to the Holy Mother and crossing himself, his windscreen adorned with crucifixes, flowers and rosary beads. She learnt to hang on tight as the buses veered round the corners, and many a time along the coast she spotted the rusty ruins of vehicles which had plummeted over the edge of a cliff on a steep bend, a testament to Malta's bad drivers and dangerous roads.

The mighty Catholic church was present in every aspect of the nation's life. Time was measured in Saints' days and celebrations and Wendy lost track of the number of times they went to Valletta on feast days to watch the colourful processions. The team paid frequent visits to the Museum of Archaeology in Valletta to identify, research and catalogue their findings, aware that Graham's ambition was for them to form part of the museum's permanent collection.

When Graham returned from his trip to Oxford he brought exciting news.

'Some researchers have found the remains of a stone circle in a place called Xaghra on Gozo. It was excavated in the 1800s but then lost and forgotten, but a new team has rediscovered it. They think it's an old burial site.'

'How old is it?' asked Emily.

'They reckon it goes back as far as 3000BC! I've suggested we go over there for a month or two to help out until the main excavations begin. It should be fascinating!'

In April the team upped sticks and moved there, renting a cottage near Xaghra close to the centre of the island. Wendy was enthused about the work and to see Gozo itself, which was more primitive and remote than Malta. 'Sleepy Gozo', they called it, and she could see why - the pace of life was slow and one had the impression that nothing had ever changed. Walking through the alleyways of the villages was like going back in time, with ancient women sitting in doorways wearing their traditional black head dress and cloak known as a Faldetta. Made from black cotton, the upper part was stiffened with whalebone sewn inside it, forming a frame around their heads. While walking, the women would gather the folds of the cloak around them, clasping it in their right hand.

Gozitan women were known for their skill in making lace and Wendy watched them, fascinated, as they sat at an upright lace pillow, their expert fingers nimbly winding cream silk thread around each bobbin, spinning the lace by twisting and crossing the bobbins under and over each other with a distinctive *click-clack*. They created exquisite patterns, often including the

Maltese Cross, making mats and decorative objects which they would sell for a few pounds to locals and tourists. Wendy bought a selection at the market to send home to her mother, knowing that she would appreciate the makers' artistry and skill.

The weather was pleasantly warm, ideal for conducting the preparatory work on the vast site, literally scratching at the surface which consisted of a series of caves used to bury the dead, surrounded by a walled enclosure. Wendy was soon engrossed in her work, happily chipping away at stones with her hammer, brushing away loose dirt and sieving through piles of earth in search of evidence of past lives.

At the weekends the team took the opportunity to explore other parts of the island. One Saturday Wendy and Emily found their way to a beach on the South side and spent the morning swimming and sunbathing, then Wendy left her friend snoozing in the shade of a beach umbrella to investigate the rocky pools by the seashore. As she marvelled at the tiny creatures that lived in the shallows she noticed a dark-haired, olive-skinned boy of about ten years old, searching among the rocks. He looked more worried than a ten-year-old boy on the beach ought to be.

'Hello!' she said, 'have you lost something?'

The boy looked up at her with his hazel eyes.

'Yes, I've lost my dap and my sister will be cross.'

'Really?' said Wendy, surprised to hear the word and looking down at the boy who was indeed wearing just one shoe. 'Let me help you find it!'

It didn't take long before Wendy saw a black plimsoll caught underneath a rock. She picked it up and gave it to him.

'Thank you!' he cried, and ran off back to the beach to join his brothers and sisters.

When Wendy returned the boy ran up to her, telling his sister, 'that's the lady who found my dap.'

'Thank you,' said the girl, who was about fifteen.

'You're welcome!' Then Wendy added, 'I haven't heard that word for a long time.'

'That's what Daddy calls it,' said the boy.

'Yes,' said the girl, 'our Daddy's English. He comes from London.'

'Really?' Wendy's curiosity was aroused.

'Are you on holiday?' asked the girl.

'No - I'm here on a dig - I'm an archaeologist. But we thought we'd have a day off on the beach. It's so lovely here.'

'We live in that house, just over there.'

The girl pointed to a house a little further along from the beach with a terracotta roof and a terrace overlooking the sea.

'Lucky you!'

'My name's Elena, and my little brother is called Alfredo.'

'It's nice to meet you. My name is Wendy.'

'I love the colour of your hair,' said Elena.

'Thank you.'

'I'm going back in the sea!' said Alfredo.

'And I'd better get back to my friend,' said Wendy. 'It was nice to meet you both.'

Towards the end of the afternoon Wendy watched as the children's parents, walking hand in hand, came to join them on the beach. The woman had long, dark hair and an amazing figure considering she'd had all those children, thought Wendy. Her husband was wearing a Panama hat and a colourful shirt, but even from a distance Wendy noticed there was something odd about the way he held himself, slightly lop-sided, and one side of his face looked strange. He was full of fun; his children obviously adored him. As he swung the youngest girl, a toddler, onto his shoulders Wendy heard him say, 'up you go, honey bunny!' then he walked to the water's edge with two girls aged around four and twelve beside him.

His other three children followed behind - Elena, a boy a year or so younger than her, and Alfredo, the one who had lost his dap. The elder boy had an arrogant air about him, as if aware that he was the most important of them all.

Wendy listened to the man talking, picking up his speech pattern in which she detected the trace of a West-country twang. He spoke as if he'd tried to lose his accent, but couldn't quite, and she recognised it because it was how she spoke herself.

After some fun and games in the sea he turned to the youngest girl, took her hand and said, 'come on, my lover, time to go home now.'

Wendy watched curiously as the family packed up their kit and walked back to their house. As they left the beach Elena turned and waved at her, and Wendy waved back.

'What's all that about?' asked Emily.

'I'm just curious about that family. The daughter said her father came from London, but I'm sure he's not - he's from Bath!'

CHAPTER 30

Bath, 1964

After forty years' service on the railways, Fred had retired. Everything was changing, with Dr Beeching's report leading to many of the old lines being cut, and the new diesel trains didn't have the charm of the old steam-driven machines. Fred felt that he'd had his day. Nevertheless he missed his job and was finding it hard to adjust, sitting at home, watching the clock he'd been presented with ticking away the seconds. He enjoyed his patch of garden - his main interest - although even that had recently been a source of frustration. He had taken his prize vegetables to the annual show, confident of his usual gold award, but this time returned home with a long face.

'Whatever's the matter?' Pat asked.

'Silver!' he cried, despondent, 'bloody silver!'

He plonked himself down in his armchair and lit a cigarette.

'And to make it worse, the bloke who beat me to the gold was a bloody German! Blum- something he was called. Honestly, Pat, it makes you wonder why we bothered fighting the war!'

Fred welcomed visits from the family more than ever, and on this particular June day they had passed an enjoyable afternoon with Susan. She was about to leave for home when she suddenly cried out with pain.

'Oh my God, I think the baby's coming!'

'But it's not due for another couple of weeks!' exclaimed her mother, 'settle down, I'll make some tea and…'

Susan cried out again, louder this time. 'I think it's decided to come early…'

'Better get you to the hospital!' said Fred, as Pat ran to the phone box on the corner to dial 999.

The ambulance arrived, Pat helped her in while the neighbours watched and Susan shouted to her father, 'call Christopher at the school!'

Its siren blaring, the ambulance departed for the short trip to the hospital in Weston. On arrival Susan was taken to the maternity ward and examined by the midwife who looked concerned.

'What's wrong?' asked Susan, beginning to panic.

'Don't worry, Mrs Johnson, I just need to fetch the doctor.'

She swiftly left the room and Susan cried out again while Pat tried to comfort her. Susan's anxiety levels were sky-high by the time the midwife returned with the obstetrician, who was none other than David Roberts.

'Susan! How lovely to see you.'

He quickly examined her then said, 'Susan, you have a breech birth - the baby wants to come out bottom first. I'll need to make an intervention. Just do as I ask and keep taking the gas and air…'

'Hold her hand, will you?' he said to Pat, 'she's going to need it…'

In the depths of her labour Susan had flashbacks to the night Wendy was born, when the bombs fell and Bath was ablaze, remembering the fear, the noise and the flames as the world exploded around her. In her lucid moments she thought to herself, 'at least this time, if I can get through this, I'll have a house and a husband to go back to.'

David Roberts, expert and reassuring, was the best doctor she could have hoped for. At last the baby was safely delivered - a healthy boy.

By the time Christopher arrived it was all over. His exhausted wife was sleeping, the baby was being monitored in a separate room, and Pat was snoozing in an armchair. He sat on the side of the bed and took his wife's hand in his; he had never felt a love so profound.

Later, after Pat had gone home, Susan awoke, relieved to see her husband. A nurse brought the baby to her, then David came to examine them and declared that all was well.

'You need to rest now. We'll keep you in for a few days to make sure everything's all right. Your wife's been through quite an ordeal,' he said, turning to Christopher, 'but it's over now, and you have a healthy baby boy. What are you going to call him?'

'I think there's only one option, isn't there?' said Susan, looking at her husband.

They said in unison, 'David!'

Malta, 1964

Wendy was excited to receive news of the baby's safe arrival and relieved that her mother was well. She wrote home immediately with her congratulations, saying she couldn't wait to meet baby David and that she missed them all. She also wrote to Cedric to tell him the news.

Another group of archaeologists had arrived to take forward the excavations of the stone circle on Gozo and Wendy's team resumed their work on the Roman site near Mdina. She was pleased to return to the mosaic floor which she had come to regard as her own, finding that the painstaking work helped to calm the thoughts she had whirling in her head about new babies and the strange man she had seen on the beach.

She received a letter from Cedric who was back in Dartmouth:

…it was a delight to hear from you. I'm so pleased you're enjoying life in Malta…Great news about your new baby brother and I'm pleased your mother is well. My mother was 41 when she had me and she survived!
…I have passed my Warfare course and am now a fully-fledged Lieutenant. I'm about to join my new ship, HMS STEVENSON, a frigate. We're going to the Med and will visit Malta at some point. When we do I thought it would be rather fun if we could meet. I would really like to see you again, Wendy, and I often think of you.
Yours, Cedric

The run ashore in Malta came more quickly than expected. STEVENSON sailed from Plymouth in August and after a short stop in Gibraltar, Valletta was the next port of call. Cedric wrote to Wendy, hoping she'd pick up his letter in time, and he was thrilled when he spotted her on the quayside, waiting to meet the ship on its arrival in Grand Harbour.

When they met they shook hands, pleased to see each other again but aware that three years had passed and a lot had happened in both their lives. She looked at him, recalling his handsome features, fair hair and piercing blue eyes, now wearing his tropical whites. He saw a more mature version of his pre-Raphaelite beauty in a skimpy Summer dress, her red hair falling about her shoulders.

'Let's go and get a drink,' she said, 'I know a nice café nearby.'

'Good idea. We've got a lot to catch up on…'

They ordered coffee and lit cigarettes, then Wendy asked, 'how long are you here for?'

'Two days, then we're sailing to Alexandria.'

Wendy, who wanted to clear the air, said, 'sorry I was so off with you. Your mother really upset me, but I do understand that you're not like her. I hope we can be friends again.'

'Of course, I would like nothing more.'

Wendy showed him around Valletta and they found their way to the Upper Barraka Gardens where they drank in the view of Grand Harbour.

'There's my ship,' Cedric pointed out, proudly. 'I say, Wendy, we're having a cocktail party on board this evening - would you like to come?'

Later in the afternoon Cedric had to return to duty, giving Wendy the chance to do some emergency shopping and buy a dress for the party. She settled on a little black number, strapless with a nipped-in waist, and some black low-heeled shoes with pointy toes.

Back at the house she changed into her new outfit and looked at herself in the mirror.

'You look lovely!' said Emily. 'You need something round your neck, though.'

'Yes, you're right,' said Wendy. 'I have the very thing…'

*

James Robinson didn't much enjoy cocktail parties but his father-in-law told him it was a necessary part of the job and a good way to make contacts. James was on the list of local VIPs to be invited to such affairs and he usually went along, even making the effort to wear a tie, despite the discomfort it gave him.

This party on board HMS STEVENSON was much like all the others he had attended on Royal Navy ships. As he stepped aboard the frigate the familiar smell of diesel oil and the throbbing of the generators took him back to his days as an Able Seaman, and he had to make a conscious effort to concentrate on the present. He was ushered into the wardroom, a place he had never entered in all his years at sea, but one he now frequented. He introduced himself to the ship's Captain, discussed business, drank a couple of gins and tonics and conversed charmingly with his hosts and other guests.

At nine o'clock the party wound up and James was about to leave when an enthusiastic young Lieutenant approached him. James wasn't interested; he'd already said all he needed to the Captain, but he introduced himself to the young man whose name was Cedric Mason. James was setting foot on the gangway when a striking red-head appeared at Cedric's side. He quickly cast an eye over her, noticing something interesting around her neck but before he could take a closer look the Captain came forward to guide him off the ship.

James glanced back, wondering if he'd really seen what looked like a pendant with a picture of a salamander, but dismissed the thought. It was probably some trinket the girl had picked up at one of the markets in Valletta.

*

After the party Cedric walked Wendy ashore.

'That man you were talking to at the end there, who is he?' she asked.

'Some local bigwig. His name's James Robinson but I didn't have much chance to find out anything else. Odd-looking chap, isn't he? He must have been in a fire years ago.'

'Yes…I've seen him before, on Gozo with his family.'

'Why the interest?'

'I don't know…just something curious about him.'

'Well, never mind him. It's our last day tomorrow, Wendy. What would you like to do?'

'Let's go to a beach and have a swim.'

'Good idea,' said Cedric. 'Now, here's your taxi. I'll see you back here at ten.'

'I'll look forward to it,' she said, and kissed him on the cheek.

The next morning Wendy and Cedric caught the bus to St Julian's where there was a small sandy beach, shaded by Judas trees. They rented a parasol, found a quiet spot and changed into their swimming costumes, each of them wriggling clumsily under a towel, Cedric finally emerging in a pair of baggy bathing trunks and Wendy in a demure swimsuit. The Maltese had strict rules on beachwear and bikinis were strictly forbidden. Wendy pulled her long hair back, twisted it into a knot and crammed it into a swimming cap. They looked at each other self-consciously, then she said, 'race you to the sea!'

They sprinted over the scorching sand, into the warm water. Cedric was a strong swimmer, as was Wendy, having learnt during her Summer holidays in Devon. They swam out onto a raft moored in the bay, Cedric heaving himself up onto it then helping Wendy aboard. As they looked around at the swimmers and sailing boats Wendy noticed a grand-looking villa at the end of St Julian's point and said, 'what a dream house. I wonder who lives there?'

'Some local millionaire, I expect. They're all crooks of course - they can't wait to get rid of us so they can make more money.'

Wendy, shocked, said, 'what makes you say that?'

'Oh - we get told these things at our briefings. Once Malta's independent we anticipate a rise in criminal activity round here - you should watch out!'

They swam back to the shore, dried themselves off and Wendy shook her hair loose, its coppery highlights glinting in the sun. They bought some lunch at a shack on the beach then laid down in the shade of the parasol. Wendy rolled over onto her stomach.

'Rub some of that cream on my back, will you?'

He loosened the straps of her swimming costume and gently massaged her neck and shoulders, caressing her smooth skin, working his way down her back while she sighed with pleasure.

Wendy fell asleep for an hour and when she opened her eyes Cedric was lying on his side, propped up on his elbow, looking at her.

'Ah, the sleeping beauty awakes!'

She stretched out and smiled, then he leant down and kissed her. She put her arms around him, drawing him close to her, loving the feel of his body against hers and wondering why it had taken her so long to realise how much she wanted him. She returned his kiss and they lay on her beach towel, entwined around each other, for the rest of the afternoon.

In the warmth of the evening they returned to Grand Harbour where Cedric was due back on board.

'It's been lovely seeing you again,' she said.

'You too.'

They kissed, lingeringly. As he walked towards the ship he turned and waved, and she called out, 'do write, won't you!'

'Of course!'

CHAPTER 31

Malta, 1964

On the 21st September 1964, after a long and complex history of being ruled by others, Malta finally gained independence. It was a day of wild celebration. A public holiday had been declared and Wendy and the team joined in the festivities, the streets crammed with people cheering and church bells ringing. Prince Philip, Duke of Edinburgh, handed over the formal independence documents to Malta's Prime Minister, George Borg Olivier, in front of huge crowds who gathered to witness history unfold. Fireworks were set off in a brilliant display over Grand Harbour, setting the sky alight with joy and hope for the future.

At a party in Valletta the Camilleri's along with other important local families witnessed this most momentous day.

'At last we are free!' exclaimed Alessandro, 'we can say goodbye to the British military that have kept us in their stranglehold for so any years. Now we can really start to expand our business interests!'

'We have escaped from the shackles of the past! Slaves to the British no more!' answered one of his associates, high on the excitement of the day and the prospects to come.

At midnight the union flag was taken down and Malta's new flag was unfurled with full ceremonial. A new era had begun.

Bristol, 1964

It felt like a new era for Wendy when she returned to Bristol for Christmas. She'd saved enough money for her air fare and although she hadn't intended to return mid-tour she felt a strong pull to home, longing to see her mother and the new baby.

Susan welcomed Wendy with open arms and the two held each other, crying with delight to be together again. At last they let go and Christopher came in, holding baby David. Wendy had never seen a man look so happy.

'Someone wants to meet you!' he said, passing the baby to Wendy who took him, carefully, ensuring his head was supported in the crook of her elbow. She wasn't particularly keen on babies but the little chap was so cute she ooh'd and aah'd, rocking him gently as he gurgled at her.

'Yes, it's me, your big sister! Oh, Mum, he's gorgeous! You must be thrilled with him!'

'I know - we still can't believe it, can we?'

Susan turned to Christopher who put his arm lovingly around her.

'He's our little miracle,' he said.

Malta, 1965

When Wendy returned to Malta, encouraged by Sandy, she bought a car. The Maltese buses were reasonably reliable and a source of entertainment, but their routes were limited. To be truly independent, one needed wheels.

Wendy had passed her test while she was at university but driving in Malta was something else. She bought herself a second-hand Ford Anglia and set about learning the Maltese driving ways. At least they drove on the left side of the road, so that was familiar, but the Maltese temperament was more difficult to get to grips with.

The usual pose adopted by Maltese drivers (mostly men, it had to be said), was to drive with their window rolled down, their right elbow propped on the window frame, cigarette in hand, and the other hand loosely on the steering wheel, removed as necessary to change gear at which point their knees would come into play. Indicators were optional, but if the driver banged his hand on top of the car roof it signalled an intention to turn left. Wendy discovered that local drivers were not inclined to look in their rear-view mirrors, saying with a Maltese nonchalance, 'what is behind, let it look out for itself.'

Rules and signs were regarded as mere suggestions - the most important safety feature was the car's horn, being blasted at every opportunity. The number of cars on the road was increasing dramatically, causing drivers to have outbursts of temper at the slightest delay, shouting at each other and gesticulating wildly.

The lanes in the old towns and in the

countryside were narrow and often unsurfaced, with semi-blind corners. Traffic could only travel down them in single file and Wendy learnt to sound her horn at every bend in the road, praying that she wouldn't meet someone coming the other way. Another hazard was the presence of deep ridges in the earth, like ancient trackways, which were widespread throughout the island.

'Be careful,' Graham warned her, 'they can ruin your suspension if you run over them. The ruts were caused by carts being driven around - some go back to the Bronze Age.'

Wendy had visions of the Maltese ancients charging about the island, and their driving hadn't improved since, she thought…

In February the museum in Valletta held a reception to mark a new acquisition of Phoenician artefacts. Graham was delighted to receive an invitation, seeing it as a step closer to getting his own team's findings from Mdina accepted into the museum's permanent collection. The directors were considering the matter and this evening may help progress his case.

Wendy and her colleagues attended the event and listened to the Mayor of Valletta's speech about the importance of the museum's role in preserving Malta's long history. Mingling at the drinks afterwards, Wendy was talking to Graham when she spotted the man she'd seen on Gozo and at the cocktail party - James Robinson. His glamorous wife was by his side, but then an older man beckoned her away, leaving James on his own, and Wendy watched as he scanned the room then made a bee-line for Graham.

'Professor Fletcher! It is good to meet you again. I hope one day we will be hosting a reception here to celebrate your work!'

'Absolutely! I'm trying to persuade your colleagues to do just that.'

'I will do what I can to help.'

'This is one of my assistants, Wendy Fowler.'

James started, hearing the surname, and shook Wendy's hand. He recognised the red-head from the cocktail party.

'James Robinson. Very pleased to meet you.'

Wendy smiled at him, aware that he was looking her over, his eyes lingering on her neckline and the pendant she was wearing which went so well with her black dress.

The Mayor appeared and ushered Graham away, leaving James and Wendy alone.

'So you're an archaeologist! How fascinating!' said James, the name 'Fowler' rattling around inside his head.

'Yes! I love it - it's so interesting, uncovering the past.'

'Indeed…'

Close to, she couldn't help but notice his scarred face and neck. The top part of his left ear was missing. He was obviously used to such attention and trotted out his usual line to put her at her ease: 'don't worry, it's not catching! I was in a fire, during the war, but it's all in the past now.'

She felt embarrassed, aware that she'd been staring, and there was something about him that put her on edge. He looked straight at her with deep blue eyes which she found attractive and menacing in equal measure.

'That's an unusual necklace you're wearing, Wendy.'

'Yes, it belonged to my mother.'

He felt his heart thumping.

'Really? May I look?'

He leaned towards her and she held the gold chain away from her body, lifting her chin so he could see the pendant more clearly. A flash of recognition crossed his face but he rapidly regained his composure.

'It's lovely,' he said, remembering the old sailor telling him he'd made many pendants like this, but only one with the extra squiggle, the 'S' for 'Susan'...

'They call it scrimshaw,' Wendy was saying, 'engraved whalebone. It was the emblem of my father's ship, the SALAMANDER. It was torpedoed during the war and he was lost at sea.'

'How tragic.'

He felt a touch on his elbow. 'Are you all right, darling?'

James turned to look at his wife who had appeared beside him.

Quickly gathering himself he said, 'yes...I was just talking to one of the archaeology team - Wendy Fowler, wasn't it? Wendy, this is my wife, Nina.'

Nina shook hands with Wendy, saying charmingly, 'I am so pleased to meet you. You and your colleagues do such amazing work.'

Then she turned to her husband. 'James, Signor Galea wants a word with you - if you don't mind...' smiling at Wendy as she led James away.

*

James couldn't sleep that night, his mind was in turmoil. He lay in bed next to his sleeping wife, feeling hot and in need of some air. He got up, tied his bathrobe around him, grabbed a packet of cigarillos and his lighter and walked out onto the terrace overlooking St Julian's bay. He lit up, inhaled deeply then exhaled, savouring the rush of nicotine into his bloodstream.

So...he had a daughter. Well, another daughter. And an amazing looking one at that. Somehow, on their wedding night at the Regina Hotel, with a shake of the genetic dice he and Susan had created this stunning, flame-haired, green-eyed beauty - Wendy. He wondered why Susan had chosen that name.

He shook his head, trying to clear his mind, but questions rushed in from every quarter.

What path had Wendy followed to lead her here, to him?

He thought back to the war. She must have been born around the same time that his ship had been hit. He imagined Susan, bringing up the baby in the bed-sitting room in Weston, visiting her parents in Oldfield Park...God, he hadn't thought of those places in such a long time. He wondered what Susan was doing now.

And what about his own mother? He hadn't given her a thought for years.

It was all too much and he lit a second smoke.

He knew one thing for sure - he wasn't going to allow Wendy to dig around into *his* past. He couldn't risk her finding out his true identity, he had too much to lose - his family, his status on the island, his businesses...

Listening to the waves falling on the shore he remembered Nina describing how she'd found him, lying on the sand, unconscious, close to death. He had emerged from the flames of his burning ship to make a successful new life for himself and wasn't going to let anyone take that away from him.

He had to get a grip and decide what to do.

Wendy was bright and intelligent - a chip off the old block! Here, on this small island, their paths may well cross again. Sooner or later she would put two and two together, and then he would be done for. He had to stop her.

He was a hard man. There was no room for sentimentality in his world.

By the time he'd smoked his third cigarillo James had made his decision. He wasn't going to risk losing everything because of Wendy Fowler. His long-lost daughter had to stay lost.

He had to get rid of her.

CHAPTER 32

Malta, 1965

The Camilleri family were holding a party to celebrate Alessandro's sixty-fifth birthday. He made a touching speech, thanking his wife and family, then said,

'As I reach this great age, do not think that I am going to retire - I'm not ready yet! But over the next few months I will hand over more work to James, my dear son-in-law, and I also want to engage my grandson Nikolai in our family business.'

Sixteen-year-old Nikolai gasped. He hadn't expected this to happen until he was at least eighteen. All the family applauded, and Nikolai stood, flattered that his grandfather held him in such regard.

Later, smoking cigars on the terrace, James spoke privately to his father-in-law.

'This has been a wonderful day. Thank you for entrusting me with your business, and for involving Nikolai too - he is thrilled! It is a good time to be thinking about the future.'

'Yes - I think you are both ready to take on more duties now.'

'Alessandro - I have been thinking about you and your legacy.'

'My legacy?'

'Yes. You are a very important man in Malta and I think it would be fitting for there to be a lasting tribute to you, something with the Camilleri name, so that future generations will remember you and what you have achieved for your country.'

Alessandro nodded, thoughtfully.

'So what did you have in mind, James?'

'When we were at the museum the other evening I was impressed with the work of the archaeologists. There is a team excavating a Roman villa near Mdina who are discovering many interesting treasures. What if we help the museum create a room for their findings and name it after you? *The Camilleri Room*. And after that, there could be more - a library perhaps, or a theatre …?'

Alessandro raised his eyebrows.

'*The Camilleri Room*…yes…I like it! What a good idea, James. Talk to the museum president - we might put a little extra funding their way. Thank you,' he said, squeezing James' arm affectionately.

*

Wendy's Ford Anglia drew up to the villa on St Julian's point just as dusk was falling. It was impressive, with white-washed walls, picture windows and a terrace running along the shoreline.

Wendy, wearing a dark blue shift dress with a lapis lazuli necklace, stepped out of her car and looked at the beautiful garden, the scent of bougainvillea filling

228

the balmy evening air and cicadas chirping. Sandy had travelled with her, then Graham arrived with the rest of the team and they walked together to the front porch where a maid showed them into a large, open plan room overlooking the sea.

James and Nina came forward to greet their guests and Graham said, 'thank you for inviting us, it's good to know you are so enthusiastic about our work.'

'My pleasure,' replied James. 'you can tell us all about it over dinner, it will help in my discussions with the museum directors.'

Wendy looked around the room which was simply furnished yet elegant. It was the place she had noticed when she and Cedric had gone swimming, but he had been wrong about one thing - there was something about James that made her wary, but surely these hospitable, friendly people weren't crooks?

The team sat down to dinner which was a relaxed affair, served by the housekeeper. There was no sign of the children. After they had eaten, James offered Graham a cigar and they sat, talking together.

Tempted by the view of the sea Wendy wandered out onto the softly-lit terrace and took out a cigarette. She leant on the rail of the balcony, looking at the red and green lights of ships in the distance and closer to shore the fishing boats with their lamps, bobbing on the calm water.

Suddenly someone was at her side, offering her a light.

'It's beautiful, isn't it,' said James.

'Divine. How long have you lived here?'

'Nina's family have owned this bit of land forever! But we had the house built fifteen years ago. Best thing we ever did.'

'It's wonderful. Thank you for hosting us tonight, Mr Robinson. We really appreciate the support you're giving our team.'

'My pleasure, and call me James. So, tell me about yourself, Wendy. How did you get interested in archaeology?'

'Well, it all started when I found a Roman coin at my grandparents' place in Bath.'

'Really?'

'I was thrilled! We were digging in the garden behind the prefab and found it there.'

'They live in a prefab?' he asked, curiously.

Wendy suddenly remembered Rosamund Mason's reaction, but this was different - not snobbishness, just surprise.

'Yes - they were bombed out of their house during the war, in the Bath Blitz.'

'Really?' He looked shocked. 'I hadn't heard about that.'

'Well, why would you?'

James tried to recover his composure. 'Were many killed?' he ventured.

'Yes - over four hundred. It was terrible. I was born in the middle of it!'

James went quite pale.

'How dreadful! So what happened to -'

But his question remained unasked as Nina appeared at her husband's side.

'Is everything all right, darling?'

'Yes...we were just talking about the museum.'

'Well, I hate to interrupt, but your guests are wondering where you are! Come!'

Giving Wendy an inquisitive look, she linked arms and led James away.

Wendy stayed for a moment to finish her cigarette, watching the sea, thinking about her host. For someone who professed to be a Londoner he showed a lot of interest in Bath, and, indeed, herself.

*

James spent the next morning in the reference library in Valletta, pouring over copies of British newspapers from April 1942. He read the reports of the Bath Blitz with horror, looking at the photographs of fire and devastation in disbelief. So many of the buildings he had known had disappeared and the chaos wreaked upon Oldfield Park shocked him to the core. In a later edition he found a list of names of the deceased, Mavis Fowler among them. So, after all these years, the city of his memory no longer existed, nor did his mother.

He sat, quietly, for a long time, while he absorbed all this information. He had more questions to ask Wendy and would soon have his opportunity. Having established that she enjoyed sailing he'd invited her out the following weekend and would seek answers to his questions before she met the unfortunate, fatal accident he was planning for her.

*

On Saturday Wendy drove to St Paul's Bay where James' dinghy was moored. He came to greet her, smiling, then drew back slightly as she said, 'good morning James! I hope you don't mind, I invited Emily along because she loves sailing too, and we don't often get the opportunity.'

James hid his annoyance, saying, 'of course, no problem! You are both very welcome!'

They climbed aboard the fourteen-foot dinghy, James untied the rope, hoisted the sail, catching the gentle breeze, then took the helm, nudging the boat out to sea. They sailed past other dinghies and brightly painted fishing boats which James said were called *luzzu*, explaining how the local fishermen worked according to the seasons, the currents and the weather. They sailed round into Mellieha Bay, where the girls remembered their new year swim, and James handed over the tiller to Wendy.

'Where did you learn to sail?'

'Off the Devon coast. I used to spend part of the Summer holidays there with a friend from school.'

'Really?'

James listened as Wendy told him about her schooldays at Colston's, intrigued as to how she had gained a place there and how she had come to be living in Bristol. He had to stop himself asking too many questions for fear of arousing her suspicions, as it was already clear that she didn't trust him - hence Emily's presence on the boat.

Wendy in turn asked James about his family, learning about his six children and their life in Malta and Gozo. Then James offered Emily the helm and she steered them competently back towards St Paul's.

Safely back ashore the girls thanked James for a lovely day, then Wendy drove back to Mdina.

'That was such fun!' said Emily, 'thank you for asking me along.'

'Thank you for coming! I just felt uncomfortable being with him on my own.'

'He certainly seems attracted to you!'

'Yes...he's a bit old for me though, don't you think?'

James stared after the Ford Anglia, wondering whether he should try to repeat his success with the bolt-croppers on Mario Vella's truck in Dingli. He felt frustrated that the opportunity of the boat trip had been wasted, but after some reflection decided upon another, more subtle, plan for his daughter's demise. He had to admit to enjoying the glimpse into her life and there was more he wanted to know, but that could wait for their next meeting when he would ensure that she came alone.

CHAPTER 33

Malta, 1965

Day by day in the heat of the sun Wendy worked methodically on the mosaic floor, carefully removing layers of earth and muck to reveal the depiction of a rural scene contained within a geometric border. A grapevine trailed over the top part of the picture and the bottom half depicted birds and animals from the local countryside - a dove, a hare, a goat, set amongst rocks and wild flowers.

The mosaic was made from cubes of local stone of varying shades with highlights in blue and green glass, a fine example of work from the period. Wendy had exposed a good two-thirds of the floor. One corner was still to be revealed - the most exciting, like filling in the final pieces of a jigsaw puzzle, which she hoped to complete before her contract was up. There was nothing like the thrill of uncovering secrets from the past.

Wendy was surprised to receive a note from James inviting her to meet Signor Borg, a friend of his from the museum who was an expert on Latin texts.

'I remember you telling me how much you love Latin,' she read, *'and thought you'd be interested in the opportunity to talk to Signor Borg. We're having lunch at the 'Alhambra' in Valletta on Wednesday and would be delighted if you would join us.'*

Her suspicions were again aroused, but the bait of lunch at Valletta's top restaurant and the chance of possible access to ancient texts at the museum were too good to resist.

When Wendy arrived at the *Alhambra* the head waiter showed her to a table by the window. James, who was alone, stood up to greet her, saying, 'how lovely to see you again, Wendy. Signor Borg should be here shortly, so I suggest we take a moment to look at the menu. I can recommend the seafood.'

He offered her a cigarette while they made their choice, then Wendy sat back and looked at her plush surroundings, the tables laid perfectly with white linen tablecloths, silver cutlery and gleaming wineglasses. James smiled at her and said, 'it is a good restaurant. I don't suppose you have been here before?'

'No, I'm afraid not. We archaeologists don't earn that much!'

'It's a shame - an attractive woman like you deserves to be wined and dined occasionally.'

He looked at her and suddenly remembered the first and last time he had taken Susan to dinner, at the Regina Hotel. He could see Wendy's likeness to her mother in her mannerisms, although she had a hard edge to her which, he thought, she had probably inherited from him.

Wendy met his gaze, refusing to be seduced by his flattery. The moment of unease was broken by the head waiter who came over, spoke quietly to James, and departed.

'I'm so sorry!' declared James, 'Signor Borg has been unavoidably delayed and will be unable to join us.'

'What a shame! I was looking forward to meeting him.'

'Indeed! We will have to arrange for you to see him another time. But…as we are here, please stay and be my guest, Wendy.'

'Very well.'

The waiter took their order, poured some white wine and while they ate their starter James said, 'so tell me about your family. You have a boyfriend, I am sure?'

'Yes - Cedric. He's a naval officer.'

James nodded. So that was how she had come to be at the cocktail party on board ship, the first time he had seen her. Then he asked,

'And how is your mother? It must have been difficult for her, bringing you up alone.'

'Oh, we managed…and she's very happy now - in fact she and her husband have a baby boy!'

'Really?! And they live…'

'In Bristol. Her husband teaches Latin at the grammar school.'

'I see!'

Things were falling into place. He had found out as much as he wanted to. Now for the master stroke.

James looked at Wendy, leaned towards her and said, quietly, 'I don't want to embarrass you, but you have something…'

He opened his mouth slightly and rubbed his little finger against his front tooth.

'…you have something green, just there…!'

'Oh!' cried Wendy, blushing, 'thank you for telling me! I'll just go to the Ladies and sort it out. Excuse me.'

James watched her go, reached into his pocket and, making sure no one was looking, released a few drops of liquid from a phial into her wineglass. It would be a quick death, showing causes akin to an unfortunate, previously undiagnosed, allergic reaction to seafood.

Wendy returned and the waiter came to clear their plates. James lifted his glass and was about to make a final toast when he became aware of a commotion behind him and mutterings from fellow diners.

Suddenly, Nina was at his side, her dark eyes ablaze.

'James! I am so sorry to interrupt your romantic lunch with *Wendy*!', spitting out the name and slapping him hard across the face.

'Nina!' he spluttered, holding his cheek, smarting with pain, 'Nina, darling, it's not what you think!'

'Don't 'darling' me!' she cried, slapping his face a second time, then she swiped her arm across the table, sending the wine bottle, glasses and plates flying, Wendy shifting fast to avoid the debris. A waiter rushed over to try and calm things down, but James stood up to face Nina, grabbing her wrists, and she struggled to free herself, shouting at him all the while, using words he hadn't even realised she knew. The other diners looked on aghast as the couple brawled, bashing into the next table, knocking over more bottles and glasses. A woman screamed, then the whole restaurant descended into chaos. The owner hurried over, apologising to his guests, passing Wendy who, amid the mayhem, slipped away, unnoticed.

*

'I never saw you as a *femme fatale*!' said Graham.

'But I'm not!' protested Wendy.

'It even made it to the *Times of Malta*!' said Ronald, showing her a short report of an incident at Valletta's top restaurant which had caused several hundred pounds worth of damage.

'Honestly, I had no idea Nina was so jealous, and there was nothing in it, nothing at all!'

'Don't worry, we believe you,' said Helen, 'although James certainly showed an interest in you!'

'Well, I wish he hadn't!'

James was summoned to Gozo to see Alessandro who despaired at the reckless behaviour of his useless son-in-law.

'James, you have been doing well, and that is why I am so disappointed in you! I thought you were learning how to deal with things, but now… I don't need to tell you how distressed we all are.'

'I'm sorry, Alessandro, I really am…'

'…you have caused my daughter much sorrow…'

'I know, and I regret it to the bottom of my heart…'

'I don't understand why you have been so keen to spend time with this woman - this *Wendy* - but it has to stop, James, it has to stop.'

'Don't worry, it has,' James replied, knowing that Nina would never let him anywhere near Wendy again.

Alessandro leaned forward, placing the tips of his fingers together, making a cage with his hands.

'So, this is what we are going to do…'

*

The owner of the *Alhambra* was honoured to receive a visit from Signor Camilleri in person, with the gift of a most generous sum of money which more than covered the costs of damage to his restaurant, even providing sufficient to fund a long-awaited upgrade to his kitchen.

*

Ester told her daughter that, as far as they could find out, there were no grounds to suspect that James had been having an affair. It was in all their interests to put this episode behind her and forgive James for his strange behaviour. Alessandro declared that the pair needed some time together to mend their marriage and despatched them to Sicily, where an old friend of his had a villa near Taormina.

'Be nice to your wife, James' he said. 'Talk to her, reassure her that you love her, that you will do anything for her. Ester and I will look after the children. Don't come back until you are reconciled!'

It took a month, until one evening, sitting on the balcony looking at the view of Mount Etna, its crater glowing orange in the twilight, Nina said, 'very well, James. I will never understand what happened, but I have decided to forgive you. I will come to you tonight.'

*

Graham said, 'great news! I've had a letter from the president of Valletta museum saying they will be delighted to accept our findings into their permanent collection. They're even going to create a special room for them - *The Camilleri Room*.'

'That's marvellous!' said Sandy, echoed by the others.

Then Graham said, 'er - Wendy, could I have a private word?'

When they were alone Graham continued, 'well, you seem to have made quite an impression out here, Wendy! The museum president was full of praise for your work.'

'Really?'

'Yes…to the extent that he suggested I help advance your career…Look, to cut a long story short, Wendy, I've spoken to one of my colleagues in Oxford who is looking for someone to do post-graduate research into the early Roman period. It would mean you leaving Malta a little sooner than planned, but it's a marvellous opportunity.'

'It sounds wonderful! Can I think it over?'

'Er - yes, although I would strongly suggest you grab it with both hands…'

He looked a little awkward.

'I think it's one of those offers you can't refuse…'

CHAPTER 34

Bristol, 1965

Susan and Christopher were pleased to have Wendy back and she in turn was delighted to see toddler David, now two years old, and to catch up with Tom who had gained a First Class Honours degree in maths and was continuing his studies at Bristol University.

'Those last few months in Malta were rather strange, but it's all worked out for the best,' Wendy told them.

'And you like Oxford?' asked Christopher.

'I love it! They've given me a room in College but I spend most of my time in the libraries and museums. They've given me access to some ancient Latin texts while I'm working on my Masters…'

'You're making me quite jealous!' Christopher exclaimed.

'I've seen my friend Pamela, from school, too - we met up the other day. She's in her final year studying Law and has got herself engaged to a medical student.'

'And what about you…?' asked Susan, realising as she said it that she sounded like her own mother.

'I'm still writing to Cedric, if that's what you mean...but there's not much point in getting engaged to someone who's never here!'

Wendy was, however, pleased to see a letter from Cedric waiting for her when she returned to Oxford.

... Sorry your stay in Malta was cut short but you seem to have fallen on your feet in Oxford, so good luck with that...This tour around Australia has been marvellous, we've been on exercise with the Aussie Navy and visited some Pacific islands, very exotic!

...when I get back next year they're sending me on the Staff Course at Greenwich. I hope it will give us the chance to see each other for more than the odd day. I would love to spend more time with you, Wendy. I still dream about being on the beach with you at St Julian's and can't wait to kiss you again...
Yours affectionately,
Cedric

Wendy read the letter, and re-read it. She was pleased to hear from Cedric, and at last admitted to herself that she wanted to spend more time with him, too, and had also dreamt about those kisses...

Bath, 1966

Fred and Pat's new year started with bad news: the small but cosy prefab they had made their home for the past twenty years was to be demolished to make way for a housing estate. The entire landscape of Bath was changing: slums and bomb sites had been cleared, modern buildings were springing up, a fancy shopping centre was planned and even the Scala cinema had been turned into a supermarket.

The Council allocated them a ground floor flat in a block on a development in Whiteway, just a mile or so from Twerton. It all felt a bit strange but Fred said, 'you'll see, we'll soon settle in all right.'

Fred was sorry to leave the old patch of garden where he'd worked so hard but had put his name on the waiting list for an allotment and hoped it wouldn't be too long before he could start afresh. For her part Pat just didn't have the same feeling about this place as she'd had with her previous homes; it seemed soulless. But she'd do her best, and the neighbours were nice enough.

Susan and Ann came to visit, leaving their husbands to look after the children.

'It's lovely!' said Ann, looking around at the large rooms and wide windows, 'better than the prefab!'

'I suppose so…' said Pat.

Susan sighed, sympathetically. 'I know, Mum, it's not the same…but I'm sure you'll make it nice.'

'We'll try,' said Fred. 'At least we've got a roof over our head…'

The four of them suddenly remembered standing outside the ruins of their house in Oldfield Park after the bombing.

'…and like I've always said, the main thing is, we've got each other.'

*

Wendy received an envelope from Malta and was delighted to find a letter from Sandy, sending best wishes from herself and the rest of the team, and enclosing a photograph of the mosaic floor that Wendy had been excavating.

'I finished work on it last week,' Sandy wrote, *'it's come up beautifully. You did a grand job and it's been a privilege to complete it.'*

Wendy looked at the large colour photograph, delighted to see the entire mosaic, the final pieces of the puzzle in place. Her eyes went straight to the area on the bottom right, the part that Sandy had uncovered. There, sitting on a rock, was a small creature, its body twisted into the shape of an 'S', its four limbs protruding at right angles - a salamander.

On Wendy's next visit to Bristol she took the photo to show her mother and Christopher.

'Look, Mum!' said Wendy, indicating the right-hand corner.

'A salamander! Like the one on the pendant, after your father's ship. How strange!'

'Well, it's not really surprising,' said Christopher, 'salamanders are native to Malta and one would expect them to be depicted in art.'

'Really? I didn't see any while I was there,' said Wendy.

'That's because they hide in the rocks most of the time, away from the sun. They only tend to come out when it rains - and I don't suppose you saw much of that!'

Greenwich, 1966

One Saturday morning in May, Wendy caught the train from Oxford to London, feeling ridiculously excited at the prospect of seeing Cedric again. He met her at Paddington and she flung her arms around him as he lifted her into the air, and they kissed. They caught the train to Greenwich and spent the day walking along by the Thames, Cedric pointing out the historic Royal Naval College where he was living temporarily while he attended his course. They wandered hand in hand through Greenwich Park, up the hill to the Royal Observatory and stood on the Meridian Line, the reference point for Greenwich Mean Time. At the top of the hill they sat down on the grass and looked at the view of the capital.

'It's lovely!' she said, 'you're so lucky to be here.'

'Yes…and I hope you'll come and visit me again.'

'I certainly will.'

He put his arm round her and they kissed, lingeringly, then he said, softly, 'do you have to go back to Oxford tonight, Wendy?'

'Not really…'

'Well, if you want to stay here I can always sneak you in…'

They said goodbye at Paddington station on Sunday evening, hating to part, still friends, and lovers at last.

A few weeks later, back in Greenwich, Cedric said, 'look, Wendy, there's something I want to ask you. I'm twenty-three, and we naval officers aren't allowed to get married until we're twenty-five. But there's nothing to stop us getting engaged. I really want you to be my wife, Wendy. Will you? Will you marry me?'

She turned and looked at him, his expression serious, intense.

'Yes, Cedric. Yes, I will!'

They embraced, then he added, 'just one thing - you'll have to meet my mother again!'

Bath, 1966

As they walked together up Lansdown Hill Cedric said, 'you have to understand, for me, growing up, the navy was everything. Father was a Captain, and my mother's father was an Admiral. My parents met at a dance in Dartmouth, but the family home was always here, in Bath. Mother and I used to rattle around the house when I was growing up. I think she wanted more children, but there was only me - she used to call me her late arrival! My father was killed before I was born, as I've told you, so mother brought me up as he would have wanted, sending me to a good school, then straight to Dartmouth. I suppose she thought I'd find an Admiral's daughter too…'

'Sorry to disappoint you!'

'Wendy, you are worth a million Admirals' daughters, believe me, I've met them!'

'And you had to live with that portrait of your father, glaring down at you.'

'Yes - it used to scare me as a youngster, but mother was always terribly fond of it. She used to sit and stare at it, with a faraway look in her eye, still does.'

'She must miss him very much.'

The visit began much as before, with a weak handshake, even weaker tea served in the drawing room with the grandfather clock ticking, and Captain Mortimer Mason glowering at them from his place on the wall.

Rosamund Mason, who had been briefed by her son, said, 'Cedric tells me you've been excavating Roman remains in Malta…,' giving Wendy the opportunity to shine.

Then Rosamund asked, 'And your family?'

'My father was killed at sea during the war, and my mother re-married four years ago, to a Latin master at Bristol Grammar. They live in the schoolhouse and are very happy there. They have a son, David - he's just had his third birthday.'

'Really?' Rosamund looked over her spectacles and nodded in semi-approval.

'...and your grandparents?'

'Their prefab was demolished, and now they live in a flat.'

'I see,' said Rosamund, hoping that was an improvement, curbing any urge to sound critical, then she added, 'what a strange impact the war had on all our lives...,' glancing up at her husband's portrait.

They conversed awkwardly for another half hour, then it was time to go.

As Wendy was putting on her coat, Rosamund took Cedric to one side and said, 'well, she's not what I would have chosen for you, but I can see she makes you happy.'

'Yes, she does. Thank you, mother - she really is a wonderful girl. You just need to get to know her better.'

Cedric and Wendy walked back down Lansdown Hill together, hand in hand.

'I suppose that went better than last time!' said Wendy.

'I tell you, she'll come round. You know it's strange, with my mother - she reminds me of someone wearing a suit of armour to protect herself from the world, but underneath she's quite vulnerable. And there are moments when I've noticed her, looking so sad...Persevere with her, won't you?'

Susan and Christopher were delighted to see Cedric and congratulated the happy couple on their engagement. When it came to meeting Fred and Pat, Cedric was charm itself, and after they left Pat said, 'he's lovely, isn't he? Nice looking, and well brought up.'

'Very posh!' said Fred, 'but I won't hold that against him!'

The final stop on Cedric's tour of introduction was to meet David Roberts. The two shook hands and made an instant connection when they found that Cedric had been to the same school as David's two sons.

'Mine are a quite bit older than you, though. Henry's in Paris, with his family - he's Air Attaché at the Embassy - and Anthony lives here, with us. He's not well, I'm afraid, but we do our best…'

Cedric spoke about his naval career, then said, 'my mother lives on Lansdown Hill - Rosamund Mason. I don't suppose you've ever come across her?'

David paused. Rosamund Mason! He hadn't heard that name for years. So Cedric was her son! He thought carefully for a moment then said, 'yes, I do remember her. In fact she was a patient of mine. How is she?'

'Quite well, thank you. As formidable as ever!'

'I'll second that!' said Wendy.

'And your father?' asked David.

'He was killed in the Battle of the Atlantic in '42, before I was born.'

'Aaah, yes,' he said, 'another tragedy of war…'

They had some tea, and David asked after Susan, Christopher and their son, and about Wendy's

248

work in Oxford, then it was time for the visitors to leave.

David stood at the window and watched as they walked away.

Yes, he thought to himself, he did remember Rosamund Mason. He remembered her very well...

CHAPTER 35

Malta, 1967

James Robinson was sitting in one of the cafés he owned in St Paul's Bay, drinking a cool cola with his eldest son, Nikolai, now eighteen. The boy was slightly taller than his father, thin and dark, aware of his good looks. James was educating him in the ways of the Camilleri family business to which Nikolai was the heir, teaching him the rules of the game as Alessandro had to James. Nikolai tried to concentrate on what his father was saying but found himself distracted by the warm sun on his face and a pretty girl walking by. James noticed and lost his temper.

'Nikolai, listen to me!' he exclaimed, thumping the table, 'this is important. You have to know these things if you are going to manage your own part of the business!'

'Sorry, Dad, I am listening, honestly!' Nikolai said, glancing up at the girl who was smiling at him.

'So,' said James, still irritated, 'your grandfather and I want you to work with Elias Attard on the new holiday apartments we are building here. He's an experienced manager and will show you the ropes. But use your initiative - you're young, you see things from a different perspective. Tell us what you think, how we can improve things.'

The girl walked away and Nikolai turned his gaze to his father.

'Yes, Dad, thank you, I would like that.'

James took Nikolai to meet Elias then drove back to Sliema, thinking about his son. Much as he loved him, he couldn't shift the thought that he had raised a lazy, spoiled brat who wanted everything handed to him on a plate. He blamed Nina for indulging him, and himself for not being there when he was needed. Perhaps it was a generational thing; at his age, James had been at sea, fighting a war. Kids nowadays were just too soft.

His consolation was Elena, his daughter, a clever girl who wanted her own career. She had developed an interest in history - James dated it to when he'd taken her to the opening of the Camilleri Room at Valletta Museum - and she was studying at Malta University. He didn't intend to involve her in the family business - that was for men only - but he was happy to support her academic ambitions and would rely on Nina to find her a suitable match when she graduated.

When James got home he sat on the terrace and lit a cigarette. He had five minutes peace, then the younger children came home from school. They ran out to see him and he reflected that he preferred them at that age; maybe that was why they kept having more. Nina placed their youngest, just over a year old, on James' lap and he cuddled her affectionately - their seventh child, conceived during that special holiday to Sicily, and named, appropriately, 'Septima'.

Cedric had completed his course at Greenwich and was back at sea, on exercise in the English Channel. In the new year he was to begin a specialist Gunnery course in Portsmouth which fitted well with plans for their wedding on the 27th January, Cedric's twenty-fifth birthday ('I'm not going to wait a moment longer!' he declared). It was to be a grand affair, held at a church on Lansdown Hill with full naval ceremonial, followed by a reception at a local hotel.

Susan was busy making her daughter's wedding gown, and one rainy Saturday afternoon in November Wendy was in Bristol to have a fitting. Christopher and Tom had gone out train-spotting, taking little David with them, so the two were alone. As Susan knelt on the floor, pinning up the hem of the dress, she couldn't help but get a little nostalgic.

'I wonder what Frank would have made of it all? His daughter, marrying an officer!'

'Strange, isn't it. And think of poor Mrs Mason - the Captain's son marrying the daughter of an Able Seaman!'

'Times change, don't they! But it was different, during the war. Who knows what Frank might have made of himself if he'd been given the chance?'

Wendy asked, 'do you still have those photos of him?'

'Yes, I'll get them if you like, when I've finished this…'

Later, Susan fetched the photos from a drawer and together, over a cup of tea, they looked at them - the wedding photos and the one taken on board SALAMANDER.

'Handsome devil, wasn't he!' said Susan.

'Yes…and he looks so young...'

'Well, he was! Of course, these photos don't do him justice. He had the most lovely deep blue eyes…'

She smiled, and went and put the photos away.

The dress fitting done, Susan and Wendy settled down to watch an old black and white film on the television. Susan said, 'I love these old movies - Frank used to take me to the pictures every Saturday. Which one is it?'

'It's called 'Blackmail!' - with Edward G. Robinson.'

'Oh yes, I remember that one - he's leading a double life but someone finds out and blackmails him.'

'Thanks Mum! Please don't tell me the ending too!'

As they watched the film, picking up the dialogue Susan said, '*honey bunny*! - that's what Frank used to call me. I haven't heard that for years.'

Wendy felt a chill run up her spine. She carried on watching the film, but in her mind another picture was forming, the pieces subconsciously slipping into place. In Bristol the rain and the wind were beating against the window, so why was she suddenly reminded of a beach in Gozo, and a man named James Robinson?

Bath, 1968

January saw heavy falls of snow and at one point Wendy was concerned that neither she, nor the groom, nor the guests, would be able to get to Bath at all. But thankfully, towards the end of the month the weather moderated and on the big day the roads were clear enough to travel, although snow was still piled up on the side and the ice on Lansdown Hill remained treacherous.

The couple's relatives and friends filled the church. Wendy's friend Pamela was her bridesmaid, little David made a charming pageboy in a sailor suit and Christopher had the honour of walking the beautiful bride down the aisle and giving her away. After the ceremony Cedric's navy colleagues in their dress uniforms formed an archway with their ceremonial swords as the couple left the church.

The guests mingled at the reception, Rosamund Mason feeling obliged to greet Wendy's family as her equals and hoping her husband would have approved of Wendy's independent spirit if not her background. Then she recognised someone she knew of old.

'Dr Roberts! I haven't seen you for years!'

'Mrs Mason! Yes - I'm at an advantage - I knew *you* would be here! I'm an old friend of Wendy's family.'

'Really?'

'Yes! She's a lovely young woman - you have a fine daughter-in-law there. And you have a fine son, as well…'

'Yes, I'm proud of him. He's getting on so well in the navy.'

'Yes - like his father…'

'Absolutely!'

'And you're keeping well, Rosamund?' he asked, leaning towards her slightly.

'Yes I am, thank you.'

She smiled at him and beneath her rigid exterior David caught a glimpse of her younger self, when she had been a beauty.

'It is good to see you again, David. I'm

surprised we haven't come across each other before. Now tell me, how are those sons of yours?'

Wendy disappeared to change into her going-away outfit, then she and Cedric said goodbye to their guests, leaving for a brief honeymoon in Brighton and the start of their new life together - apart from the small snag that Cedric was based in Portsmouth and Wendy in Oxford.

Noticing Wendy looking wistfully out the window of the Common room one afternoon, her tutor said, 'I suppose you're missing your new husband?'

'Yes, I am!'

'Actually...an excavation team in Chichester has requested some expertise on the early Roman period. Would you like to go down there and help them out for a bit?'

Wendy jumped at the chance. She and Cedric rented a small terraced house in Portsmouth for the duration, excited at the prospect of living together. They soon settled in and spent the weekends exploring the rolling Hampshire countryside. They were blissfully happy, but while they were out walking one Sunday Wendy seemed pre-occupied and Cedric asked her what was wrong.

'I don't want to tell you because you'll think I'm mad!' she said.

'Oh, go on!'

'It's just that...working on the site in Chichester reminds me of when I was in Malta, excavating the Roman villa in Mdina. I keep thinking about it - it's three years since I left, and I had a wonderful time...'

'I know, I was there with you on the beach at St Julian's!' he interrupted.

'Yes! But - it's only since I've been away that I've thought about how strange it all was, especially those last few months.'

'What do you mean?'

She hesitated.

'James Robinson. You remember - the man who was burned in a fire. He was at the cocktail party on your ship, then he kept appearing at the museum, and there was that weird lunch when his wife turned up and they had a fight…It was as if he engineered meetings so he could see me on my own, and not because he fancied me - it was something else.'

She paused.

'Cedric, I think he's Frank Fowler - my father!'

'WHAT?!' Cedric stopped in his tracks and turned to her. 'What on earth makes you say that?'

'I don't know…lots of little things. It's hard to recognise him from old photos because his face has changed so much, but there's definitely a similarity. And there's that Bath accent he tries to hide, and the questions he asked when he saw my pendant, the interest he showed in my family…it's driving me daft, and I don't know what to do about it!'

'It all sounds terribly far-fetched, Wendy. I think your imagination is working overtime!'

'I know, but the more I think about it, the more it makes sense - to me, anyway. I'm even wondering if he was trying to bump me off!'

'Now, that is ridiculous. But…I suppose if you want to do something practical you could check him out at Somerset House - see if they have any records of a James Robinson who fits the bill - it's a fairly common name, though. And you could find out more about the SALAMANDER at the Maritime Museum in Greenwich.'

Wendy nodded. 'That's a good idea, Cedric. At least then I'll feel I'm doing something…'

'You haven't told anyone else, have you?'

'No.'

'Thank God for that. I don't want everyone to think I've married some crazy woman!' he said, pulling her towards him and kissing her.

Wendy's research at Somerset House drew a blank. There were several James Robinsons, but she could find none that were about the right age and from London. Maybe that pointed towards a false identity? The Maritime Museum proved interesting in that the helpful curator showed her the records of HMS SALAMANDER and pointed out Able Seaman Frank Fowler's name on the crew list. He confirmed that the ship had been sunk off the coast of Malta with the loss of all hands, a great tragedy.

'Have you ever heard of someone surviving in such circumstances?' Wendy asked.

'Well - it does happen,' said the curator, an old Royal Navy man himself. 'We used to hear stories of sailors getting washed up on the shore. And there have been examples of men being found, years later, leading a new life. A few came out the woodwork in '53, when deserters were pardoned.'

Sitting on the train on her way back to Portsmouth Wendy reflected on what she had learnt. She would never be able to prove that James was really Frank. And, even if she could, what good would it do?

It would destroy his family and the life in Malta he'd obviously worked hard to achieve; Susan would be distraught to discover that the man she thought had been killed had, in fact, deserted her; and what did she, Wendy, hope to gain? She had managed without a father all her life, and if she needed any paternal guidance she had Christopher who was such a dear man, and she would hate him or her mother to be hurt.

The best thing she could do, she concluded, was to leave things alone and concentrate on her career and her new life with Cedric. The rhythm of the train on the tracks spelt it out for her as if in confirmation: leave it alone, leave it alone, leave it alone…

CHAPTER 36

Bath, 1973

Dr Wendy Mason was thrilled with her new job. Having gained her Doctorate at Oxford she had been invited to join a team of archaeologists working in Bath where a programme of clearance and excavation was underway at the Roman Baths and the Pump Room. New parts of the structure had been exposed, revealing fresh insights into the Baths and those who had used them. Wendy's expertise in identifying and dating artefacts was required and she was soon immersed in the ancient world that she loved.

Changes were underway above ground as well. Wendy was excited to move back to the city of her birth at a time when many new buildings were under construction and the older ones were having their stonework cleaned, restoring them to their former glory. A new shopping centre in Southgate had opened and the place was alive with new ideas, the University was bringing younger people into the city and trendy restaurants and cafés were on every corner. There was even a pub called The Salamander, she noted, wryly.

As Bath would be their base for the foreseeable future Wendy and Cedric decided to make their home there and settled on a Victorian semi-detached in Lower Weston, close to the house where Wendy had been born, lost to the bombs. Susan loved coming over from Bristol to visit her daughter in this familiar location, rediscovering her old haunts. They went to Whiteway to see Fred and Pat who were delighted to have their granddaughter living back in Bath. Catching up on the family news, Pat told them the latest from Ann and Brian.

'The cigarette factory at Bedminster's closing and they're moving production to a new factory in Hartcliffe. It's only a few miles away, but it means Ann and the family will have to find somewhere else to live.'

'Can't they rent a house from Wills?'

'No - it's not like when you first moved there. It's all different now...'

'What a shame!' said Wendy, remembering the place she'd grown up, sad to think that the community she'd once been part of was being dispersed. She hadn't been there for years, but it made her feel as if part of her past was being taken away from her.

During the Summer, Susan and Wendy visited David Roberts who had just celebrated his eightieth birthday and was in good health, still with a keen interest in life. He told them about his family and how, thanks to a scientific breakthrough, his younger son Anthony was able to communicate and had married Gilda, the woman who cared for him.

'It's remarkable! Due to his illness Anthony can't speak, but he can blink his eye and indicate what he wants to say using a spelling board. That's how he took his wedding vows.'

'That's incredible!' said Susan, 'you must be so happy that he found love, in his circumstances.'

David listened avidly as Susan told him about her son David's progress at prep school, Tom who was now studying Computer Science, and how Christopher doted on them all. For her part Wendy spoke about her work at the Roman Baths and her husband's promotion to Lieutenant Commander.

'He's just taken command of his first ship, a minehunter, and he's thrilled about it.'

'That's marvellous - and quite a responsibility. His mother must be very proud...Rosamund...'

'She certainly is! I go and visit her occasionally - we get on better nowadays...'

David was thoughtful for a moment, then said, 'I delivered him, you know.'

Wendy wasn't sure whether she had heard correctly.

'You delivered Cedric?' she asked, to make sure.

'Yes. Rosamund Mason was my patient. I monitored her throughout her pregnancy.'

Susan and Wendy looked at each other.

'We had no idea!'

David smiled. 'I haven't mentioned it before, but I know I can rely on you both to be discreet. Rosamund was an elderly primigravida, having her first child at the age of forty-one.'

'Not easy!' said Susan, recalling the birth of her own son.

'Absolutely! It was long-awaited…'

Susan's curiosity got the better of her.

'Er - so did she have trouble…'

'Conceiving? Yes…'

David hesitated; he shouldn't betray patient confidentiality, but it was all so long ago…

'I treated Rosamund for many years. She was desperate to have children, poor woman, but it just wasn't happening. I did all the tests I could and found nothing wrong. But that is nature for you: at the last, she became pregnant. It shows that one must never give up hope. Although…'

Knowing he had already said more than he should, he paused, then asked Wendy, 'and all is well with you, I trust?'

'…in that department? Yes, thank you. Cedric and I don't want children yet - our lifestyle isn't settled enough.'

'Well, don't leave it too late!'

Malta, 1973

Ester wandered out onto the terrace of her home in Gozo to join her husband who was snoozing in the sun. She gently touched his shoulder to wake him, but he didn't respond. She touched him again and his head fell to one side.

'Alessandro, what is it?'

Ester screamed.

Her daughter Maria heard her and came running out of the house. Ester was on her knees, frantically shaking her husband, shouting his name.

'Mama, what is it? Shall I fetch the doctor?'

'No,' cried her mother, sobbing, 'it's too late. Fetch the priest.'

Alessandro's sudden death, due to heart failure, left a void in his family that could never be filled. In accordance with Catholic tradition, Alessandro's funeral was held the day after his death. The whole of Gozo went into mourning. Alessandro's associates travelled from Malta to pay their respects, as did his old rival George Galea. Ester, swathed in black, led the funeral procession as it snaked around the island, finally arriving at the church where the great man was laid to rest. That evening, surrounded by her family, Ester, deep in her grief and with immense dignity, addressed James.

'My husband Alessandro...' She paused to gather herself. 'My husband Alessandro wished you, James, to be his heir. You are now head of the family and the Camilleri business. We will give you all our support and put our trust in you to continue Alessandro's work in the way he would have wished.'

She approached James who stood up to face her. Ester took her hands in his and kissed them, then kissed him on both cheeks. She turned to Nina who kissed James in the same way, then they stood to one side as each family member followed suit.

James was overcome by this extraordinary ritual. He felt like a king being crowned, a Roman emperor having a laurel wreath placed upon his head. Feeling the weight of responsibility he declared,

'Thank you. You do me a great honour. I will try to uphold Alessandro's work to the best of my ability, and to respect his legacy.'

Then, addressing Ester and Nina, he said, 'I owe all that I have to you. Without you and Alessandro I would not have survived. I can never thank you enough.'

That night James lay awake in the heat, listening to the crickets chirping and the waves breaking on the shore. As Alessandro's chosen successor he was now one of the most powerful people in Malta. Not bad for a butcher's boy from Bath...

The day after the funeral, with a shiver of excitement, James entered Alessandro's study, now his own. He went through the desk, looking at papers and account books which were full of notations and comments which he didn't understand. Alessandro had told him the combination of the safe which James had never dared use, but now he opened it. Inside he found wads of several thousand Maltese pounds, along with incriminating letters and photographs relating to some of Malta's top people which James presumed Alessandro had used as leverage. This mine of information was worth its weight in gold, and he must guard it carefully. He closed the door and spun the lock.

Alessandro had been involved in many deals over many years, not all of which James had been party to. He had to tread with caution. When he felt sufficiently prepared he met Alessandro's associates in Valletta to discuss the future. Out of respect to Alessandro they made a show of accepting James into the fold and agreed that 'business as usual' was the best approach. James told them he intended to continue his work in Sliema, leaving his son Nikolai managing St Paul's and his younger son Alfredo to look after the family's farming and fishing interests on Gozo.

Afterwards James held a separate meeting with George Galea and they each agreed to uphold the amicable arrangement he and Alessandro had had in place for some years. It was James' personal view that they should put the old hostilities behind them - there was plenty of business to go round and it was time to herald a peaceful new era.

James returned home, pleased with his day's work, confident that he had held his own with these Maltese barons and having convinced them he was up to the challenge of continuing Alessandro's business.

But to the Maltese James would always be an outsider, and behind his back they still called him *Ingliż* - the Englishman. They knew that James had only survived all these years because Alessandro had protected him. But Alessandro wasn't there anymore.

CHAPTER 37

Bath, 1975

Susan was on the train to Bath, looking out the window at the countryside rolling past. It was late September and the trees were just beginning to turn to their Autumn gold. She hadn't been to Bath for a while and was looking forward to her day out, especially as she was meeting a friend that she hadn't seen for a long time - Jean Daniels.

Jean, recently retired from Bayer's and with time on her hands, had got in touch with Susan, suggesting they might visit the Museum of Costume together. Susan was also enjoying some new-found freedom now that her eleven-year-old son David had started at Bristol Grammar under the watchful eye of his father, so Jean's idea was timely.

The train sped past the chocolate factory at Keynsham, then slowed down as it went through Oldfield Park on its approach to Bath Spa. Susan recalled her time living at Jean's after the war when Wendy was a baby, and how grateful she'd been to her former boss for giving her a job and a home.

Jean was there to meet her at the station. They hugged and looked at each other.

'You haven't changed a bit!' they both said, although, of course, they had.

Together they walked up the hill towards the Assembly Rooms where the Museum of Costume is housed.

'I haven't been up to this part of town for years!' said Susan.

It was good to see Bath thriving again with shoppers and tourists from all over the world swarming in the streets, but the legacy of war and re-building during the 1960's was ever present. The bombsites had largely been cleared, replaced with ugly, cubist office blocks and high-rise flats. Some of the older buildings bore traces of the air raids, with gouges taken out of the stone by shrapnel and bullets from low-flying planes, and many remained blackened by soot from the fires that had raged.

After the war the Assembly Rooms had been restored to their former glory and re-opened in 1963, complete with the original chandeliers which had been recovered from storage. Susan glanced at the building opposite, once the site of the Regina Hotel, split in half by an explosion, now lost to memory, rather like the honeymoon she and Frank had spent there.

It was Susan's first trip to the museum and Jean led her around the collection of fashionable dress for men, women and children from the sixteenth century to the modern day. The two expert seamstresses enthused over the embroidery and intricate work on dresses, suits, gloves and shoes, then Jean said, 'here's what I really want to see! The dress of the year!'

This year's winner of the annual fashion award was a wedding dress and veil in cream silk organza. With their experience of making wedding gowns they appreciated the skill that had gone into the design and the execution of the garment and spent ages admiring every detail.

'At least they didn't have to use parachute silk!' said Jean.

Needing a sit down they went to the café. Jean lit a cigarette and Susan asked after Frances.

'She's very well, and sends her love. She's just been promoted - she's one of the most senior women in the Ministry in Bath now. And how's Wendy?'

'Very happy - she's working on excavations at the Roman Baths and loves it. She came back early from her job in Malta, I'm still not sure why. Sometimes I wonder if there's something she's not telling me...' Susan trailed off, then said, 'but she's very happy with her husband, Cedric.'

'The younger generation are so lucky. It shows one can be happily married and have a career.'

'And you and Frances...?'

'Yes...we're fine.'

Jean lowered her voice. 'We live discreetly, as ever. But sometimes, Susan, I just want to be able to hold her hand as we walk down the road without people staring. Will that ever be possible, I wonder? That's why we enjoy going abroad for our holidays, things are more relaxed...We're going to Greece next year - Lesbos.'

'Of course!'

Malta, 1976

Nikolai Robinson was in a good place: his nightclubs were flourishing, giving him access to as many girls and as much drink and cocaine as he could handle, and his new casino in St Paul's was a great success. He planned to open a chain of them in the resorts which were blossoming across Malta, seizing opportunities afforded by the gradual easing of the gaming laws and stealing a march on his rival, Giacomo Galea, grandson of George Galea.

Alfredo, Nikolai's younger brother, was content to manage the family's farming and fishing interests on Gozo. This suited Nikolai perfectly; that side of the business bored him but Alfredo loved it and Nikolai found it provided good cover for some of his illegal import/export activities. Gozo's secluded coves and bays were perfect for transferring goods away from prying eyes and Alfredo's knowledge of the currents around the island and the vagaries of the weather was invaluable. Moreover Alfredo would do whatever his big brother told him to, without question.

James hadn't been too keen on Nikolai's plans - he wasn't sure it was a good route for the family business - but had to concede that his son's nightclubs and casinos were proving profitable. Perhaps he was mellowing as he grew older but James had become less obsessed with making money at all costs, and with his father-in-law gone he no longer felt obliged to follow the old ways. In the three years since Alessandro had died James had secured some decent deals, all legal and above-board, with Italian businessmen who had helped keep Malta afloat during the economic crisis it had endured since becoming independent and a republic.

Nowadays James found more satisfaction in continuing Alessandro's benevolent work: the Camilleri Room at Valletta museum had been joined by the Camilleri Library and the Camilleri Theatre. (George Galea, rather put out, had founded the Galea Concert Hall.) Whatever the means by which he had achieved his fortune, Alessandro had bequeathed a fine legacy and James was keen to maintain it.

His particular favourite was the Camilleri Foundation which provided financial aid to enable bright children from poor families to attend Malta's top private school. He was in regular contact with the school, attending events and awarding prizes at the end of term. He couldn't help but think of his daughter - the one he could never acknowledge - who, thanks to a benefactor, had attended grammar school and made a successful career as an archaeologist. Sometimes he remembered with a shudder just how close he had come to ending her life. What sort of a monster had he become, to want to kill his own flesh and blood? Surely education, not violence, was the key to success.

However, there were other, more pressing matters giving him concern. Valletta was not what it used to be. Illegal drugs were infiltrating the island; just the other day he'd seen a report in the *Times of Malta* about a young girl from Sliema who'd been found dead in a shop doorway having overdosed on heroin. He heard that cannabis was freely available if you knew who to ask, and lectured his own children on the dangers of using drugs. He had also noticed more prostitutes on the streets in Valletta - nowadays they ventured further than The Gut (as British sailors had christened it) and were undoubtedly linked to the drugs trade.

James called a meeting with his associates to discuss his concerns and took Nikolai along with him. When Nikolai stepped into the room he was warmly welcomed and exchanged greetings with the men in Maltese. James was shocked; this had never happened in Alessandro's time when, out of politeness, they had always spoken in English. James, asserting his authority, said, 'thank you for welcoming Nikolai. Now, we will continue in English,' which they did, although James noticed his son trade an amused glance with the others.

The meeting considered the drugs issue, but no one seemed to have any idea who was behind it, or how it could be stopped.

'We had a word with one of the Italians but he denied any involvement,' said the banker, shrugging his shoulders. 'But business is changing - there are many new faces and these activities are more difficult to control than in the old days.'

Then Nikolai said, 'I can ask around if you like. The Galea family may know something…'

'Thank you,' said James, pleased to see his son taking the initiative, although inside his head an old voice warned him, 'summat's up. There's something they're not telling you.'

Things were changing on Gozo as well. Since Alessandro's death Ester had worn the Faldetta, the traditional black head dress and cloak, and only left the house to go to church. Nina spent much of her time with her and had also taken to wearing black, and with her greying hair pulled back into a bun she looked older than her fifty years. She still loved James, but in a different way - with their family complete, she was aware that her fiery passion for him and her possessiveness had waned. Instead, she found pleasure in her children and she adored her new grandson (her daughter Maria had married a Gozo farmer and produced a beautiful boy). When she saw James she had the impression he was losing control, suspecting that Nikolai and Alfredo knew more about what was happening in the business than their father. She was pleased her sons got on so well together and occasionally came across the two of them deep in discussion. She cherished her youngest daughter, Septima, who was her joy. Her only worry was Elena who was so consumed by her teaching career that she showed no sign of wanting to marry and start a family. She couldn't relate to her at all.

James was also aware of his changing relationship with Nina. They would often spend days apart, and when they were together there was a different dynamic between them, as if she had lost respect for him. He found solace in alcohol and took to drinking at least a bottle of wine every evening, followed by a couple of whiskies to help him sleep.

One hot night, back on Gozo, he was restless and awoke in the early hours, aware of lights out at sea and people speaking in hushed tones in a foreign language. He had a sudden memory of his early days on the island when they were still at war, when he had lain in bed listening to the voices of the enemy. When he awoke the next morning he thought he must have been dreaming, and blamed the whisky.

CHAPTER 38

Malta, 1979

Lieutenant Commander Cedric Mason RN successfully navigated his minesweeper, HMS GRAFTON, into Grand Harbour. The setting hadn't changed - those golden cliffs, aglow in the early Spring sunshine - but the fleet of Royal Navy ships which had previously filled the harbour had gone, replaced by merchant vessels, tankers, and warships from Russia and Libya.

Malta was due to celebrate its Freedom Day in four weeks' time, on 31st March, marking Malta's attainment of full independence and the closure of British military bases on the island. GRAFTON was there to monitor the situation and, covertly, to follow up reports of illegal activity in the surrounding waters. Cedric's first appointment was to pay a courtesy call on the Mayor of Valletta, followed by an intelligence briefing at the British High Commission.

Wendy flew out to join her husband who had rented an apartment in Sliema for the month. Having a break from her work at the Roman Baths she had cleverly taken up an invitation to deliver a series of lectures on archaeology to Malta University and timed her visit perfectly. Cedric met Wendy at Luqa airport, both of them finding it strange to be back in Malta after fourteen years. In his hire car Cedric whisked her back to their apartment where they went straight to bed, still crazy for each other; their times apart heightened the pleasure they had when they were reunited.

The next day, while Cedric took his ship to sea on patrol, Wendy met her contact at the university to discuss the lecture programme. Afterwards she had a free afternoon and decided to visit the site near Mdina where she had worked on the dig. It was impressive: the place had been transformed into a visitors' centre and Wendy joined the guided tour, surprised to see how far the site now extended.

For Wendy, the highlight was the mosaic floor - *her* floor - which looked in incredibly good condition, just as she had seen from Sandy's photo, and there, in the right-hand corner, was the salamander. Seeing it reminded her of James, and she could no longer ignore the thought that was playing at the back of her mind. Her belief that he was her father had been gnawing at her heart for too long. All these years she had left well alone, but now another opportunity had come her way. Their paths were likely to cross and this time she had decided to confront him, regardless of the consequences. She had to know the truth.

*

Cedric said, 'we've been invited out on Saturday night to a casino! Guests of the High Commissioner. Should be fun. Have you been to one before?'

'No, I haven't.'

'You'll need to wear something glamorous!'

Wendy went shopping and in a fashionable boutique in Sliema she chose a white silk jumpsuit with bell-shaped sleeves and a low V-neckline which only someone with a figure as slim as hers could get away with. A pair of wedge-heeled sandals completed the look, and around her neck she wore her mother's scrimshaw pendant on the gold chain. For his part, Cedric was looking very smooth in his DJ.

The casino in St Paul's was a grand affair. They entered a vast, high-ceilinged room, over-decorated with gilt and crystal chandeliers, and there was an excited buzz about the place. The High Commissioner greeted them with champagne, then at a booth they exchanged a few Maltese Pounds for gaming chips. They had a flutter at the roulette table and Wendy watched as a suave, good-looking man worked his way around the room, meeting and greeting his guests, slapping men's backs, putting his arm around women's waists. A charmer, he oiled his way towards them and introduced himself.

'Nikolai Robinson. Welcome to my casino. I trust you are having a pleasant evening?'

He scanned Wendy with his dark eyes, noting her cleavage, not her pendant.

'We are, thank you,' said Cedric.

The Commissioner introduced his guests, then Nikolai continued his tour.

'One of the island's playboys,' said the Commissioner. 'Owns a chain of casinos and nightclubs…' He lowered his voice. '…a cover for money laundering, we suspect. He's up to all sorts, but we've never been able to pin him down.'

'He's James Robinson's son, isn't he?'

'Yes, he is!' said the Commissioner, surprised at Cedric's knowledge. 'James was an important businessman in Malta, although not as influential as he used to be.'

'Really?' said Cedric, looking at Wendy.

'It's his sons who call the shots, now, apparently. And we've got our eye on them…'

Elena Robinson attended Wendy's lecture at Malta University. She listened, enthralled, admiring this clever Englishwoman and trying to place where she'd seen her before. When Wendy finished speaking Elena introduced herself and said, 'that was so interesting. I teach history and have always loved the Roman period. You make it come alive!'

'Thank you, it's always been a passion of mine.'

Then Elena said, 'I think we have met before?'

Wendy had recognised the name. 'Yes, we have. I saw you on the beach on Gozo, a long time ago when I was first working here. And you may have seen me at Valletta museum when we were putting our collection together.'

'Yes…I remember now. You're the lady who found my brother's dap! I remember your lovely red hair. You said you were working at a dig on Gozo, but at the time I didn't even understand what that meant.'

'The early days of my career! So, what are you doing now, Elena?'

The two went to the café and had a coffee together. They chatted easily, forming a connection through their love of history, and Wendy kept looking at her, thinking, 'if I'm right, she's my half-sister.' More worrying was the thought that, by the same token, Nikolai was her half-brother...

When James heard that the director of Valletta museum had invited Dr Wendy Mason to speak as part of her Maltese lecture tour, he knew it must be *his* Wendy. Thinking back to when he had last seen her, fourteen years ago, he appreciated how much things had changed - her star had risen, and his was falling, rapidly. The power he'd once wielded had been gradually eroded by his sons and he found himself weakened, excluded from what had once been his domain. He had tried to re-assert himself but the mighty Maltese machine he came up against was too powerful for him; he was out of his depth. His relationship with his family and business were on the point of collapse; he had taken to eavesdropping on his sons' conversations to find out what they were up to, and what he learnt filled him with horror. Rather than avoiding Wendy he decided to make a point of seeing her, because even if she figured out his true identity it didn't matter to him now; he had little left to lose.

James went to hear Wendy deliver her lecture. She spotted him in the audience and afterwards he approached her. Wendy was shocked by his appearance. He didn't look at all well - he'd lost weight and confidence - the swagger, the bonhomie, gone, although when he greeted her his eyes lit up.

'Welcome back to Malta, Wendy, or Dr Mason as I should call you!' he said, coming forward to shake her hand. 'That was fascinating. I'm pleased to see your career is flourishing. And you married your naval officer!'

'James! It's good to see you again. Thank you, and yes, Cedric and I are married.'

Looking around, and remembering the incident at the restaurant, she said, 'I hope this won't be as dramatic as the last time we met!'

'Indeed! A regrettable misunderstanding…' Slightly embarrassed, he added, 'er…my wife is on Gozo at the moment, with her mother. May I buy you a drink at our café?'

'Thank you, James, that would be nice. We have a lot to catch up on.'

As they talked Wendy looked into his deep blue eyes, comparing his features with those in her mother's old photographs, surer than ever that her instincts were correct. But she also saw that recent years had not been kind to him. Something was wrong.

'Things have altered since independence,' he was saying. 'There is less - well, - *deference*, for want of a better word. In fact, being English out here is a disadvantage these days, and with Freedom Day coming up I can only see it getting worse…'

'I suppose it was bound to happen.'

'Yes…but since my father-in-law died - well, times have changed. My family…' He hesitated. 'Let's say, things are not what they were…'

He looked into his coffee cup, unhappy.

'The museum is doing well, though. You have some wonderful collections.'

'Yes,' he said, brightening a little, 'I spend most of my time here now - it gives me some solace. My days of wheeler-dealing are over.'

Wendy began to appreciate just how much his situation had altered. She sensed that he was ready to make a clean breast of it, but this was neither the time nor the place. She leaned closer to him and said, 'James, there are some things I'd like to talk to you about - in confidence. Would you like to come round to our apartment for supper one evening?'

He looked into her eyes. 'Yes. Thank you, Wendy, I would like that.'

They parted and as he watched her walk away he said to himself, 'she's worked it out. She knows.'

James returned to his house at St Julian's and sat up all night, thinking. He couldn't face life any longer - the lies, the loss of status, his distrust of his family - it was driving him insane. He had to make a plan, and by the time the pink dawn rose around the bay, he knew what he must do.

CHAPTER 39

Malta, 1979

Wendy awoke early. She turned and looked at Cedric sleeping peacefully beside her, his smooth, tanned chest rising and falling with his breath. Much as she desired him, there was something else on her mind - this evening James was coming to their apartment and she intended to confront him with the truth. She stretched out in bed, aware of an unfamiliar coolness and an unusual sound coming from outside, so got up and went out onto the balcony. It was raining.

She leaned on the balcony rail, looking at the puddles forming in the street under a rare grey sky. The place was deserted and on a whim she decided to go for a walk, knowing that Cedric wouldn't wake for at least another hour. She made her way to the seafront and onto the beach, following the narrow stretch of sand that lay between the rocks and the sea, enjoying the refreshing rain on her face.

Out the corner of her eye she spotted a small, lizard-like creature on a rock, also appreciating the rain. She cautiously moved closer, not wanting to scare it away. It was in the shape of an 'S', black and shiny with vivid yellow markings, its four limbs projecting at right angles to its body. A salamander.

When James arrived that evening Cedric could see straightaway what Wendy meant - he was a shadow of his former self. The couple welcomed him and while Cedric served drinks they talked about how Malta had changed in recent years.

'It's the Libyans and Russians who wield the influence nowadays,' James told them. 'Business isn't what it used to be. My sons deal with everything now.'

'We met your son Nikolai at his casino,' said Cedric, 'it's an impressive place!'

James sighed.

'Yes - he enjoys it, and it certainly makes money! I do have some concerns, though ...'

Cedric looked at Wendy, both feeling the tension beneath their talk. He knew that she and James needed to be alone and made an excuse to go into the kitchen. Wendy sat next to James on the sofa and took a deep breath.

'I'm pleased you came round tonight, James, because there's something I want to say. After I returned to England I kept thinking about you, and now I've seen you again I'm sure I'm right. You don't have to pretend any more, I know who you are. You are my father - Frank Fowler.'

Even though he had been expecting this, it came as a shock to James to hear his real name spoken for the first time in nearly forty years.

His automatic reaction was to deny everything.

'I don't know what you're talking about! Whatever makes you say that?'

'Lots of things - photos Mum showed me, things she told me about you. I couldn't understand why you were so interested in me, then it began to make sense. And there's that Bath accent you try to hide! I didn't piece it all together until I got back to England, but you knew, didn't you, as soon as you saw the pendant.'

He shook his head and sighed. There was no point in fighting it, and besides, he was ready to come clean.

'You're right. I did know who you were but I couldn't say anything, I had too much to lose, back then.'

Her relief at knowing the truth was suddenly overtaken by anger.

'You tried to kill me, to keep me quiet!'

A chill ran through him as he remembered how close he had got.

'I'm so sorry, Wendy. I was a monster. But everything is different now, I promise…'

'And did you ever think of Mum and me, while you were making your new life?'

'Of course I did! But you have to try and understand - it was the war, I was badly injured. I couldn't face going back to Bath, I just couldn't. I was given the chance to start over and I took it. I can't say I regret it, but I am sorry for hurting you and Susan. Can you ever forgive me?'

'It's too soon for that! And I can't speak for Mum - she knows nothing about this.'

He looked at her with tears in his eyes.

'I don't know what led you here, but I'm pleased you found me. My long-lost daughter - my beautiful Wendy...'

He gently touched her face with the backs of his fingers. For all his faults and evil deeds, (and she suspected that she didn't know the half of it), Wendy felt a connection with this broken man sitting beside her. She looked at him, his disfigured face, and knew he had suffered. A deeper instinct overrode her anger, and putting aside the hurt he had caused she reached out to him and gave him a hug, father and daughter united at last.

Reckoning he'd given them enough time, Cedric returned to find the two together on the sofa, both in tears. He waited until they had recovered their composure, then Cedric asked, 'so, what are you going to do?'

James exhaled.

'I'm going to turn myself in. I was already thinking about it before seeing you tonight, and now I'm sure. I'm ready to go back to England, to face whatever I'll have to face.'

'But you'll go to prison! Fraud, deception, bigamy - they're serious charges...'

'Yes, I know. But I'm prepared for that, and to be honest with you I don't know how long I'll last if I stay here...'

Then James said, 'look, I have some information for you, but first there is something you can do for me.'

Cedric was suspicious. This was more like the old James.

'What do you want?'

'I want you to vouch for me, with the authorities - to tell them that the information I'm about to give you helped capture some of the most serious criminals on the island. Then at least they might reduce my sentence. I think it's the best I can hope for.'

'So what is this information?'

'There's a big drugs operation planned for Freedom Day. There's a boat coming from Libya with the goods and they're going to rendezvous off Gozo at midnight.'

'And how do you know all this?'

'Because I've heard my sons, planning it.'

*

On Freedom Day the Robinson family awoke early at their home on Gozo - a busy day of celebration lay ahead. Nina and the younger children were staying there to take part in local festivities, while James was to attend a function at Valletta museum. He casually said goodbye to his family, who barely looked up, and without a backward glance he got in his car, drove to the ferry and made his way to Wendy's apartment in Sliema. She was expecting him.

'Everything going to plan?' he asked.

'Yes. Cedric sailed at dawn.'

'Good. Now, we must act as normally as possible for the rest of the day. You'll be catching your flight tomorrow?'

'Yes - I'm all packed up, ready to go.'

'I never thought I'd say this, Wendy, but I'm looking forward to seeing England again. I need to get away from here, and so do you.' With that, he kissed her on the cheek and left.

The celebrations began with a ceremony near the war memorial at Floriana, just outside Valletta, followed by parades through all the main towns, culminating in a festival in the crowded streets of the capital and a regatta in Grand Harbour. James stayed at the museum until the evening when he emerged to meet Elena. Together they stood among the rejoicing crowds and at midnight watched the impressive firework display as people celebrated Malta's full freedom at last. Elena was excited about it, but aware that her English father had his doubts. He had been in a strange mood lately.

'Are you all right, Dad?' she asked him.

'Yes, I'm fine.'

She gave him a hug and said, teasingly, 'don't worry, I know you're English but I still love you!'

He held her for longer than he should, and said 'I love you too, Elena.'

With a massive explosion which lit up the sky the firework display came to a glittering end. Some colleagues from the museum joined the party and James looked at his daughter, chatting and laughing with them. He knew it was time for him to disappear and said to her, quietly, 'I just have to go and see someone for a moment...'

Elena smiled and nodded, then James walked away, out of her life.

*

Just off the coast of Gozo HMS GRAFTON intercepted a ship they had been tracking from Libya which was about to rendezvous with a Maltese fishing boat. Exercising the authority vested in him, Lieutenant Commander Mason addressed the Libyan vessel through a loud hailer, ordering its captain to stop and allow his officers to come aboard to conduct a search on suspicion of illegal activities. In the beam of strong searchlights the ship slowed down, and when the two were close enough Cedric's men climbed on board.

Another officer pulled over and searched the fishing boat, the two Maltese on board protesting their innocence, saying they were simple fishermen going about their night's work. Then the officer wound in a fishing line which had been cast over the side to find a waterproof bag attached, containing wads of several thousand US dollars.

'A good catch!' he declared.

The search team on the larger vessel were well-experienced and knew all the best hiding places for illegal goods. While the captain and crew claimed to know nothing, the men were below deck, sifting through the cargo which largely comprised crates of fruit, tobacco and boxes of cheap jewellery. Then the team leader noticed a bulkhead which was out of alignment.

'Over here!' he shouted.

They demolished a false partition wall to expose a stash of goods wrapped in polythene, crammed tightly into the concealed cavity. The officer opened one of the packets to reveal a white powder which he recognised to be cocaine.

'Arrest them!' he ordered.

The smugglers were no match for the Royal Navy and put up no resistance. GRAFTON towed the vessel containing the drugs and the fishing boat into Grand Harbour where the police awaited them.

*

James arrived at the High Commission, told the official at the desk that he had an appointment with the Commissioner and was shown into his office.

'I'm pleased to say that the information you passed us proved correct,' the Commissioner said. 'Tonight, HMS GRAFTON apprehended a Libyan ship with the largest haul of cocaine we have ever seized in these waters and we have also taken into custody the Maltese fishermen who were about to buy it.'

He leant forward on his desk and looked at James.

'You have satisfied your side of the bargain, and we will fulfil ours. Tomorrow one of my officers will escort you by plane to London where he will hand you over to the police, with our recommendation that you be dealt with leniently.'

'Thank you,' said James.

'My pleasure, Mr Robinson - or should I say - Mr Fowler.'

PART FOUR

CHAPTER 40

Bristol, 1979

The Judge at Bristol Crown Court gave his verdict. Taking into account Frank Fowler's plea of guilty to charges of deception, fraud and bigamy, and in view of his cooperation with the security services, he sentenced him to be detained for seven years. He was taken down and sent to HM Prison, Bristol.

Wendy was in court. Frank caught her eye as he was taken away in handcuffs and they nodded at each other in acknowledgement.

Afterwards, Wendy left the courtroom and pushed her way through the crowd of waiting journalists, ignoring their questions and heckling. She quickly got into the waiting car and Cedric drove off at speed. They were both astonished by the attention the case had received.

'I wish he'd stayed out there!' said Cedric. 'Honestly, Wendy, your family…how on earth am I going to explain this to my mother?'

Wendy was too stunned to speak. She was pleased the truth was out, but hadn't reckoned on the speed of events and Frank wanting to give himself up and return to England. Once that decision was made there was no going back.

*

It had been the worst moment of Wendy's life. Susan welcomed her home and asked how the lecture tour had gone, then Wendy said,

'The tour went well, thanks, but Mum, there's something else I've got to tell you. Something really important…I think we should sit down…'

As gently as she could, Wendy broke the news that Frank was alive and had been living in Malta since the war.

'Don't be silly, love, he died before you were born! I've always told you…'

Wendy repeated what she had said, explaining that Frank had taken a false identity but had now given himself up, and was back in England to stand trial.

Susan couldn't comprehend what Wendy was saying to her.

'He was terribly injured, Mum - he nearly died. His face is badly scarred from the fire on the ship - that's why I didn't recognise him at first…'

'No,' Susan repeated, 'this isn't right, Wendy. Frank's dead. I still have the telegram! If you keep on with this nonsense I'm going to get angry…'

She got up and started walking around, twisting a handkerchief in her fingers. Wendy also got to her feet and, facing her, said, 'there's something else, Mum - he married again…'

Susan covered her face with her hands.

'I don't believe you! I don't want to know!' she cried, hot tears forming in her eyes.

Christopher came in to find the two women, Susan shaking, her face contorted with pain, in an atmosphere you could cut with a knife.

'What on earth is going on?'

'She's lying!' shouted Susan, pointing at Wendy, 'she's a lying little bitch!'

In a frenzy Susan thumped Wendy with her fists, screaming, 'why are you doing this to me?'

Wendy tried to fend her off, shouting, 'it's the truth! I don't like it any more than you do, but it's true!'

Christopher weighed in to separate them, then Susan, distraught, ran from the room.

'What the hell is this all about, Wendy?'

Wendy, breathless with the stress and tension, said, 'it's my father - Frank Fowler. He's alive…'

'Oh God,' said Christopher, and ran to comfort his wife.

*

After the trial Christopher told Wendy, 'your mother had better not go anywhere near him. She'd kill him. Or your Aunty Ann for that matter - she's absolutely furious!'

Fred and Pat were shocked and devastated by the news. Pat remembered the day the warden had carried Susan into the church hall after her collapse having received the news that Frank was lost at sea.

'And all these years he's been alive! And married with seven children!' Pat exclaimed.

'I hope they lock him up and throw away the key!' said Fred.

The press had a field day.

David Roberts couldn't believe the news which even made the nationals.

SECRET LIFE OF EX-SAILOR IN THE SUN

All this time - poor Susan. His heart went out to her, and to Christopher. And how did Wendy feel, finding her father after all these years?

Another ex-sailor, Alfie Jenkins, was at home in Corsham with his wife Julie, reading the report in the *Bath & Wilts Chronicle* with disbelief.

BATH MAN CAUGHT AFTER LEADING
DOUBLE LIFE

'…and it says here, he had seven children! Seven!' exclaimed Julie, who personally thought the five she had were quite enough.

'…*living a life of luxury in his million-pound villa by the sea*…Doesn't sound too bad to me!'

'Look at his face, though,' said Julie, more sympathetically, 'he didn't fake that, did he?'

Alfie put down the newspaper, pulled his wife onto his lap and put his arms round her.

'I don't think I could have coped with all that drama. He's welcome to his millions. I'd rather be here with my Jules,' he said, kissing her.

In their house in Oldfield Park, Jean Daniels read out the reports to Frances.

'Poor Susan! How humiliating for her, knowing that Frank was living in luxury all those years with a new family, while she was battling to bring up Wendy, alone!'

'She did a good job, though, didn't she? That little girl always had spirit.'

'True...maybe he did her a favour, staying away - they were better off without him!'

'Well that's men all over, isn't it...' said Frances.

Cedric hated seeing Wendy so distressed; they had both underestimated the effect that Frank's reappearance would have on Susan and the family.

'You must let him go, Wendy,' he told her. 'He's got the punishment he deserves. All he wanted from us was a safe passage home. I don't want you to have any more to do with him.'

Malta, 1979

It took a couple of days for Nina to realise her husband hadn't come back from Valletta after the Freedom Day celebrations. Elena, who had returned to Gozo, said she'd last seen him when they were watching the fireworks.

Then Nikolai turned up, incandescent with rage. He tore through the house, found his mother and shouted, 'where is he? Where is that son of a bitch?'

Nina was terrified. She'd never seen Nikolai like this. He grabbed her shoulders and screamed into her face.

'If you're hiding him you'll regret it!'

Nina became hysterical, and Elena ran in to see what was happening. Nikolai took a breath and said, 'that lying Judas has betrayed our family and our business. I swear by the Holy Mother, if I ever get my hands on him I'm going to kill him...'

The younger children stood back, terrified to see their brother so angry, then he stormed out.

Nikolai and Alfredo were taken in for questioning by the police but they had planned their drugs operation very carefully; although they were the brains behind it, other people had carried out the work including a young, gullible member of the Galea family. All the evidence the police could muster pointed to him, and the brothers were released. They agreed to lie low for a while, then re-group and resume their activities without their father around to get in their way.

It was only later that the rest of James' family grasped the fact that he had left them, for good. Nina was at a loss to understand what had happened. Although they hadn't been so close recently she still loved her husband and went to her mother who held her as she sobbed, unable to accept that the man she had been married to all these years wasn't James Robinson at all, that he was somebody else. And that woman, Wendy, who had made her so jealous, was his daughter! When Nina was ready to listen, Ester, elderly and wise, said, 'it is God's will. We found him, on the seashore. We didn't know who he was. He chose to stay here, to be with you, Nina. He loved you. He gave you seven children! The Holy Mother brought him to you, and now she has taken him away.'

Bristol, 1979

In his prison cell Frank lay on his bunk, oblivious to the maelstrom he had provoked. In the end he had had no choice; once he decided to betray his sons he was dead meat, and his life in Malta was finished. Returning to England had been his only hope and it was fortuitous that Wendy and Cedric had been on the island at the right time to smooth his path.

At the age of fifty-seven he had seven years to reflect on what had happened, be contrite, re-build himself, learn his lessons. He would see what opportunities prison afforded him. He was, after all, the ultimate survivor and had overcome worse than this.

James Robinson was no more, but Frank Fowler was back.

CHAPTER 41

Bristol 1979

The press interest faded after a few weeks. Frank was safely behind bars and just as well - there were a lot of people outside who wanted to get their hands on him. Two months into his sentence Wendy decided to visit him in Bristol Prison, conscious that it was only a couple of miles from where she had spent her formative years - Bristol Museum - and close to her mother's home.

She didn't tell anyone she was going, knowing it would cause too much distress. Her mother and Cedric didn't want her to have any contact with Frank, but she felt it was something she needed to do. In Malta she had sensed that she was getting to know the man - he was her father, after all - and following the drama of his departure from the island, leaving behind his home and family of nearly forty years, and her own role in discovering him, she felt an obligation to see how he was faring.

Wendy walked into the prison visitors' room in trepidation - it wasn't a place she'd ever expected to be. She spotted Frank and sat down at a table opposite him. He looked thin and pale - his previously permanent suntan had faded - and he was subdued, so different from the successful businessman with the millionaire's lifestyle, as one of the newspapers had put it.

'How are you?' she asked.

'Not too bad. I keep myself to myself.'

Something about his attitude made her wish she hadn't come and she felt her anger rising.

'Have you any idea of the hurt you've caused? Mum's distraught! She wants to kill you! And she's not best pleased with me, either, for finding you...'

'Oh God...I'm sorry, Wendy. I never expected to be welcomed, exactly, but I thought there might be some who would be pleased to know I was alive...'

'No! It was better when everyone thought you were dead!'

'Well, I'm not, and now they'll have to get used to it. I suppose you wish you'd left me alone.'

'It has crossed my mind...'

Wendy took a moment and looked at him, her feelings about him confused and uncertain. He leaned forward on the table which separated them, fixed her with his deep blue eyes and spoke softly.

'I couldn't stay in Malta, Wendy. My sons will never forgive me for betraying them. At least here I'll be safe. I'm grateful to you and Cedric for helping me find a way out. I'm really sorry about everything, and you can tell your mother that, for all the good it will do. I don't want to do any more damage. I've been given my punishment, and I'll serve my time.'

In spite of all the pain he had inflicted she felt that connection again, an empathy. She leaned towards him and touched his hand, getting a telling-off from the prison warden. He smiled at her, then the bell rang for visitors to leave.

'Thanks, Wendy, for coming to see me. I do appreciate it. But I'll understand if you don't want to come again.'

She nodded. 'We all need some time. And I won't tell anyone I've seen you. So, I'll say goodbye -'

She hesitated.

'I don't even know what to call you!'

'Frank,' he said.

'Yes…goodbye, Frank.'

Frank's proximity was not wasted on Susan who told Christopher, 'I can't stand the thought that he's there, just up the road, in his cell. I just can't. We're going to have to move.'

'Don't be ridiculous! You can't let him drive us out of our home!'

'But it's not the same anymore!'

'Now let's not rush into things, Susan. We've got to be sensible about this.'

Christopher had found this the most trying period of his entire life. Susan was in a terrible state, often in tears, raging against Frank and at her daughter for finding him. It took all his patience and understanding to calm her, reminding her daily that if Frank had returned after the war, they - Susan and Christopher - would never have met.

'So you see, my love, it's all for the best,' he tried to reassure her. 'He had his family in Malta, and we've got our family here - you and me, and Wendy,

Tom and our own David. Frank being back isn't going to change any of that.'

Deep down Susan knew he was right but she was a long way from accepting it.

'I still hate it, that's all - the thought of him, just up the road...' and off she went again.

Cedric also had a job on his hands with Wendy, whom he could see was a whirl of emotion, worried for her own relationship with her mother, and unable to unravel how she felt about her father. He advised her to throw herself into her work to try and take her mind off it. He also had his own mother to contend with, who made it clear that she'd always known Wendy was a bad lot with a questionable background, and now with a father who was a common criminal! He was relieved when his next posting came through, sending him back to sea.

After many fraught months it was Fred's eightieth birthday that brought the family together. Pat was keen to make a special occasion of it and hired the upstairs room of their local pub for the celebration. Susan came, with Christopher, Tom and David; and Ann and Brian were there with their four, all grown-up now and with babies of their own. Cedric was home on leave so accompanied Wendy to the bash. It was Fred's big day, and for his sake everyone tried to be civil to each other. Pat had invited some of Fred's old colleagues from the railway, plus neighbours and friends from the allotment. Fred was the last remaining Bishop of his generation, his sister Elsie and her husband Edward both having passed away a few years before.

It was a day of celebration and remembrance, and the only word that was forbidden to pass anyone's lips was 'Frank'.

They all had such a happy day, and when at the end of it Pat said to Fred, who was asleep in his chair, 'come on love, it's time to go to bed,' and he didn't respond, it was a terrible shock, but everyone said, 'what a lovely way to go…'

Pat hated being on her own and missed Fred desperately. She'd never really settled in the flat in Whiteway and, being there alone, all the things she didn't like came into focus - the noise from upstairs, the children crying next door, all contributed to her unhappiness. She complained to the Council who did nothing, and told her daughters who couldn't do much either.

*

Tom came home with some news.

'I've been offered a job at Bath University,' he announced. 'A Professorship in their Computer Science department.'

Christopher was stunned. He knew his son had been doing some sterling work at Bristol, but this…

'That's wonderful!' he exclaimed, calling to Susan to join them.

'Congratulations, Tom!' she cried, resisting the temptation to hug him because she knew he disliked being held.

'So - they've met you? - I mean, you never mentioned an interview…'

'Yes - one of their Professors was with us the other day. He said he was impressed with my work and

302

wants me to join them. It's all to do with the computer programme I've been developing which helps people who have no voice, to speak. They seem to think there might be something in it.'

'Brilliant! I'm so proud of you, son.'

'It was Susan who gave me the idea.'

'Whatever do you mean?' asked Susan, shocked.

'You told me about David Roberts' son using a spelling board. I've been thinking about it ever since.'

As Christopher approached his sixty-second birthday he knew it was time to make some important decisions. The new headmaster was keen to recruit fresh blood to the school and Christopher felt his days were numbered. They could only stay in the schoolhouse as long as he worked, and he began to think Susan was right - maybe it was time to move and make a new start. He had saved several thousand pounds over the years and could afford to retire and buy a modest property. He broached the subject with Susan who was thrilled with the idea.

'We could move to Bath!' she exclaimed, 'we could get somewhere near the University for Tom, there's plenty of good schools for David and…'

Christopher looked at her, waiting.

'…would you mind if Mum came to live with us?'

Susan told her sister Ann and Wendy about their plans. Ann thought it was a marvellous way to care for their mother, but said, 'I will miss having you in Bristol - we've both been here such a long time…'

'But you're settled in your house, Ann - you're happy in Hartcliffe, aren't you? And you've got all your family nearby. I won't be far away, and I'm so excited about living in Bath again!'

Susan went house-hunting and brown envelopes from estate agents were posted through their letterbox daily. Christopher had been quite clear about what they could afford but invariably the places Susan liked were a little over budget. Finally, Susan found somewhere promising and asked Wendy to go with her to have a look. The pair were on speaking terms again; Susan had told Wendy, 'he's your father, and if you want to be in contact with him, that's up to you. Just don't involve me in any of it.'

House-hunting was a useful diversion and a way of bringing them together. The property at Claverton Down on the South side of Bath, near the University, had a separate 'granny annex' and matched Susan's requirements perfectly, apart from the price - the house was two thousand pounds above budget. The estate agent thought they may be able to negotiate a small reduction, but it was still too much.

Susan looked so low, and Wendy said to her, 'let me help. She is my grandmother, after all. I've got savings, Mum - one benefit of not having children!'

'You can't do that!'

'Yes I can!'

CHAPTER 42

Malta, 1981

Elena was struggling to come to terms with who her father was and what he had done. She kept thinking about the last time she'd seen him at the Freedom Day celebrations, remembering how he had held her a little too long, knowing now that he was saying goodbye. He had deserted his home and his family, betrayed his sons to the authorities and, on a personal level, had deceived *her*.

She had read the reports in the newspapers; she had learnt about the pregnant wife he had abandoned in England during the war and that his real name was Frank Fowler. And she had worked out that Dr Wendy Mason, the woman she had admired and made a connection with, was his daughter - her own half-sister.

However, she was in agreement with him as far as her brothers' criminal activities were concerned. Their dealings in illegal drugs and prostitution were getting out of hand, a disgrace to the family name. She knew Nikolai and Alfredo distrusted her and she kept her contact to a minimum, only seeing them at gatherings on Gozo with their mother. She yearned for the past when her father and grandfather had managed to maintain a balance of power with their rivals, but now Nikolai had got into this crazy competition with Giacomo Galea and she feared how it would end.

Elena immersed herself in teaching and managing her grandfather's legacy projects, but she remained anxious. The Headmaster at her school knew the pressure she was under and made a suggestion.

'Elena - there is a vacancy at the University of London for someone to assist research into mediaeval history. Why don't you take a Sabbatical for a year? It would do you good to get away from Malta. I'll keep your job open for you for when you come back.'

Elena thought about this and spoke to her mother, who was so devastated by her husband's departure that she was losing a grip on reality. Sitting on the terrace of her house in Gozo she said, 'do what you think is right for you, Elena. I am in good hands - I have my Mama and your sister Septima here to look after me.'

So the decision was made, and Elena headed for London.

Bath, 1981

With Cedric at sea Wendy took his advice and thew herself into her job. The excavation of the Roman Baths and the Sacred Spring was reaching an exciting stage - areas of mud and rubble which had been dismissed by earlier teams of archaeologists had revealed secrets which had been hidden for two thousand years. Rough paved surfaces sandwiched between layers of sediment contained evidence of the final years of the temple of the goddess Sulis Minerva, a significant discovery not just for the academics but for the city as a whole. Wendy felt privileged to be playing her part at such a significant moment, as well as being grateful for the distraction.

In her moments away from the Baths Wendy spent time helping her mother organise the new house at Claverton Down and making sure her grandmother, Pat, was as comfortable as possible. Pat needed all her effort to cope with widowhood and appreciated the support of her family, feeling fortunate to live in such a lovely part of the city.

'What would my Fred have thought, me living up here!' she said, a hundred times a day.

When Wendy received an envelope addressed to her from the University of London she assumed it concerned her job, so was surprised to say the least when she opened it to find a letter from Elena Robinson who had traced her through the university network. Intrigued to find that Elena was in London, Wendy accepted Elena's invitation to meet her at the British Museum, a suitable venue for the two historians.

Wendy caught the train and made her way to the museum where she and Elena recognized each other straight away. They went directly to the café where they could talk, Wendy listening keenly as Elena told her about life with her father and sharing what she knew about his last months in Malta. She said how her brothers loathed him, but that she still struggled with his sudden departure, not giving her time to say goodbye properly, and leaving her mother distraught.

Listening to Elena, Wendy felt a stroke of jealousy, knowing that her father's other family had had the benefit of his best years. She remembered watching them on the beach in Gozo, fun-filled days, the love he felt for his wife and all his children clear to see. She couldn't help but feel there was a side to her own life that had been missing, one that she would never be able to get back.

Wendy told Elena how she had gradually come to determine their father's true identity, although he had worked out who she was some years before. She explained how they had only acknowledged their relationship just before he left Malta, and described her own mother's distress at his re-appearance. He certainly had a lot to answer for.

'Have you seen him?' asked Elena.

'Just the once - when he was first in prison. I haven't told anyone.'

Conspiratorially, Wendy leaned towards her and said, 'do you want to go and visit him, Elena?'

*

Frank was overwhelmed to see his daughters, together. Compared to the last time Wendy had visited him, two years ago, he looked well, had gained some weight and recovered his self-confidence. He listened to Elena, keen to know the news from Malta, taking on board the situation with his sons and the family business. He knew that Nikolai in particular hated him and would kill him if he had the chance. He was concerned to know that Nina wasn't coping. His biggest regret was leaving her, but what could he do?

Wendy told Frank that her mother had moved to Bath and hoped it would mark a fresh start.

'She doesn't want anything to do with you.'

'I don't blame her,' replied Frank, 'although it would be nice to see her, just once, after all these years…'

'No!' said Wendy, 'that is not a good idea!'

Elena asked how he spent his time.

'There's a good library here and I've been reading a lot of history. Thought I'd try and understand why it gets you two so excited!'

Then he added, 'I can't tell you how proud I am of you both. And to see you here, together! My beautiful, clever daughters! I'm sorry for causing all this trouble - I don't deserve you, do I?'

Visiting time ended and as the two women got up to leave Frank asked, 'can I write to you?'

They both said 'yes,' then said goodbye as their father was put in handcuffs and led away.

Back in his cell the prisoner lay on his bunk and lit a cigarette, his head a whirl of memory and emotion. He would replay that visit in his mind a thousand times. From Bath to Malta, from butcher's boy to sailor to businessman, he had led an extraordinary life. He had done some terrible things and was genuinely sorry for the trouble he had caused, but at least in these two women there was something he could be proud of, and he was pleased they had become friends.

Wendy took Elena to Temple Meads and saw her off on her train to London. They agreed to stay in touch, the two half-sisters who shared an extraordinary bond and a secret - that in spite of everything he had done, they still felt an attachment to their father and were glad they had been to visit him in prison.

*

A couple of months later Wendy was back in Bristol to attend a special Old Girls' reunion. Colston's Girls' School was celebrating the ninetieth anniversary of its foundation and prompted by her friend Pamela, Wendy decided to go along. The bash was being held in the Grand Hotel in the city centre, where she booked a room for the night.

Entering the reception room felt surreal, like going back in time, seeing faces which looked vaguely familiar, but older - teenagers suddenly grown up, hair greying, weight gained, and a lucky few who seemed not to have changed at all. Wendy hadn't seen Pamela for some years and was pleased to catch up with her news from Oxford. Some of Wendy's classmates had become successful academics and businesswomen, others had given up careers to be full-time mothers. Not many, though, could boast a father who'd come back from the dead and was now in Bristol prison, provoking a scandal that had won the attention of the gutter press. If any of her ex-schoolfriends remembered reading about it and made the connection they discreetly said nothing.

There was a speech from the current Headmistress - not much older than themselves - giving thanks to their benefactor. However, in addition to the usual words she added a codicil:

'An increasing amount of attention is being paid to how our founder, Edward Colston, acquired his wealth. We will never know the extent to which he was involved in the slave trade, but we know that his ships transported thousands of men, women and children from Africa to the Americas, contributing to human suffering. And yet, here in his home city, his memory has been celebrated for centuries.

'We have to remember that Colston was a man of his time; many of his contemporaries followed the same path. When he died two hundred and sixty years ago he bequeathed his wealth to charities, and his legacy and name are still seen on Bristol's streets, memorials and buildings, and in our school. We who have benefitted should continue to be thankful for his legacy. Let history be the judge of his actions.'

The speech sparked a discussion and Pamela said, 'yes - things are changing. In Oxford they're starting a campaign against Cecil Rhodes. It's as if all our past heroes are under attack.'

'Indeed!' said another woman, 'but the problem here is, it's hard to find any historic Bristolians who weren't connected to the slave trade in some way or another. There's Colston, and the Wills family...'

'It's good to have the debate, but we'll never know,' interjected another woman. 'The slavery connection to Wills isn't that strong.'

'If it's true, it's dreadful, but you can't change history and you can't judge the past using today's standards,' contributed Wendy. 'Just think what the ancient Romans got up to!'

'Some people think the name Colston should be eradicated!' said another.

'That's ridiculous!'

Then Wendy thought of what Elena had told her about names of streets in Valletta being changed since independence. Perhaps it wasn't such a far-fetched notion after all, but she couldn't see anything so radical happening in her lifetime.

CHAPTER 43

Bath, 1981

Wendy was overjoyed when Cedric came home after a year away at sea, carrying out exercises in the Indian Ocean. They went straight to bed, as they always did after so long apart, and this time seemed extra special - there had been so many changes since they were last together, and Wendy's emotions were heightened. She loved her husband and wanted him desperately. Cedric, too, was overjoyed to be back. It had been a busy deployment and they'd had their share of fun ashore, but he desired his red-head more than ever.

They made love with a passion, for hours, and it was only later that Wendy thought, 'I've been off the Pill'. Life had been so intense after the return from Malta and visiting Frank with Elena had been emotionally draining. With Cedric not there she just hadn't got round to renewing her prescription. Then she thought, 'to hell with it, I'm too old to get pregnant anyway!'

But she wasn't.

After a trip to the doctor she found herself saying to David Roberts, 'yes, I know, I'm elderly primigravida. It seems to be quite common around here!'

Cedric and the family were shocked but delighted to hear the news, and even Rosamund Mason wasn't too hostile, telling Wendy about the joys of being an older mother.

'Good job I'm getting promoted!' said Cedric, about to take up a new post as a Commander.

'And when's it due?' asked Susan.

'Next May.'

Cedric joined HMS INVINCIBLE, an aircraft carrier, at Portsmouth, the largest ship he had served on. They were due to be away for six months. As they kissed goodbye he held her close and said, 'look after yourself won't you, darling. By the time I get back you'll be so huge I won't be able to get anywhere near you!'

*

It was the end of March and Wendy was big and feeling exhausted. She'd had to give up her job - it was impossible for her to work in the confined spaces at the Baths and her concentration had gone. She sat on the sofa next to Cedric who was back for a couple of weeks' leave, moving around, trying to get comfortable.

'For goodness sake stop fidgeting!'

'Well I'm sorry but I can't help it!' she replied, irritated.

The news was on the television and towards the end of the bulletin came a report about some

Argentinians who had set up camp on a place called South Georgia in the South Atlantic and laid claim to the territory.

'Bloody cheek!' said Cedric, 'who do these campers think they are?'

'Where is it, anyway?'

'It's a small island near the Falklands.'

The next day Cedric received a telephone call.

'Sorry, Wendy, duty calls. Looks like this Falklands business is getting serious. I've got to go back to Portsmouth and join my ship.'

Wendy went with Cedric to the railway station that afternoon to see him off. Standing on the platform he kissed her goodbye, saying, 'I'll be back as soon as I can, and if this one can't wait -', touching her belly, 'I'll look forward to meeting them. Good luck with it all...'

As the train approached, Wendy had a sudden sense of dread. It dawned on her that this wasn't a normal tour of duty; Cedric was going to a potential war zone. She kissed him once more then he climbed aboard, the whistle blew and he was gone, Wendy staring after him, powerless, as the train motored away into the distance.

From then on, every evening Wendy would be glued to the news bulletins as reports came in of the Fleet's progress South. While the politicians argued and international talks took place, the British military were strengthening their position, preparing to re-capture the islands which the Argentinians called the *Malvinas* and claimed as their own. By the end of April South Georgia was restored, but that was only the start.

Wendy's fortieth birthday came and went without fuss - she couldn't celebrate properly knowing her husband was in danger.

In May the war began in earnest and each evening's report gave a grim summary of the day's events, with numbers of ships attacked and personnel killed on both sides. Wendy knew that Cedric was at the centre of the action, carrying out the duties he had been born to and trained for.

News came in that HMS SHEFFIELD had been sunk - the first Royal Navy ship to be sunk in action since the Second World War - and the reality hit home. Wendy realised this was how it must have been for her mother, pregnant and anxiously waiting for news of Frank on the Malta convoys. When Susan next came to see her Wendy asked, 'how did you cope?'

'Well, you just take it, day by day. Although it was different, then, because the whole country was involved. Now we're just a bunch of civilians looking on while the professionals do their work. Don't forget that, Wendy - they know what they're doing.'

The mention of Frank was only a breath away. At last Susan said, 'he did go through an awful lot, your Dad. He must have been very brave. It really was a miracle that he survived...'

It was the first kind thing she'd said about him since he'd returned.

Wendy set up a support group for local naval wives to help each other through the difficult days and keep up morale. Having always followed her own career, she now understood that being a naval officer's wife gave her another role. She was pleased to help others and equally, to receive support from her new friends, as being pregnant made her feel vulnerable in a way she'd never experienced before.

By contrast Rosamund took a 'stiff upper lip'

approach. 'I had this for years, with my husband,' she told Wendy, 'one gets used to it.'

Speaking to her niece on the phone, Ann could tell her anxiety levels were rising and offered to come and stay with her.

'Your Mum and I are worried about you. Susan's needed at home, but my lot won't miss me.'

Normally Wendy wouldn't have dreamt of putting her aunt out like this, but these weren't normal times. The baby was due any day and she really didn't want to be on her own, so she accepted, and found having some company was a real help.

As more British ships were sunk or damaged by enemy action, Wendy's concern for Cedric's safety transmitted itself to the baby. One night in mid-May she awoke crying out in pain, and Ann was with her in an instant.

'I'm calling an ambulance,' she said.

The hospital was only a few minutes away. Ann went with Wendy then rung Susan who joined them and stayed with her daughter all night, throughout her labour. In Wendy's more lucid moments she said to her mother, 'at least there isn't an air raid going on! How on earth did you manage with that as well?'

'It was all right - those bombs helped keep my mind off it!'

At last the baby was born - a healthy girl with a strong pair of lungs and fine, fair hair.

The next day Ann joined Susan, Wendy and the new arrival in the maternity ward. As they cooed over the baby Ann said to her sister, 'do you remember when we were here, after the raids? I'd broken my arm and you were nursing Wendy. Then Mum found us. What a relief it was to know we were all safe! We were so lucky to come through it all. And now we have another little girl to love!'

Wendy was thrilled with her beautiful daughter and wrote to tell Cedric the news, but at the same time she had a fear of history repeating itself - that something awful might happen and he might never know.

Wendy left hospital and went to stay at her mother's at Claverton Down, ready to receive visitors. Cradling her great-niece, Ann said, '*Romilly*. That's an unusual name. I like it!'

'It means *Man of Rome*', said Christopher, 'or, in this case - woman!'

'We chose it before Cedric left,' explained Wendy. 'I wanted something connected to Roman times and it's a name for a boy or a girl, so it seemed perfect!'

'And she's perfect, too - my great-granddaughter,' said Pat. 'Oh, I wish Fred could see her!'

David, nearly eighteen, wasn't particularly interested in his new niece, but looked up from the newspaper where he was avidly following the progress of the war and said, 'I suppose she is quite sweet.'

Then he added, 'Mum, I think I might join the Royal Navy when I leave school.'

'Don't you dare!' said Susan, 'I couldn't stand the stress!'

CHAPTER 44

Malta, 1982

Nikolai Camilleri was lying on a sun lounger on the terrace of his villa on St Julian's point, smoking a cigar. He was wearing swimming trunks and the gold medallion around his neck nestled in his black chest hair.

He put down his copy of the *Times of Malta* where he was following the progress of Britain's war with Argentina, wondering why they were making so much fuss over crop of half-barren islands in the middle of nowhere. He would never understand the British mentality when it came to their colonial pride.

He was ashamed to be half-English and hated his father with a passion, making it his mission to eradicate the name 'Robinson' from Malta. Just as 'Kingsway' in Valletta had become 'Republic Street', Nikolai had re-branded all his father's restaurants and properties, proving it was possible to re-write history.

On the instructions of his brother, Alfredo had also changed his surname to Camilleri, the name of their mother and grandfather, a Maltese name to be proud of. Three of their sisters had married, so the only remaining Robinsons were their mother, Elena and Septima. Nikolai had tried to persuade his mother to revert, but for all her misgivings about her husband she refused. Her own mother, Ester, had recently died and now Nina spent all her time sitting on the terrace of her home on Gozo, wistfully looking out to sea, with Septima her only consolation.

It was Elena who caused Nikolai most concern. He didn't trust her. He suspected that while she'd been on her Sabbatical in London she may have made contact with their father and the woman called Wendy Mason, who it turned out was his half-sister - the scandal he had to live down on that account! At least now that Elena was back home he could keep an eye on her, although he didn't think she was foolish enough to betray him and he kept her well away from his business interests. He decided to leave her be, for the moment. He needed to concentrate his efforts on what mattered most - his war with Giacomo Galea.

A stunning dark-skinned girl wearing a bikini emerged from the house, presented him with a cold beer and kissed him, lingeringly, on the lips. He squeezed her breasts, then she lay down on the sun lounger next to him.

'Is everything all right, *caro*?' she asked.
'Yes,' he replied, 'everything's fine.'

The South Atlantic, 1982

Cedric was up on the bridge, the ship at action stations. Reports had come in of an attack being launched on them by six Argentinian aircraft. INVINCIBLE stood ready to defend itself but the atmosphere was tense.

Thankfully, the tactics they deployed were successful. The position of the carrier was disguised, the enemy fooled, and the aircraft were shot out of the sky by other ships in the group before they could launch their deadly weapons.

That night Cedric thought of his lovely wife and wondered if she'd had their baby yet. The irony wasn't lost on him - he knew that both his and Wendy's mother had been pregnant while their husbands were at sea, at war, and now he was putting his own wife through the same torture. He wanted to see her desperately, but, for now, his job had to come first.

Bristol, 1982

In his prison cell Frank listened to the news reports on the radio, following intently the progress of the Fleet, unbelieving that another generation had to go through all this. He learnt with increasing horror about ships being sunk and men being killed and injured but remained confident that the enemy would be defeated. The disaster at Bluff Cove with the loss of many Welsh Guards hit him the most; seeing pictures of helicopters hovering in thick black smoke, winching survivors from burning decks while others fought for their lives in a blazing sea brought it all back to him and he felt the heat of the raging fires around him, heard the screams of the injured men.

He lay on his bunk, his face and left side throbbing, his injuries hurting as they always did when he was stressed. These men's sufferings became his own, and he wept. He no longer had Nina to soothe his wounds. For the first time since his return to England he allowed himself to think about the life he had once enjoyed, missing his Maltese home and family, longing for the past, for the warmth of Nina's arms and the love of his children.

*

Wendy took Romilly to meet her other grandmother, Rosamund, who welcomed them both. Wendy gave her the baby to hold and as she cradled her, gently stroking her fair hair, Wendy noticed an expression on Rosamund's face that she'd never seen before - a happy memory, a faraway look in her eye.

'Does she remind you of Cedric when he was a baby?'

There was a hesitation, then Rosamund said, 'yes, Cedric, of course. So fair…! And those eyes…so blue…'

Handing the baby back to Wendy she said, 'thank you, she's lovely. And such a pretty name, too.'

Then Rosamund's usual stern exterior returned. 'You'll need to put her name down for prep school. You have to do it early to secure a place at a decent one, you know!'

Romilly's arrival turned Wendy's life upside down. On a sea of hormones she veered between elation and exhaustion, but most days were good and she took pleasure in taking her daughter out and showing her off to friends and colleagues.

David Roberts was high on the list, admiring the new arrival but also taking a professional interest in mother and child.

'Very wise that you gave up smoking while pregnant. Try not to start again, won't you.'

'I'm finished with the weed! And so is Cedric. I might fancy the odd glass of wine, though…'

They paid a visit to Jean Daniels and Frances in Oldfield Park where the two women, both retired, greeted them enthusiastically. They avoided the subject of Wendy's father, instead asking after Cedric and discussing the Falklands campaign. Frances reassured Wendy that all would be well.

'Our navy really is the best, you know. And I'm still in touch with my old colleagues here in Bath who are working flat out to make sure they get the supplies they need.'

'You enjoyed your time in the Wrens during the war, didn't you, Frances?'

'Yes, very much. One had a sense of being involved, of doing something useful. In other circumstances I might have stayed on. But it's different for women nowadays. There's a proper career structure and more opportunities, although of course you have to leave if you marry, or get pregnant.'

'I wonder if they'll ever have Wrens at sea?'

Frances snorted.

'There's no reason why not, they're just as capable as men. But there's always excuses - having to build new facilities, problems with fraternisation… These things take a long time to change. Maybe by the time Romilly's old enough to join up things might be different!'

Wendy looked at her baby girl and a chill went through her as she tried to imagine her going to war. Then she had a vision of a pretty Wren working in close proximity to Cedric on a ship and felt an irrational rush of jealousy. It occurred to her that, in seeking equality with men, women might be their own worst enemies.

In June the focus of battle shifted to land as the Army and the Royal Marines bravely fought their way to Port Stanley, the Falklands' capital. At last the Argentinian forces surrendered and the union flag was raised. The whole country rejoiced while mourning more than two hundred and fifty British dead and many more badly injured. This most unexpected, unanticipated war, was over.

Wendy was relieved beyond measure but knew that nothing could be taken for granted at sea and couldn't rest until Cedric was safely back with her.

When he finally returned they embraced, then, holding his baby daughter he said, 'I have never, ever, been so pleased to be home.'

CHAPTER 45

Bath, 1984

After another, less eventful, tour at sea, Cedric was posted to Greenwich to undertake a year-long course. It suited perfectly, as he was able to return home most weekends to see 'my two favourite girls' as he called them. Romilly was an active toddler, into everything, a fair-haired cherub one minute and a howling devil the next. For the sake of her sanity Wendy found a child minder and returned to work part-time, wondering whether older mothers were less tolerant of their screaming offspring. Much as she loved her daughter she was thankful to have been of the Pill generation, not being cut out to have a large family. She threw herself into her work, brushing up her skills to assist in dating the findings emerging from excavations of the temple near the Sacred Spring, pleased to be back in familiar surroundings and the company of her colleagues.

In the final week of Cedric's course, just before Christmas, Wendy was invited with the other wives to attend a formal dinner in the College's ornate, historic, Painted Hall. She was pleased of the diversion, and leaving Romilly with Susan overnight, caught the train to London and made her way to Greenwich to meet Cedric. They both felt nostalgic, remembering Wendy's first trip there, making love in Cedric's bunk. They had come a long way since then, but their passion hadn't waned and at least this time there was a larger bed.

Afterwards, they got dressed for the evening, Cedric looking handsome in his mess dress uniform and wearing the South Atlantic medal he had been awarded for his service during the Falklands campaign. Wendy was wearing an elegant, low-cut, black evening gown.

Cedric said, 'I have a present for you.'

Wendy unwrapped the box from a London jeweller to reveal a sizeable emerald pendant on a gold chain. She gasped; it was exquisite. Cedric stood behind her, fastened it and kissed her neck.

'But why...?' asked Wendy.

'Because you deserve it!' he said. 'And it matches the colour of your eyes. I've wanted to buy something like this for you for years.'

He looked at his wife, her hair, still the colour of flame, cascading around her shoulders, and clasped her by the waist.

'*Over my head his arm he flung against the world.*'

'What?'

'It's a quotation written on the frame of a picture I saw in Bristol Art Gallery, years ago - 'The Guarded Bower'. It depicts a beautiful pre-Raphaelite woman, like you, with her lover and protector.'

'You old romantic!'

'It's a lovely painting. Next time we're in Bristol we'll go and look at it.'

'I'd like that.'

'I think, Wendy, what I really want to say, is - I love you.'

They entered the Painted Hall and took their seats at the long dining table. A member of the directing staff noticed Wendy admiring the spectacular Baroque ceiling and wall decorations.

'Wonderful, isn't it. It is such a privilege to work here and dine every day in these beautiful surroundings. They call it 'Britain's Sistine Chapel'. What you have to do, of course,' he said, leaning towards Wendy confidentially, 'is count the number of breasts you can see!'

Wendy countered by telling him about the erotic frescoes in Pompeii, after which the two got on famously. The meal was followed by speeches, toasts to the Queen and glasses of port, and the drinking went on until the early hours.

Wendy and Cedric awoke the following morning with a slight hangover and went down to breakfast which was taken in silence, the custom being not to converse. They were working their way through bacon and eggs when a steward approached Cedric and quietly informed him that he was wanted on the telephone. Cedric excused himself and got up from the table. A few moments later he stood at the entrance to the room, looking ashen, and Wendy went to him.

'What is it, darling?' she asked, anxiously, worried that something had happened to Romilly.

'It's my mother,' said Cedric. 'She's dead.'

*

Rosamund's housekeeper had found her, collapsed on the bathroom floor. It was too late; her heart had given out and no one could have saved her. She was eighty-one but had the air of someone who would go on forever, and Cedric was devastated. He took leave while he and Wendy made the funeral arrangements, both of them in shock. In her will Rosamund had left everything to Cedric, and as they sat in the drawing room at The Oaks, Mortimer Mason staring down at them from the wall and the grandfather clock ticking, Wendy said, 'what on earth are we going to do with the house? Do you want to sell it, or do you want to live here?'

Cedric put his head in his hands.

'I don't know.'

She'd never seen him like this, so lost, so indecisive. She needed to be patient.

They traced Rosamund's few remaining relatives and friends, including David Roberts, and invited them to the funeral service and wake. Wendy was curious to meet Cedric's extended family and spoke to his elderly aunt who said, 'I didn't see my sister often - my husband was in the Army and we spent a lot of time abroad. But I always wished Rosamund could have had a happier life.'

Intrigued, Wendy asked, 'what do you mean?'

'Mortimer gave her security, but not the warmth and love she needed…'

The aunt turned to speak to another guest, leaving Wendy dying to know more, but unable to ask.

*

In the new year Cedric took up a new appointment in London, entrusting Wendy with the daunting task of sorting through his mother's papers and the worldly goods she had accumulated during her long life. She was helped by the housekeeper, Eileen, who had lived in the house opposite The Oaks until the Blitz destroyed her home and her parents with it. Rosamund had taken her in as a fifteen-year-old orphan and she had served her, loyally, ever since.

Rosamund had never thrown anything away: paperwork, bills, bank statements were neatly filed in order, going back decades, and upstairs her wardrobe was overflowing with clothes. A sudden thought struck Wendy.

'There's the portrait of Mortimer, but I haven't seen any photographs of him. Not one! I wonder why?'

'They're all up in the loft,' said Eileen, 'I remember her putting them up there, years ago, when Master Cedric was a toddler.'

Together, they ventured into the dusty loft which hadn't seen the light of day for decades. Shining a torch around, Eileen located the box and they brought it down. They looked through photographs of Rosamund with her parents, then with Mortimer as a young Lieutenant. They made a handsome couple on their wedding day, but in the later photos she had a sadness about her and there weren't many pictures of the couple together.

The next day Wendy was in the drawing room, looking up at the portrait above the mantelpiece and, in an action which felt almost sacrilegious, took it down from the wall, laid it on the sofa and examined it. It was a fine oil painting, skilfully executed, conveying the subject's strong character, and in the corner were the artist's initials, *M.W.*

'So, what were you really like, Mortimer?' Wendy asked of the portrait.

She turned the painting over and noticed a piece of paper tucked into the back of the frame which she removed, carefully. It was a carbon copy of a receipt which read:

Portrait of Captain Mortimer Mason. £30 paid to Michael White, artist, 25th April, 1942.

Wendy recognised the date straight away - the day before her birthday, the start of the Bath Blitz. The artist, Michael White, must have brought the finished portrait to the house that very day and received his payment - quite a lot of money in those days - and that night, the air raids had begun. Wendy wondered what had happened to the artist, hoping he had survived to enjoy his hard-earned cash. She would love to find out more about him, but that would have to wait for another day - there was a mountain of paperwork to sort out and letters to write. So, she hung the portrait back on the wall but kept the receipt and put it safely in her handbag.

CHAPTER 46

Bristol, 1985

One Saturday in March, Susan, Wendy and Romilly paid a visit to Ann and her husband who lived in Hartcliffe, where the cigarette factory had its new premises. It wasn't as nice as Bedminster - the old sense of community was gone - and the whole area was basically a huge post-war council estate. Ann and Brian lived in a decent-sized semi-detached house on one of the quieter roads and made the best of it. Their youngest was still living at home and had a job at the factory but the other three were married with families of their own.

'And how's little Romilly?' asked Ann, stooping down to talk to the three-year-old. Taking her hand she said, 'shall we go into the kitchen and see what Great Aunty Ann's made for you? Look - a chocolate cake!'

'I like cake!' said Romilly, happily.

Susan updated Ann on their mother who had been in hospital for routine surgery and was making a good recovery.

'She is a worry,' said Ann, 'I'm so pleased you and Christopher are there for her.'

'Yes, it's worked out well, and she loves being with us. She'll always miss Dad, though.'

Ann talked about events in Bristol, and Wendy mentioned the discussion they'd had at her school reunion about Colston and Wills. Ann listened with interest but was more concerned about recent unrest in the streets than injustices from the past. Like many other large cities, Bristol had been the scene of rioting in recent years and she was worried about racial tension which was spilling into the area where they lived.

'I'm not happy here,' she told Susan. 'It's not such a good place to live any more. In fact,' she said, looking at her husband, 'when Brian retires we're thinking of buying a bungalow in Clevedon. It's not too far away and the grandchildren would enjoy coming to see us by the sea.'

Brian nodded in agreement. 'We've had enough here. It's time for us to find somewhere nicer...'

He caught his breath and erupted into a coughing fit. Ann went to him but he waved her away.

'I keep telling him to go to the doctor's, but he won't!' she said, exasperated.

'It's just a cold!' he said. 'Stop nagging, there's nothing wrong with me!'

While Susan took Romilly out to play in the garden, Ann quietly asked Wendy, 'what's happening with Frank?'

'I haven't seen him for ages - it must be four years since I last visited him. Don't tell Mum - she doesn't know, and neither does Cedric - he doesn't want me to have anything to do with him. We write to each other though. He was interested in Cedric serving in the South Atlantic, and I had to tell him about Romilly - she is his granddaughter, after all, and he said he loves kids...'

'Yes, we know - seven of them, he had in Malta! Look, Wendy, I know he's your Dad, but I never trusted him. Even as a youngster he was always taking advantage of Susan's good nature. You really must be careful where he's concerned...'

Later, Ann asked, 'how's Cedric bearing up? Are you keeping his mother's house, or selling?'

Wendy sighed. 'It's been so difficult - he hasn't been able to decide. He doesn't want to sell, but he doesn't want to live there either, so once we've finished sorting it out we're going to let it for a while. The housekeeper, Eileen, still has her own rooms there, so she's keeping an eye on things for us. It has been strange, though, going through Rosamund's things - like uncovering somebody's life.'

'That's what you archaeologists do all the time, isn't it?'

Wendy laughed. 'Yes, I suppose it is!'

When the visitors left they gave Brian a hug. He coughed again and Susan said 'take care, won't you...'

'I'll be fine,' he replied.

Ann shook her head. 'I have tried, Susan, but he won't listen to me! Anyway, give my love to everyone and tell Mum I'll come over and see her soon.'

*

In North Bristol, not a million miles away from Ann and Brian's, Frank was lying on his bunk in his cell, smoking a cigarette and thinking. When he'd first gone to prison he had been relieved to be safe, protected from the long list of people who wanted his head on a plate. But after six years he'd had enough of being locked up. He reckoned that by now tempers would have cooled and as long as he kept away from those who wished him harm he might yet live to a ripe old age. He had a plan to become a new, rehabilitated version of Frank Fowler, upright citizen.

He had learned how to play the prison game. His behaviour was exemplary, he avoided trouble, read a lot of books from the library, worked in the kitchens and generally kept his head down. He expressed genuine regret for his past misdeeds at every opportunity and assured those in authority that he had no intention of repeating his crimes.

He often thought of his daughters, replaying their visit in his mind, and kept in touch with both of them by letter. He had hoped Wendy would come and see him again, but understood that it was difficult for her, especially since she'd had Romilly - his granddaughter. He would love to meet her one day.

His Parole Board hearing was due next month and he intended to demonstrate that he was a reformed character who presented no threat to the community. If he played his cards right he'd get out on early release and could start to build a new life for himself. He was good at doing that.

CHAPTER 47

Bath, 1985

On a bright April afternoon, Wendy took Romilly to call on David Roberts. Now past ninety years of age he was physically frail, but his mind was as sharp as ever and he was delighted to see them both. He asked how things were going at The Oaks.

'It's a bit of a nightmare, to be honest with you! Rosamund was certainly a hoarder. There's loads of paperwork and other matters to sort out.'

'Not an easy task after all those years! So, have you discovered anything of interest?'

Wendy told him about bringing the photographs down from the loft with the help of the housekeeper, then said, 'and I found this.'

She took the receipt for the portrait from her handbag. 'There's a portrait of Captain Mason in the drawing room which Rosamund used to sit and stare at. I took it down and found this in the back of the picture frame. Look at the date - the artist, Michael White, was paid for the portrait on the same day as the first air raid. I wondered if you'd heard of him?'

'Well, I can't say I know the name, but I do remember students from Bath School of Art working in the city during the war. There was an exhibition some years later - a marvellous record of how Bath used to be. Some students may have painted portraits of local people to earn some extra cash.'

David thought for a moment, then said, 'my granddaughter's friend is an art teacher in Bath. I'll ask her if she knows anything about Michael White.'

'Thank you, David. It would be interesting to know more about him. I hope he survived the raids.'

*

When Wendy received a letter with familiar handwriting and a local postmark she opened it with a sense of foreboding.

'Oh my God!' she exclaimed, 'he's out!'

'Who? What?' asked Cedric.

'Frank! He's been released, a year early. And he's living in Oldfield Park!'

'I don't believe it!'

She read out his letter.

Dear Wendy,

I'm just writing to let you know that the Parole Board approved my early release. I'm living at the above address...You don't need to contact me, unless you wish to. I have all I need - a roof over my head and a job. I was grateful for your visits. It was good to see you and Elena - I've written to her as well to tell her I'm out. Wishing you and your family all the best, Yours, Frank Fowler

'Hang on a minute...' said Cedric, 'so you went to see him? And what's all this about Elena?'

Wendy had to confess.

'It was ages ago, while you were away...Elena was in London and she got in touch. We went to see him together.'

Cedric started to pace around, angrily.

'I'm surprised you thought he was worth the effort! What else haven't you been telling me, Wendy?'

'Nothing!' she said, guiltily.

'Well, just make sure Frank stays well away from us. That man has given us nothing but trouble.'

'But he is my father!'

'I know, but you managed without him for years and you can manage without him now. It's not as if he was a father you could look up to...'

For a moment he visualized Mortimer Mason, glaring down at him from the drawing room wall.

'...he's a convicted criminal. I don't want you getting involved with him, Wendy, and keep Romilly right out of it. And think of your poor mother! I wish we'd left him in Malta!'

*

Frank's plan had worked; the Parole Board were satisfied with his case for early release. As his last address had been in Bath (albeit more than four decades ago) he was returned there and his probation officer found him a bed-sitting room to rent in the basement of a house in Oldfield Park. She fixed him up with a job at a local supermarket and it was only when Frank got there that he realised it was the old Scala cinema. 'The wheel is come full circle' he thought, remembering something he'd read in the prison library. He got on with stacking shelves and doing as he was told, his colleagues keeping their distance from the odd-looking fellow.

Frank soon adapted to his new routine of going to work, coming home, letting himself in through his own front door and putting a meal in the new-fangled microwave oven. Afterwards he would sit in his armchair with a glass or two of whisky, watching TV and smoking cigarettes. It was freedom of a sort, and for the moment, it was enough.

*

Wendy told her mother that Frank was out of prison.

'So, he's back in Oldfield Park...bit of a come-down for him, after his 'millionaire's lifestyle'!'

'Better than being inside, though.'

'Well, I was happier when he was behind bars. Thanks for telling me, Wendy, but I really don't want anything to do with him. If you want to see him, that's up to you, but please leave me out of it. I've spent this long learning to accept that our lives took different paths, and I'm very pleased with how mine turned out. I've no wish to go delving back into the past now. At least I'm unlikely to come across him up Claverton Down!'

Malta, 1985

Elena was surprised to hear from her father, glad to know he was a free man again. Since she'd seen him in prison they had exchanged the odd letter, but she hadn't dared breathe a word to anyone, especially her brothers. She wrote back, wishing him luck in his new home, and asking him to let her know how he was getting on.

Following her Sabbatical, Elena's academic career had gathered pace and she had gained a Doctorate in mediaeval history. A job in London beckoned and she was tempted, but she couldn't leave her mother who was becoming increasingly unstable.

She was grateful that her youngest sister, Septima, still lived with their mother on Gozo, but couldn't let her have all the responsibility of looking after her. Elena had plenty of work to do, managing the Camilleri Room at the museum and her grandfather's legacy projects, the part of her family's business that she could be proud of. Maybe one day she would return to England and see her father again, for despite all he had done, she still cared for him, but for the moment she was needed here.

Bath, 1985

To take her mind off Frank, Wendy returned to The Oaks to see how Eileen was getting on with clearing out the house in preparation for letting it. She had done some sterling work, sorting the contents of Rosamund's wardrobe into neat piles for the charity shop, to sell, or throw away, and had found some exquisite pieces of jewellery which Wendy insisted Eileen should keep.

In the study Wendy found another drawer full of paperwork and, sifting through it, came across Mortimer's record of service. She made herself a coffee and settled down to read it, fascinated by his career which mirrored Cedric's in many ways, starting in Dartmouth and undertaking tours of duty at sea interspersed with courses at Greenwich College.

During the war he was Captain of HMS ALBERT, a destroyer on the North Atlantic convoys which was damaged by enemy fire in February 1942. According to the record he had taken four weeks' leave while the ship was in dock being repaired and had re-joined her at Scapa Flow in the Orkneys at the end of March 1942.

'That must have been when he sat for his portrait,' thought Wendy, imagining Rosamund organising it as a surprise, something to amuse him while he was at home.

The final entry stated that HMS ALBERT was sunk following enemy attack in December 1942 and its Captain had gone down with his ship.

'What a tragic way to end his career,' thought Wendy, 'and Cedric was born at the end of January, so Mortimer never knew he had a son.'

She reflected on the echoes with her own life, being born while Frank was away at sea and his ship torpedoed by the enemy. But in this case there was a difference.

Rosamund had always said that Cedric was her late arrival, and with a shock, Wendy understood what she meant...

CHAPTER 48

Bath, 1985

David Roberts found himself at the centre of a difficult situation. He had faced some surprising revelations within his own family in recent years, and just as he began to think his time was done, that every day would continue much the same as the one before, a new challenge had presented itself. He sat in his study and lit his pipe while he considered what to do. As ever his dear wife was watching over him.

'He needs to know the truth,' she said, 'and you're the right person to tell him.'

David telephoned Wendy.

'I have some interesting information for you about the artist you asked me about - Michael White. I…' He hesitated. 'I think you and Cedric should come over.'

'Thank you, David, we will. And since I last saw you I've discovered something as well…'

Wendy and Cedric went to Eagle House, Cedric curious to know what this was all about and Wendy feeling nervous, anticipating what David was likely to tell them. Gilda, David's daughter-in-law, now widowed, showed them in and brought them some tea.

Once settled, David said, 'Cedric, I knew your dear mother for many years. She was my patient. Now she is no longer with us I feel able to tell you her secret, that she kept all her life, because she loved you.'

Cedric leant forward. 'What are you talking about, David?'

'It's about you, Cedric - you, the son that she adored. Rosamund desperately wanted a child, and over many years I conducted tests but could find nothing wrong. When she finally conceived she was overjoyed. She always swore that she became pregnant in March, while her husband was home on leave. That would mean her baby was due in December, and in January she started saying the baby was late. But I monitored Rosamund throughout her pregnancy, and I knew the baby was to term. Cedric, when you were born at the end of January - and it was I that delivered you - you were of normal weight and size. You weren't late.'

'So…'

'Rosamund conceived in April, after her husband was back at sea.'

'What?!'

Cedric shook his head. 'I don't understand. Are you trying to tell me that Mortimer isn't my father? And if he isn't, who is?'

David exchanged a glance with Wendy and proceeded to the next piece of news.

'Wendy asked me if I knew anything about Michael White, the artist who painted Mortimer's portrait. I asked a friend of my granddaughter - Lizzie James, an art teacher in Bath - to see what she could find out. Now, Lizzie loves a mystery - she helped us with a family matter some years ago - and, I have to say, she has come up trumps again… Here is her letter.'

Dear David,

Thank you for your letter, it was lovely to hear from you and I'm pleased you are keeping well.

I've managed to find out about Michael White. He studied at Bath School of Art before, and during, the war. He couldn't join up because he suffered from migraines, but carried on working, taking on commissions for portraits of local people, very fashionable at the time and quite lucrative for him. It rang a bell with me because by chance there was an article about Bath Society of Artists in my Art & Craft magazine recently which mentions him - I enclose a copy for you. Sadly Michael and several other students were killed at the School's premises in the city centre at Green Park, during the third air raid on Sunday 26th April, 1942.

I hope you find this useful. Please give my regards to Wendy and her husband. Yours, Lizzie James

'Well this is all very interesting, and I'm sorry to learn that Michael was killed in the raids, but what's it got to do with me?' asked Cedric.

David took the magazine from the envelope and showed him the article about Michael White, alongside a reproduction of his self-portrait.

Cedric gasped. The young, fair-haired man with piercing blue eyes was his double.

After a silence which lasted an eternity, David said, gently, 'I'm sorry, this must be a terrible shock for you, but it is best that you know the truth.'

Wendy took Cedric's hand in hers.

'I found Mortimer's record of service when I was looking through your mother's papers. I read that he re-joined his ship at the end of March and I could see where it was leading. I told David what I'd found, and now, with this information about the artist - well, it makes sense.'

'It doesn't make any sense to me at all!' said Cedric, standing up.

'Thank you, Doctor Roberts, but I need to have some time to think about all this. Come, Wendy - we're going home.'

Feeling embarrassed, Wendy whispered her thanks to David and followed her husband out of the house.

Cedric was in turmoil. All his life his mother had told him stories about his brave father, fighting in the war, and his illustrious naval career. He'd worshipped him, held him in awe - Captain Mortimer Mason. And now David had told him that biologically he was the fruit of a young artist, the result of - what - a casual fling? - an affair? with his mother! There was no questioning the reality of the dates. And that self-portrait of Michael in the magazine - they looked so alike, there could be no doubt.

He realised that his whole upbringing had been orchestrated to demonstrate that Mortimer was his father. His mother had over-compensated by her attitudes, her snobbishness, to deflect anyone from suspecting the truth.

Every day on his commute back and forth to London, Cedric looked out the train window thinking back over his life, looking for a hint of what his mother had hidden from him. She had certainly done a good job - as far as he knew, no one had ever suspected. Then he recalled her vulnerability, that faraway look. He wondered whether Rosamund had had feelings for this young man - half her age! When she used to stare at the portrait, was she thinking about the subject, or the artist?

He wondered what Mortimer had really been like, knowing his parents' marriage may not have been as happy as he'd always assumed. There were so many questions and he was beyond frustration that the only person who knew the answers was no longer there to ask.

He said nothing to his colleagues and was grateful that he didn't have to face details about his personal life being reported in the press, as Wendy had experienced with Frank.

Wendy left Cedric in peace, knowing he needed time to come to terms with the truth. One Sunday he went out for a long walk on his own and returned, ready to talk. He opened a bottle of wine and said, 'I'm sorry - I'm finding all this really hard to deal with. I feel I'm not myself - it's as if someone else has invaded my body and my mind. I can't explain how it feels, Wendy, to discover that your father isn't the person you thought he was…'

'Cedric,' she said, 'I am one of the few people you know who understands *exactly* how that feels…'

CHAPTER 49

Bath, 1985

Frank was enjoying living in Oldfield Park and in his spare time he walked the streets, familiarising himself with his old home turf. He was struck by all the changes, although in over forty years it was to be expected. He couldn't believe the number of cars on the road that lined every foot of space outside the rows of terraced houses. He searched for the house where he had lived with his mother, grasping the fact that it had been completely re-built, and found the same had happened to the Bishop family's former home. Drewitt's butcher's shop was long gone. He tried to imagine the devastation after the bombing raids and how hard it must have been for everyone to start over and build new lives. And he'd been oblivious to it all.

He walked over to Victoria Park, rediscovering the places he used to know. It was May, and the cherry blossom trees had never looked so good - it took being locked up in a cell to make you appreciate the beauty of the outside world, he thought. A memory came back of being here with Susan - Boxing Day, wasn't it, when he'd told her he was joining the navy. How the war had changed everything, for everybody.

On his way back home he took a diversion to Lower Weston. He knew Wendy's address and walked past her house, not intending to call but just to see it. He was disappointed that she hadn't tried to contact him since he'd been out and suspected her husband had warned her off. A child was playing with a ball in the pathway at the side of the house. She didn't notice him, and he didn't approach her, but he knew the pretty little girl with long fair hair must be Romilly, his granddaughter.

*

The next time Wendy was at The Oaks she sat down with Eileen and told her what they had learnt about Cedric. Knowing her loyalty to Rosamund, Wendy broke the news gently. Eileen listened as Wendy showed her the dates on Mortimer's record of service, although she wasn't convinced Eileen had understood - she was a good housekeeper, but Wendy had observed that she wasn't the sharpest tool in the box.

Wendy proceeded to show her the magazine article about Michael White, and when Eileen saw the self-portrait she said, 'yes, I remember him.'

'What?!'

'I remember him. I saw him a few times, going to the house.'

'Really?'

'Yes - he used to walk along the drive, carrying his easel and paints. Nice looking chap he was...'

Wendy listened, rivetted.

'I was fifteen - living at home with my parents in the house opposite. My mother told me he was an art student. The last time I saw him was on the Sunday morning, after the first two raids. It had been a terrible night, with the bombs falling and fires everywhere - it was horrible. I was outside our house with my mother, sweeping up broken glass, and then I noticed him, walking out the driveway opposite. It was odd because there was all this awful damage around, yet he looked happy. My mother said something which I remember because she said it in a funny way which I didn't understand. I can see her now...she arched an eyebrow and said, 'looks like she had someone to keep her company during the night...'

Eileen stopped talking and looked at Wendy.

'Oh...I think I've just realized what she meant!'

Wendy caught her breath.

'But, Eileen, all the time you were with Rosamund, did you ever wonder? Did she ever say anything about the artist?'

Eileen went quiet, then said, 'our house was hit in the third raid, on the Sunday night, and my parents were killed. I was buried under some wreckage and a warden found me. I suffered a head injury and, with that and the shock of it all, I don't think I was quite the same again. It's only talking to you now that's bringing it all back.

'Mrs Mason was kind enough to take me in, and I just stayed. It was a very sad time and I think we were company for each other. When she got the telegram telling her the Captain was lost at sea she sat in her chair, quiet, staring at the portrait. She didn't cry. Then when Master Cedric was born she was so happy, took on a whole new lease of life. She used to say to me, 'Mortimer would be so proud of his fine son.' It never occurred to me to think otherwise, all these years.'

Then she looked at Wendy and said, '…and quite honestly, I don't see any need to think any different. You can say what you like, but to me, Mortimer will always be Cedric's father.'

Wendy relayed the conversation to Cedric, then said, 'you should talk to Eileen - she's one of the few people you can share your memories with.'

'I suppose she is,' he replied, still reeling from this latest piece of evidence. 'I never paid her much attention when I was growing up - she was always there, cooking for us and cleaning the house. Maybe she and mother were closer than I knew. She was certainly a loyal servant. I'm beginning to wonder what else mother kept from me. I had no idea parents could be so difficult…'

'You don't need to tell me that!' exclaimed Wendy. Then she added, 'people are never quite who you think they are. Everyone's got secrets - there's just different degrees of it…'

Cedric considered these words, then took his wife's hands in his.

'Perhaps I've been too hard on you over Frank - he is your father, and I'm just beginning to learn what that means. If you really want to contact him, I won't stand in your way.'

Then he qualified his remark by adding, 'I don't want him getting involved with Romilly, though,' feeling a surge of protection towards his own daughter.

'All right, Cedric. Perhaps I will go and see him, but I'm in no rush. You're the priority now. I'll wait till things have settled down with you.'

'So, do you have anything else tucked up your sleeve?'

'Well...there's just one thing. I'm nine months older than you and I can't help but think that the night I was born, during the air raid, when the bombs were falling and Bath was on fire, a mile or so away you were being conceived...'

Wendy felt ready to share the news about Cedric with her mother and Christopher, who listened, fascinated.

'I thought it was strange that there were no photographs of Mortimer in the house, but I guess that was why,' said Wendy. 'It wasn't him that Rosamund wanted to remember.'

'How extraordinary! And she was such a snob! So, all that time, nobody knew...'

'Well, David Roberts knew that Mortimer wasn't Cedric's father, but it's only now that we've found out about Michael White.'

'Did you have any inkling, Wendy?'

'Not really. Although, when Rosamund first held Romilly I saw a glimmer of something... I imagined she was remembering Cedric, but now I wonder whether she was thinking of Michael...'

Christopher was concerned about how Cedric must be feeling.

'He's gone out today on one of his country walks,' Wendy told him, 'he said he needs space to think.'

'I can understand that. I used to do the same

after I lost my first wife. He's suffered a huge shock. You'll need to be patient, Wendy, but with your support he'll come through. He needs to come to terms with the past, but you and Romilly are what matters now - you are his future.'

Wendy returned home with Romilly, made her tea and put her to bed. Cedric still wasn't home, and as darkness fell on the Summer evening she grew concerned. He had never been out this late and she hoped he hadn't had an accident, imagining him lying in a field with a broken ankle, or falling down a gully somewhere. She was thinking about ringing the police when, at last, she heard him come in.

'Where have you been?' she asked, by now frantic with worry.

'I'm sorry,' he said, coming over to give her a kiss. He smelt of alcohol.

'You might have phoned!'

'I'm sorry,' he said, again. 'I went to see David Roberts, to apologise for being so abrupt with him that day. He was very understanding - he invited me in and we had a long chat - and a few whiskies…Anyway, he ended up telling me all about his family, and the war, and the night Susan came to see him to ask if she could name her baby - you! - after his beloved wife. Then we spoke about my mother, and Michael White. David told me the main thing was to remember that she loved me and always wanted the best for me. He's a marvellous old chap isn't he, Wendy? We and your family owe him so much!'

CHAPTER 50

Gozo, 1985

Nikolai Camilleri drove over to Gozo, causing quite a stir on the car ferry - it was the first time a Ferrari had been seen on the island. He drove it fast up to his mother's house with the radio blaring, the engine roaring as he accelerated around the bends in the narrow roads. Finally he screeched to a halt in the driveway where Nina and Septima were waiting to greet him, having heard the car at least a mile away.

'Nikolai!'

Nina kissed him and he gave his sister a hug.

'Come in, come in,' said Septima, 'we've prepared your favourite lunch - swordfish stew!'

She took his arm while their mother followed behind, more slowly.

Nikolai told them his news, bragging about how he'd beaten the Galea family to reach a lucrative deal with some Libyan businessmen (omitting to mention it was a cover for smuggling women into Malta for prostitution). His other interests were flourishing so he'd awarded himself a bonus - hence the car.

While they ate, Nina told him the latest about his sisters and their children.

'And you, Septima?' he asked, looking at his attractive nineteen-year-old sister.

'I'm very happy, here with Mama.'

In the afternoon the three of them relaxed on the beach in the late Summer sunshine, Nina sitting in the shade of a parasol, enjoying the company of her elder son and her youngest daughter. Most of the tourists had gone and Gozo was peaceful again. Nikolai lit a cigarette and looked out to sea, knowing it did him good occasionally to get away from the bright lights of his clubs and casinos and return to the place of his youth with its simple pleasures. He remembered the good days - the grandfather he had hero-worshipped and his father, whom he had loved, until he'd changed, gone soft, and betrayed them all…

Septima went inside to prepare drinks. When she came back she said, 'Nikolai - would you let me drive your car? I've passed my test! Just a little way - I'd love to see how it feels.'

He was reluctant but said, 'all right - but I'm coming with you…'

'Thank you!'

She went indoors and picked up the keys which he'd left on the table. Nikolai followed her and watched as she ran ahead, opened the car door and got into the driving seat.

Out of the corner of his eye he noticed a man in the distance, running away.

His mind in overdrive he screamed out, 'NO!' as Septima started the engine. With an almighty boom the bright red car exploded in a violent fury of flames and smoke sending debris flying, leaving his treasured vehicle a blazing wreck and his beloved sister, blown to pieces.

*

The death of her daughter was beyond Nina's comprehension. She couldn't bring herself to grieve, because she couldn't accept what had happened. Septima's funeral was held the day after her death and her coffin was laid beside those of Alessandro and Ester, her grandparents. Nina returned home, numb, confounded. In the night she arose, put on a dress with large patch-pockets and walked down to the beach, her long grey hair hanging loose down her back. The air was balmy, the sea calm, the waves lapping gently on the shore. In the light of the full moon she filled her pockets with rocks then walked steadily into the sea. The water passed her waist, then reached her shoulders, her neck, then covered her mouth and her nose. She carried on walking, unafraid, for she was delivering herself into the care of the Holy Mother.

*

Nikolai knew he had been the target of the car bomb and was distraught at what had happened to his sister and, in consequence, his mother. Drastic action was required and he reacted in the only way he knew how, meeting violence with violence.

He feared for the safety of the rest of his family and instructed Alfredo to tell his sisters' husbands to take extra care of them. He handled Elena himself.

Although he didn't trust her, he had to admit that her hard work maintaining the Camilleri legacy projects had given the family an air of respectability which provided a useful cover for his own illegal activities. He didn't wish to see her harmed and spoke to her on the telephone.

'You need to get out, Elena, it's too dangerous here. Go to London, take the job. Mama's gone now and you don't need to stay. But I warn you - don't go near that so-called father of ours, I don't want you having anything to do with him. This is all his fault. If he'd acted as a true Camilleri, as our grandfather taught him, rather than a weak-livered Englishman - if he'd fought the Galea's as he should have done - all this might not have happened.'

Elena fiercely disagreed but said nothing. There was no reasoning with Nikolai when it came to his hatred of their father. She was devastated at the loss of her sister and mother and felt there was no choice but to do as he said. She quickly packed her things and took the next plane to London.

Knowing that his family were as safe as possible, Nikolai took the first step in his plan to avenge the deaths of his sister and mother.

It was well known that Signor George Galea, well into his eighties, enjoyed going out in his boat on Sundays to do a bit of fishing. But the next time he took to sea, accompanied by his little great-grandson, a bomb that someone had secretly placed on board exploded, sending them and the boat sky-high.

The loss of George Galea, the elder statesman, and his great-grandson, his ultimate heir, was too much for the Galea's to bear. Nikolai met Giacomo Galea and the two agreed that enough was enough; it was time for a truce before the rival families obliterated each other completely. For the moment, at least, Nikolai was the undisputed Emperor of his underworld, and with his brother Alfredo they would ensure that the Camilleri name was the most powerful and the most feared in Malta. It was a sweet feeling.

Then came the next step.

Nikolai let himself into Elena's apartment. It was untidier than usual and clear that she had left in a hurry, as he had instructed. He looked around until he found what he was looking for - an envelope postmarked from England. His suspicions were proved correct - Elena was in touch with their father. He read the letter which was signed 'Frank Fowler' and noted the address in Bath. So, he was out of prison!

Nikolai could put in place the second part of his plan. His thirst to avenge his father was stronger than ever, and now he knew where he lived.

CHAPTER 51

Bath, 1985

Susan went over to Wendy's for the day to spend some time with her and Romilly. They had received bad news - Ann's husband Brian had succumbed to lung cancer like so many of their contemporaries.

'By the time he finally went to the doctor's it was too late,' Susan said, sorrowfully. 'I went to see Ann yesterday - she's bereft, poor soul. Thirty-seven years they were married. Her children are with her, so at least she's got some company. The funeral will be held next week.'

'That's so sad, he was a lovely man. Will Aunty Ann stay in Bristol?'

'Yes, for now. They were planning to move to Clevedon and she said she still might, but it's too soon for her to decide anything yet.'

After lunch Romilly was fidgety and Susan offered to take her out for some fresh air. It was a warm day in early September, just right for a walk, and

Susan watched as Romilly happily ran ahead along the pavement, then turned and ran back towards her. Before they knew it they were walking over the footbridge onto the South side of the river towards Oldfield Park, Susan's old stamping ground. She hadn't been over there for years, and as they passed rows of houses re-built since the Blitz, she doubted whether the new generation growing up there even knew it had happened.

As they turned a corner Susan took Romilly's hand and said, 'now, this is where we used to live - me and your Great Aunty Ann, and your great-grandparents. We lost our house in the bombing...'

It was a quiet afternoon with hardly anyone around, most people being out at work. Then Susan noticed a man walking towards her, quite tall, but holding himself in a lop-sided way. He was wearing jeans and a jumper, and his hair was cropped short. As he grew closer she felt her blood run cold. A few yards apart, they stopped in their tracks and looked at each other.

'Susan!'

'Frank!'

She caught her breath at the sight of him, noticing the scarring on his face and neck. After a long moment of silence Susan said, 'Wendy told me you were out.'

'Yes - time off for good behaviour! And this must be Romilly!' he said, coming closer and squatting down to speak to the little girl on her level.

'Leave her alone!' cried Susan, instinctively pulling her away from him.

Frank stood back, raising his hands and the child stared up at him, curiously.

357

'Okay, okay, I'm sorry, I don't want to scare her. I love kids.'

'Yes, I gathered that…'

Calming herself, Susan said, 'yes, this is Romilly, Wendy and Cedric's daughter.'

'And you look well, Susan.'

'A bit older than when you last saw me…'

She remembered waving him goodbye at Weston station on his way to join his ship.

'After our honeymoon…' he said.

Her throat tightened and she felt on the verge of tears.

'I couldn't come back, Susan. I'm sorry, I just couldn't. I nearly died, but then I had a chance of a new life…'

'And you did very well out of it, by all accounts - enjoying your millions!' she said, her anxiety turning to anger. 'And your seven children…!'

'You've been all right, though, haven't you? You've got a husband and son…'

'Yes. That's the only good thing you did, Frank - give me the chance to do something better than live here with you!'

'Look, Susan, I've done my time. Can't you at least be civil?'

'Not really, Frank - no. There's been too much hurt. I moved on from you a long time ago. I'm happy with my life and I don't want you back in it.'

'But what about Wendy? She's my daughter too - not that I've seen her since I've been out…And now we have a granddaughter!'

He stooped down again, facing Romilly who gripped her grandmother's hand tightly, anxious about this stranger.

'Don't touch her!' cried Susan, beginning to feel scared. There was something sinister about him that hadn't been there before.

Frank exhaled. 'We can't do this here. Can we go somewhere and talk?'

'No, Frank. No, I don't want to talk to you. It's too late…it's all too late…'

He took a pace towards her and fixed her with his deep, blue eyes.

'Susan…'

'NO!' she said, stepping back from him.

'Goodbye, Frank. I really don't want to see you again.'

She turned and walked away quickly, dragging Romilly along with her, the child struggling to keep up. Susan's eyes were stinging with tears, and she didn't look back.

Frank hadn't been home long when there was a knock at the door. He got up to answer and for a fleeting moment wondered if Susan had changed her mind and followed him, wanting to talk, but when he opened it a man wearing jeans and a leather jacket was standing there.

'Frank Fowler?' he asked.

'Yes.'

'I have a message from your son Nikolai.'

CHAPTER 52

Bath, 1985

The knife had been inserted under Frank's ribcage and up into his heart, a professional job, the police said, and the perpetrator was never found.

Frank was cremated in Bath, his body finally consumed by fire. Wendy and Cedric attended the service with Elena who had travelled down from London. They laid a wreath of white chrysanthemums at the crematorium and stood, solemnly, together.

Looking down at the wreath Cedric said, 'Frank Fowler, James Robinson, whoever you are, may you rest in peace.'

Wendy said, 'Farewell, Frank.'

Elena said, 'goodbye, Dad. The Holy Mother will take care of you now,' and she crossed herself.

In their house on Claverton Down, Susan and Christopher sat quietly together, knowing that Frank was out of their lives for good.

Elena returned to London, her permanent home. In a few years she would marry and the name of Robinson would be no more.

Back home after Frank's cremation Cedric took refuge in his study, shocked by the violent way Frank's life had ended and sorry for his wife's loss, but relieved that he had gone.

Wendy sat on the sofa with Romilly and cuddled her, seeking comfort in her daughter. The child wriggled around to get comfortable, then reached up and touched the necklace her mother was wearing.

'What's that, Mummy?'

Wendy hadn't worn the scrimshaw pendant for years, but today, thinking of Frank, it had seemed appropriate.

'Your Grandad Frank gave this to Granny Susan, and when I was twenty-one she passed it to me. It was made by an old sailor - scrimshaw, they call it - carving on whalebone. Pretty, isn't it?'

'It's very smooth,' said Romilly. 'I like the lizard.'

'It's a salamander - that was the name of Frank's ship. One day I'll tell you all about it.'

'And what's that squiggle, there?' asked Romilly, tracing the mark with her finger.

'Frank asked the old sailor to carve that, especially for her. It's an 'S', for 'Susan'.'

Epilogue

On the fiftieth anniversary of the Bath Blitz the Mayor of Bath dedicated a memorial garden in Oldfield Park to commemorate those who had lost their lives during the bombing raids in April 1942. The location, outside the Scala, was chosen because it was the site of the public air raid shelter which received a direct hit, killing so many in the place where they had sought safety.

The small, circular garden has a plaque on a stone plinth and trellis work from which wreaths can be hung. It is a tranquil place to come for remembrance and contemplation, to stop for a moment to think of those whose lives were changed forever by those nights of blitz and fire, when Bath was ablaze.

Bath Ablaze

Original artwork by Maggie Rayner

About the Author

Originally from Kent, Maggie moved to Bath at the age of eleven and lived and worked in the city for many years.

She is now retired and lives in Wiltshire.

Also available from Amazon:

'When Bombs Fell On Bath'

The first part of the 'Bath At War' series.

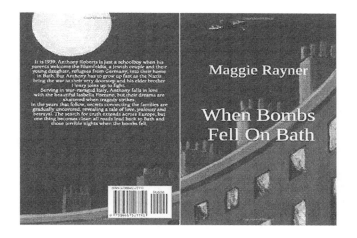

Original artwork by Maggie Rayner

Also available from Amazon:

'Moonflight and Other Tales from Wiltshire and the West'

Original artwork by Maggie Rayner

Printed in Great Britain
by Amazon